I0746653

FOUR GUNS AND
SIXTEEN TRAILS

LAWLESS TRAILS PRESS is an imprint of

Hydra Publications
1310 Meadowridge Trail
Goshen, KY 40026

Cover art by Julia Dreams.

ISBN: 978-1-958414-80-4

First Trade Paperback Printing: October 2025

FOUR GUNS AND SIXTEEN TRAILS

Short Western Fiction From

JOHNNY D. BOGGS
MICHAEL ZIMMER
VONN MCKEE
MICHAEL KNOST

TABLE OF CONTENTS

"A short story can pierce the heart in a way a novel cannot, for it has no time to dull the edge."
— Ian McEwan

The Sum of My Inheritance

Michael Knost

Certain men build a life, and others inherit one like a debt—I reckon that was the sum of my inheritance, though I did not appreciate it at the time. My name is Eli Maddox, and I have laid my head in many places that would not be called fit quarters by any reasonable person—tents with rotted seams, railroad culverts black as stovepipe, and once in a stable where the mule objected to my presence with an attitude I took to be personal.

My father was Clay Maddox, known to some as a road man, though he disliked the term on principle. He said it sounded like something a greenhorn newspaperman would write to frighten store clerks. He preferred "operator" or sometimes "freebooter." These were just hats he put on, but the head was the same—shrewd and contrary and forever measuring the odds in silence.

I never knew my mother. I asked him about her once, and he looked at me as if I'd inquired after the state of his soul. He said she perished in travail and was gone before she could hold me. That was the only statement he ever offered on the matter, and I learned to hold my tongue about such questions.

My father rode with men who carried rifles wrapped in canvas and wore their hats low, men with permanent squints from a life outdoors and a tightness about the mouth that came from too many lies told in too many places. When they spoke, it was in the manner of a ledger—short entries, no elaboration.

I was born to that life and grew up in it like a weed between wagon tracks. My mother's sister and her husband took me in those early years, raising me under their roof until I was old enough to be claimed back. They said a boy ought to know his own blood and learn his place in it, however hard the lessons proved.

My earliest memory of my father was of him lifting me onto the back of a piebald mare, telling me to sit still or else, and then stepping away to confer with a man who had a red bandanna over the lower part of his face. I did not know at that time that this was called robbing a coach. I took it as ordinary business.

By the time I was thirteen my father began to show signs that the life had worn thin on him. He told me he had one job left, and after that, we would go north to Wyoming, to the land he came from . . . a homestead up in the scrub hills where he said an apple tree had grown thick and tall.

"It's up there yet," he said one night while we sat fireside near Pinedale. "It don't look like much, but that tree is older than me and my brother put together. When I was a boy, it gave us all the fruit we could eat. Apples so red they looked painted, but they had a bite you'd feel in your jaw. Then, after you chewed a spell, the sweetness came."

He dug out that flat stone from his coat pocket—the one he admired from time to time—and handed it to me. "I got this from the creek near that tree," he said. "Maybe it will bring you better luck than it's brung for me."

I put the stone in my boot, under the arch of my foot, where I knew it would stay if things went wrong.

The job he had in mind was said to be simple, which is always a bad sign, and I think he knew it too. He told me the details in that same even voice he used when the matter was serious.

A rail payroll wagon was making its way from Cheyenne up to the Medicine Bow camps. It was due to pass a certain bend in the canyon road where the pines crowded the track, and the grades were steep enough that the horses could not make any quick dash if a tree was dropped across the way. The money was meant to pay the poor souls who laid track without repose.

"You're staying back," he said without meeting my eye. "Ain't no need for you to witness the mess. Just keep your head straight. If things go sideways, you head north."

"What if you don't come back?"

He raised his eyes to mine. "Then you go to the place I told you about. There's a shack under the hill, with the boards painted green. My brother Ephraim lives there. You tell him who you are."

At first light, we broke camp. My father moved with a deliberate calm that I had learned to distrust. When he grew quiet and slow in his movements, it meant the stakes were higher than he wished to admit. He tied down the packs with a care he seldom showed, cinching each knot twice, checking the girth strap on the mare, then re-checking it though it had not slipped an inch.

He had arranged to meet two men who would ride along for the job. One was called Sutton, a bony fellow with a mustache the color of sand and a raw-looking scar that started at the corner of his mouth and cut across his cheekbone. The other was named Cole, dark-eyed and soft-spoken in the manner of a man who believed it best to keep his sentiments to himself.

We found them waiting under a ponderosa whose limbs drooped nearly to the ground. They had a bay horse between them and a mule for the strongbox, but no extra saddle horse. My father's mare would have to carry us both when the going turned rough.

Sutton nodded to my father but did not rise. "You're late," he said.

My father did not dignify this with a reply. He set down his pack and straightened up slow, as if to say he would tolerate no fuss over matters of punctuality.

"Boy," Sutton said, looking at me, "you know how to use that little rifle?"

I had a single-shot .32, its stock worn smooth. My father had given it to me on my ninth birthday with no ceremony beyond the remark that a man ought to have his own piece, even if he was not full grown.

"I can hit a jackrabbit if it's not moving," I said.

Sutton grinned. "Well, that's fine, long as the rabbits don't shoot back." He looked to my father. "You sure about bringing him?"

"He won't be in the thick," my father said. "I've told him where to wait."

Cole, who had been watching the sky, finally spoke. His voice was soft and low. "If we do this clean, there won't be no thick."

We rode out single file, not a word spoken, not a glance shared.

We came to a halt when we approached a rise looking over the canyon road. My father dismounted and tied the mare to a sapling, and the others followed suit.

Sutton took a spyglass from his coat and trained it downslope. "They'll be along in an hour. I seen the dust."

"Then we best set up," my father said.

They had brought a coil of rope and a crosscut saw. I was set to keeping lookout while the three of them picked out a pine that leaned already at an angle. The saw bit in with a noise like tearing cloth.

My father did not acknowledge it, but I knew he was aware of my gaze. It struck me then that he had spent his whole life this way—measuring a man's capacity for violence no different than a banker tallying a ledger.

When the tree was near to falling, he waved me back to the hillside, where I found a place to sit and watch the canyon road. The quiet was uncomforting yet relaxing in a confounding way.

Time drew out like a wire as my father, Sutton, and Cole waited, hidden away out of sight. None of them moved nor made any noise that I could tell at all. I watched the road until my eyes watered.

At last, I saw them. Four horses drawing a covered wagon with ironbound wheels, their flanks white with sweat. The driver sat bent, a wide hat pulled low, and beside him rode a man in a brown coat with a shotgun across his thighs. Two more men on horseback followed, keeping an easy distance.

The wagon reached the bend where the tree stood propped on its last inch of holding wood. Sutton gave a whistle like a quail, and my father stepped up to the trunk with a pry bar. With a single motion, he levered the tree loose. It tumbled across the road with a crash that set the horses dancing.

For a few breaths, there was only confusion—shouting, hooves stamping, the driver hauling at the reins.

Sutton rose from his cover, his revolver lifted. "Drop them guns!"

Swinging his shotgun toward the sound, the man in the brown coat jerked and fell backward into the dirt as Cole's shot beat him to the trigger. One of the outriders kicked his horse to flee up the slope, and the other tried to draw his carbine, but Sutton fired, and the man tumbled off the horse like a sack of grain.

I sat frozen, the .32 clutched in my hands, though I knew there was nothing I could do to alter any of it.

Below, my father strode forward, revolver in hand. The driver had dropped the reins and raised his palms in surrender.

"Take it easy," my father said to him. "Just do as you're told."

Sutton and Cole began unloading the strongbox from the wagon bed. I watched them strain from its weight while the horses stamped and tossed their heads in panic.

When the box was clear, my father tossed the driver a small pouch. "For your trouble," he said.

The driver did not move to catch it. The pouch hit the boards and lay there like a dead thing.

"Let's go," Sutton said.

Hoisting the box between them, they grunted under the strain and made for the trees. My father lingered a moment, surveying the bodies in the road. For a time, he did not move. Then he turned away, climbing the slope to where I waited.

We did not speak as we picked our way back to the horses. My father moved ahead of me, and I watched his back with a feeling that was not quite fear and not quite pity, but something of both.

Sutton and Cole had set the strongbox down to catch their breath. Sutton's face was red as cookfire, and he cursed the weight under his breath.

"That's what comes of the railroad paying in coin," he said.

"No time to jaw," my father replied. "Help me get it settled."

They split the strongbox open, packing the coin into bags and loading them in panniers across the mule's back, binding them with three lengths of rope. I stood by, trying not to look at the flecks of blood on Cole's boot.

Sutton wiped his brow. "They'll send riders from Cheyenne when that wagon don't show," he said.

"Then we'd best be out of the canyons by sundown," my father said. He turned to me then. The lines in his face looked deeper than before. "You good?"

Nodding, I clenched my hands tight until the trembling passed.

We set out along the ridge as quiet as we arrived. No one spoke a word, as was the usual. The only noise was that of the mule's labored breath, provoked by its substantial burden.

After an hour, we reached a cut in the slope where a creek ran thin over rust-colored stones. Sutton called a halt.

"Rest the animals," he said. "We can spare ten minutes."

He took out his makings and rolled a paper of tobacco as though he'd just come from the barber chair. Cole washed his hands in the creek while my father paced the clearing, holding his gaze to the trail behind us.

I took off my boot to rub the soreness from my foot. The stone my father had given me was warm now, pressed against my skin all morning.

"You think they'll follow us?" I asked.

Cole looked up, water dripping from his fingers. "They'll have to gather a posse first," he said. "That takes time."

"You ever been to Cheyenne, boy?" Sutton laughed, though there was no humor in it. "They keep deputies there like fleas on a dog. Give it an hour, and they'll be on our trail."

My father came to stand over me. "We will be far from here in an hour."

Dusk came on as we reached the high meadows past the canyon. The woods peeled back, leaving nothing but hills and grass. The mule was flagging under the load, and Sutton insisted we stop to camp.

"We can't push her all night," he said. "She'll founder."

My father looked at the sky. At last, he nodded. "One night," he said. "No more."

Building no fire, we made do with cold biscuits and jerked beef.

When the stars came out, Cole wrapped himself in his blanket and was soon snoring. Sutton sat propped against the mule's pack saddle, his revolver across his knees. My father did not lie down— he just sat, scanning the area. I studied him a bit, thinking a word might come, but none did.

Sometime or other, I must've nodded off. Dreamed I was standing in an orchard. The trees were tall and bent with red fruit. I saw my father standing a ways off, but he paid me no mind no matter how I called out.

Waking to darkness and the movement of boots, I thought the posse had come, but it was only my father, moving among the horses to check the cinches.

"Can't sleep?" I asked.

He did not look up. "Never did rest easy before a ride," he said.

"Do you think they'll find us?"

He paused, his hand on the mare's withers. "They'll try," he said. "But they'll break before we bend."

He came to sit beside me. For the longest time, we said nothing. The night was quiet but for the insects.

"When I was your age," he said at last, "I thought I'd be a farmer. My old man had a patch of ground up near Laramie. Every spring we'd dig the rows and plant seed, and come harvest there'd be enough to get us through. I thought that was how a life ought to be—simple, honest."

"What happened?"

He let go of a sigh. "I was young. I got the notion that there was quicker money to be made. A man tells himself it's just for a while, till he has a stake to buy land of his own. But the while turns into years, and the stake never seems quite enough. Then one day you look around and realize you've spent your best days in the company of men who'd watch you burn just to warm their hands."

At first light, we struck out north across the meadows. In places, elk trails braided through the sedge, and once we passed the bones of a bull picked clean but for a rag of hide over the ribs.

When we paused to water the stock, I helped Cole tighten the mule's straps. His face had gone the color of old wax. He was pressing a hand to his side.

"You hurt bad?" I asked.

He turned his eyes to me. They were the dullest gray I ever saw, like river clay.

"Bullet nicked me yesterday," he said. "Thought it weren't much."

"You tell my father?"

He shook his head. "He's got troubles enough."

Come late afternoon, a stack of clouds pushed up out of the west. By the time we hit the saddle between two peaks, the wind was up, and the rain had started to spit.

"Need shelter," Sutton said. "She won't go much farther in this."

There was no arguing. The mule dragged her feet, ears laid back. That's when we found a break in the rock that opened into a sheltered hollow. A stand of juniper grew there, their trunks twisted like old men's fingers.

We got the animals in under the overhang as the rain set in earnest. Sutton removed the mule's panniers to the ground with a grunt.

Cole sank to a seat against the stone wall. His breath came ragged. My father crouched by him, lifting the edge of his coat.

The shirt beneath was black with blood.

"Damn it," my father whispered.

Cole's eyes fluttered. "Don't waste time," he said. "Soon as this rain lets up, you've got to move."

"You're coming," my father said.

Cole shook his head. "Can't ride. Can't make it."

Sutton stood off, arms folded. "Leave him. If we don't get over the divide before nightfall, we're as good as caught."

My father turned, slow, and looked at him. His face was blank. "You'll hold your tongue," he said, "unless you want me to cut it out."

Sutton looked away. "I seen men die before. Doesn't mean I like watching it."

My father put Cole's revolver in the man's hand and pulled the blanket to his chest. After a time, he stood and brushed at his coat. "Help me get the mule loaded," he said to Sutton.

An hour after making our way along the slope, Sutton drew alongside. "We're near the head of Dry Creek," he said. "If we follow it, it'll take us east of the old stage road. Might shake pursuit."

My father studied the valley below, his face unreadable. "You sure of it?"

Sutton shrugged. "Sure as I am of anything."

My father's hand shifted on the reins. "All right. Take the lead."

Sutton pushed forward, the mule plodded after. My father set our mare to follow, and I held tight to his belt.

Dusk was coming fast when we hit the flats past Dry Creek. The sky looked near spoiled, the clouds thinning out in strips. We kept to a shallow cut that opened at last into a wide basin hemmed in by old cottonwoods. The earth there lay broken and mean, scored with dry runs and sinkholes enough for any man to melt away unseen. Sutton drew up where the ground leveled and swung down.

We did not linger. The mule was near give out, her breath harsh in the stillness. My father took her by the lead rope, and I came behind on foot, tripping now and again over dry roots that veined the basin's hard ground. We made camp under a leaning cottonwood whose branches reached as low as a stooped man. There was no fire. Sutton sat against an embankment on the far side as my father rubbed the mule down, whispering to her in a tone I had never heard him use with any living creature.

I retrieved the stone from my boot and listened to his soothing whispers.

When he finished, he came to sit beside me. "You're tired," he said. I nodded.

He took the stone from my hand and turned it over in his palm.

"When we started," he said, "I thought it was the last time. Just one more stake, enough to set us up right. I told myself it was for you."

His eyes stayed on the stone like he thought it might speak back to him. "But the plain fact is, I had no notion how to quit."

He finally set the stone in my palm again.

We sat in that stillness for a while, the wind whispering through the leaves overhead.

At dawn, we mounted up. The mule stumbled as we set off, but my father spoke to her soft, coaxing her forward. We made for the rise that would take us north into the rough country, where he claimed no lawman would care to follow.

We had not gone a mile when I heard it—a faint drumming behind us like rolling thunder. I twisted to look back. Over the rim of the basin came six riders, their coats lashed by the gallop, rifles and pistols drawn.

Sutton met my father's eyes. "Get him clear of here." He glanced at me. "The boy ain't chose none of this." He then drew his Colt and took toward the riders.

We tore up the slope, earth flying under the mare's hooves. The mule trailed behind, lurching. My father rode at her flank, turning in the saddle to fire.

The first shots cracked past us. I heard a whicker as a bullet split the air by my ear.

Halfway up the rise, the mule faltered, her legs folding. My father dismounted and removed his rifle.

"Ride on!" he called out.

I swung up into the saddle, fighting to draw a good breath.

"Go!"

I looked him square and saw he was in dead earnest.

I kicked the mare on, tears blurring the world. Behind me, I heard the last exchange of gunfire—single reports, spaced out like nails driven into a lid.

When it ended, the silence was worse than the shooting.

I recollect little of those first days on my own. Just tatters of memory linger—slivers of cool shade under scrub junipers, creek water so cold it set my teeth to aching, the smart in my thighs where the saddle rubbed them near raw. Now and then I came upon chokeberries or wild currants, just enough to keep my belly from gnawing itself hollow. The mare grazed what little she could find between stops.

I crossed into Wyoming by way of a low pass. There was no marker to say I'd crossed from one stretch of land to the next, yet I felt it just the same. The ground turned lonelier, wide open in a way that set a man right with how small he truly was.

I kept north, minding that line my father once spoke of, with nothing but his words to steer me. Nights, I scarcely shut my eyes, straining for hoofbeats that never showed.

Come the seventh day, I made the place.

It was edging toward dusk, the sun dropping and shadows running long over the grass. I come over a low swell and saw it then—a house of old green boards, the roof stitched up with scraps of canvas.

I rode down slow, though every part of me wanted to gallop the last stretch. The mare was near done for, her head hung heavy and low. As we drew close to the yard, a dog slunk out from under the porch, letting into a startled bark.

The door opened, and a man stepped onto the stoop with a rifle. He was older than my father by ten years at least, with hair gone to white at the temples. His shoulders were broad still, though age had set its hand on him.

I swung down and stood there, unsure if my legs would hold me. "My name is Eli Maddox," I said, watching his face. "My father was Clay Maddox."

He was silent a long moment. Then he came down the steps, studying my face. "You look like him," he said at last.

I nodded. "He told me," I began, but my throat closed up. "He told me to come here."

He looked past me at the mare. "You better bring her in," he said. "We'll see her fed and watered. You hungry?"

I nodded.

Stepping into the dim room, I smelled woodsmoke and bacon grease. My legs near gave out when the warmth hit me.

Ladling stew into a cracked bowl, he hummed something softly before sitting across from me, elbows on the table. "You can stay," he said. "As long as you need."

I wasn't fit to give a word in reply.

Later, we made our way out the back door, where he led me around the corner of a split-rail fence.

And there it stood.

It rose from a bare spot of grass, trunk thick as a keg, branches stretched wide. Against the dimming light, the leaves looked dark, the fruit pulling down the boughs heavy.

I stepped closer. The apples were just as my father had told it— red-skinned, firm to the touch. I reached up and took one. It came free with a twist.

Taking a bite, I found the tartness bright on my tongue. A moment later, the sweetness rose behind it. Something in my chest burned.

I did not cry. Not quite. But I stood there a long time, chewing slow, thinking of the life my father had chosen . . . and the life he had tried to give me in the end. I also thought of Sutton and the way he'd turned back toward the gunfire without being asked. I reckon he went down facing trouble, same as he lived—but for once, he did not do it for himself.

Taking the stone from my boot, I gently placed it among the tree's exposed roots.

Some men build a life. Some inherit one like a debt.

I figure I'd been handed both.

Anthony's Ride

Johnny D. Boggs

"There's nothing to it. The horse does all the work."

Those words from Ian Rountree rang through Anthony Benton's head, so many dust-clouded miles, so many bone-jarring hours later, as the bay horse carried him across an endless prairie of sagebrush.

His thighs felt raw, while the wind blasted his numb face. His eyes burned. Sand coated his tongue. It even hurt to swallow. Every bone, every organ inside his body seemed to have been rattled loose. He wanted to stop, to sleep, yet he kept riding.

He ought to be feeding horses or mucking stables, not risking his life to deliver letters to people he didn't know, mailed by people he had never met.

This was Ian Rountree's job, but Ian had broken his leg two days earlier. Mr. Kruger, the station master, didn't worry. Jules Koch would fill in, and when a high fever kept Jules in bed, Mr. Kruger merely said, "Coop Richardson will just have to ride to the next station." Only when Coop Richardson galloped to Midway Station just before dawn, he collapsed from the saddle, clutching his stomach.

"Drank bad water." Pain racked Coop's voice. "Sick . . ."

Anthony had been holding the reins to the fresh horse. He constantly marveled over how fast those riders—many no older than he was—could exchange a 20-pound mail sack, called a *mochila*, from one saddle to another. Midway was a home station, where a new rider was supposed to take over, but at relay stations the rider would leap on a new horse with the *mochila* and disappear, often without a chance to say hello or goodbye.

Mr. Kruger was already putting the mail on the fresh horse, yelling at Anthony. "Get on, kid! You got to make this ride!"

"But . . ." Anthony tried, but Mr. Kruger lifted Anthony's leg, guided his foot into a stirrup and shoved him onto the eager-to-run black horse.

"No choice!" Mr. Kruger shouted. "I'm too old and fat, and you center a horse good as anyone. Just get to the relay station. Somebody can take over there."

Mr. Kruger slapped the horse's rump, and Anthony almost fell off immediately. The burst of speed shocked him almost as much as being in the saddle. His hat blew off. He didn't try to catch it, just gripped the reins.

Oh, Anthony could ride. Practically every 14-year-old boy in Nebraska Territory knew how to ride. The Central Overland California and Pike's Peak Express Company—commonly called the Pony Express—had hired him because he knew horses, but he was a stable hand, not a rider.

"This is our most important run ever!" Mr. Kruger yelled. "It's in your hands!"

Ten miles. Anthony could stay on a galloping horse for that long. *Just follow the river, keep your balance. Like Ian told you, let the horse do all the work.*

Ten miles . . .

But the men at Gilman's Station didn't give him a chance to explain, just helped him off one horse and onto another, and he was back in the saddle, riding west, already aching. Sagebrush, miles and hours dashed by.

Three horses later, he thundered toward Fremont Springs, knowing he would find a new rider at the home station, could climb out of the saddle, and collapse. Yet as he neared the station, a bearded man waved his hat frantically, and Anthony realized there were no horses—none!—and no new rider to relieve him.

"Stock's been run off!" the man yelled. "Keep riding! Keep riding!"

Anthony didn't have time to think. He kicked the horse's ribs, and loped back to the trail, riding on . . . and on . . .

"Watch out for Indians," said the boy holding a fresh horse at O'Fallon's Bluff.

Indians!

For five miles, Anthony scanned the horizon. In addition to the *mochila*, riders carried water and a revolver. That was all. But Anthony wasn't a regular rider. He wore no gun. What would he do if he ran into a bunch of Indians? Slowly, he relaxed. Maybe the boy had been teasing him.

Then he saw the brave, two hundred yards off the trail, mounted on a paint horse, gripping a lance in his right hand. Fear gripped Anthony as the Indian turned his horse and began loping west. Although he kept his distance, the Indian was definitely following him.

It's not my mail, Anthony thought. *I'll quit. Next station, I'll just get off this horse and quit.*

He didn't, though. He couldn't. "This is our most important run ever!" Mr. Kruger had said. Sure, Mr. Kruger told every rider that same thing every time on every run. It didn't mean anything. "But he said that to *me*," Anthony said. "*Me*. It's in *my* hands."

Before he reached the next station, the Indian vanished. Yet after Anthony had changed mounts and covered another mile, the Indian was back, following him, a little closer now.

So it went. The Indian would fade into the sagebrush when Anthony neared a relay station, then reappear on the westward trail.

Since Frontz's Station, where he had picked up the bay horse, he hadn't seen the Indian. *Probably got bored*, he thought, but now Anthony faced a new problem. The trail was washed out. He would have to ease his horse into a gully, climb out on the other side. He could do that. Just lean back in the saddle, give the bay plenty of rein. They were halfway down when the horse stumbled. Quickly, Anthony kicked his feet from the stirrups, felt himself catapulted.

He hit hard, sagebrush slashing his arms and face, sand scraping his palms. Groaning, Anthony stumbled to his feet. The horse rolled over, snorted, and rose as Anthony quickly caught the reins. "Easy, boy," he whispered. Kneeling, he checked the bay's legs, and sighed with relief. Bleeding and bruised—just like Anthony—but nothing broken. They could make it to Julesburg, only a mile or so away.

After leading the horse out of the gully, he swung back into the saddle—and saw the Indian.

This time, the brave wasn't alone.

Anthony nudged the bay into a walk, making sure the horse was all right. He eased into a trot, then started loping, riding straight for those twenty Indians—he didn't know what tribe—blocking the trail.

Turn back? No, he wouldn't do that. Besides, he couldn't outrun them, not on this horse. Probably not on any horse. He galloped toward them. Closer . . .

Anthony closed his eyes.

Hearing the yells, he opened his eyes to find the Indians moving out of his way, lifting lances and bows over their heads. Cheering him. Honoring him. Saluting his bravery.

Stunned, he thundered past them and toward the sinking sun.

Ahead of him lay Julesburg Station. He saw a rider and horse ready to take the *mochila*. Anthony had done it. He had covered 150 miles, twice the distance of a normal run.

Everybody would ask how a stable hand had been able to make such a hard ride. As the bay carried him the last few yards, Anthony found his answer:

"There's nothing to it. The horse does all the work."

Eddie and the Stranger

Vonn McKee

Sheriff "Fat Jack" Jennings didn't even look up from his newspaper when two cracks of gunfire echoed from up the street. The man seldom heaved himself out of his chair unless things got truly ugly. It was said there'd been seventy-two murders in Pioche, Nevada, before the first death by natural causes occurred, and already the cemetery was the fastest growing part of town.

Pioche was young and cocky, swarming with glinty-eyed speculators who laid claim to swaths of Treasure Hill outside town, hoping for a piece of the silver mining action. For every investor, there were hundreds of threadbare laborers, risking their lives in the creaky shafts underneath the mountain for a dollar or two a day. Common thieves, claim jumpers, and general troublemakers rounded out the town's population.

Hearing three more gunshots, Fat Jack huffed and slapped the paper on the desk. He shoved his chair back. "Spence, I s'pose we'd better go check on things. Sounds close. Lynch's Saloon maybe."

Deputy Spencer Melton had just finished passing out plates of cabbage and beans to the inmates. The Pioche jail hadn't been empty since the day it was built. "Well, if there's any left standing, I don't know where we'll put 'em," he said, hanging up the oversized key ring.

"Just shoot 'em. That's my creed."

Indeed, Fat Jack had lead-poisoned plenty of men since he took office. And he had taken bribes from plenty others who could buy their way out of his jail. He was called "Fat Jack" for the bulk of his wallet, and not necessarily his middle age paunch.

"You'd think these hell raisers would eventually all shoot each other dead," said Spence, grabbing his hat. "Wouldn't be nobody left to bury 'em, I guess."

"Wouldn't that be nice?" said Fat Jack, slamming the door behind them.

The sheriff guessed right. Two men carried a blood-soaked body, boots first, through the doors of Lynch's Saloon and crossed the crowded street to the undertaker's office. A man, surrounded by a ragtag group of miners, sat on the edge of the boardwalk with his head in his hands.

"Who's the shooter?" Fat Jack asked, to nobody in particular.

"Him," said John Lynch from the doorway, pointing to the hunched figure on the boardwalk. The saloon owner looked disgusted, maybe even a little pale. "The two of 'em got in a tussle over something. Couldn't hear what about. They'd had a few . . . well, too many, I reckon. This one turned mad out of his head. Grabbed somebody's pistol and shot the fellow twice in the face. Then . . ." Lynch wiped his brow and blew out a deep breath. "Then he stood over the man, who was done dead, for sure. Shot him a few more times square in the chest. Out of control, he was. Just kept shooting. Biggest damn mess I ever saw. And I've seen some." Lynch motioned over his shoulder. "How the hell I'll get that floor cleaned up, I don't know. Then there's the bullet holes."

Fat Jack and Spence stood at each side of the crazed killer, who was no more than a small heap.

"What's your name?" Fat Jack grabbed the man's shoulder and straightened him up so he could see his face. He was a miner, slightly built—probably a Basque, wearing a shabby flat-crowned hat. His face, coat, and overalls were embedded with dark reddish mine dust. His eyes were squeezed shut and he didn't answer.

"Maybe he don't speak English," said Spence, turning to the other miners. "Who is this fella? Somebody speak up."

The laborers looked sorrowful. Finally, one said, "That's Eddie. He would not . . . it is not like him to do this kind of thing."

"I did *not* . . ." The quavering, pitiful protest came from Eddie. "I did not . . . I did not," he continued weakly. His small grimy face was now streaked with tears.

"Well, Shorty, a saloon full of men say you did." Fat Jack grabbed Eddie's arm and dragged him to a standing position. The miner couldn't have stood more than five feet tall. "Keep your gun on him, Spence. He looks like a tough one."

Fat Jack grinned, revealing a big gap between his front teeth. The sheriff somehow managed to maintain a frown, even when smiling.

Edarto Luken—or Eddie—was by far the quietest prisoner in the Pioche jail, except for when he had nightmares. The first night, he woke up the whole place with his thrashing and babbling.

It would be a pretty cut and dried conviction, Fat Jack thought, although it would be over a week before the next court date. The sheriff was always a little peeved when he had to follow legal procedures. If the little miner had put up a fight, there would have been grounds for putting a bullet in him and ending the matter.

"What came over you, Eddie, that you went and killed a man?" asked Fat Jack, locking up a cell after the release of a sobered up drunk. Eddie had a cell of his own, at Deputy Spence's request. He didn't think the little man would last long with any one of the current cellmates.

Eddie sat on his narrow bunk. He'd washed up—his face, at least—and Fat Jack guessed him to be about twenty. "Sheriff, I did not commit this terrible act."

"Yeah, you keep saying that. If you didn't, then you wanna tell me who did? You were the only one standing over that fella with a gun in your hand."

Eddie rose and walked to the cell door. He wrapped his fingers around the bars and looked imploringly at the sheriff. "Sheriff, I will be needing—what do you call? One who argues the law." Fat Jack cocked an eyebrow.

"A lawyer? You wanna get a lawyer? You think you got a prayer of getting off with murder?"

"You must believe me. I was not the one responsible! It was . . . someone else."

"And just who might that be?" The sheriff was interested to see where this was going. Eddie swallowed hard.

"It is hard to explain. Sheriff, I really am not a man who would do this. You may ask anyone at the mines."

The sheriff recalled hearing the miners outside the saloon saying that very thing. Surely, Eddie did not believe he was innocent! He let the man keep talking.

"I do not myself touch strong drink. I do not believe in harming another. I am a religious man, Sheriff Jennings."

Fat Jack was getting impatient with the little man. "Five shots, you liar. At close range. That man's face and chest were shot to a pulp when you got through with him."

Eddie buried his face in his dirty sleeve, choking back sobs. After a minute, he looked Sheriff Fat Jack Jennings straight in the eye. "I am not the one who fired the shots. It was . . . it was the stranger."

Fat Jack had heard a lot of wild tales. A man behind bars would say just about anything to save his hide. This was a new one. "The stranger? Didn't hear anybody mention a stranger."

Eddie gripped the bars again and wedged his face between them. "The stranger is a terrible man. He has done terrible things. Things I would never do. I swear this to you," said Eddie, placing a hand over his heart, in oath.

"And where do you reckon this stranger is now?" Fat Jack was playing along. A look of pure misery washed over Eddie's face. He slowly moved his hand from the left side of his chest to the right.

"He is here," he said.

The sky outside the sheriff's window was gray with the approaching dawn. Water for coffee heated in a pot on the wood stove.

"Gawdamighty, sheriff. Can't you do something about this little Turk, or whatever he is? It's hard enough to sleep on a board without some fool jabbering in his sleep." Hobie Smith was a frequent guest at the Pioche jail, due to his love of a good brawl. He gingerly rubbed a swollen eye with his big paw.

Fat Jack was good and tired of Eddie's nightmares and the complaints from the other prisoners. He grabbed a fire poker and stalked to the back, then slammed the poker a couple of times against the bars of Eddie's cell. "Wake up! Enough of that caterwauling!"

Eddie jumped up from his bunk and looked around wildly. Like a storm cloud swallowing the sun, his face turned angry and his eyes sparked hate. He rushed to the cell door and poked his skinny arms through the bars, reaching to grab Fat Jack by the throat. His small hands were locked into rigid claws. "Get over here, you coward! I'll squeeze your fat neck to mush."

Fat Jack took a step back, the iron poker hanging forgotten in his hand. "Eddie?"

Eddie strained to get a grip on the sheriff. His hair stuck up in messy spikes, framing his frightful countenance. Profanities in at least two languages spewed from his mouth. Apart from Eddie's tirade, the jail was dead silent. Fat Jack's brow furrowed as he considered his next move. Eddie continued to claw the air between them. Finally, the sheriff propped the poker against the wall behind him. He lowered his head and charged toward the cell door, with his big fist drawn back. He connected neatly with the bottom half of Eddie's face, but not before the miner grabbed his shirt. The jail echoed with the sounds of ripping fabric, the smack of the punch and Eddie's body sprawling heavily onto the bunk behind him. He lay motionless, eyes closed.

Fat Jack picked up the poker and walked back to his office. He sank into his chair, waiting for his heart to slow down. On the stove, the coffee water boiled vigorously. Spence came in the door, ready for breakfast duty. He froze when he saw Fat Jack sitting like a statue, shirt ripped, staring at the pot clattering on the stovetop.

"You all right, chief?"

Doctor William Kent sat beside Sheriff Jennings at the Capitol Saloon bar. He was not a frequent patron at the Capitol, or any saloon, but Fat Jack invited him there to ask his opinion on something.

"It's the damndest thing I ever witnessed." Fat Jack wiped the beer foam from his mustache and clunked the empty glass onto the counter.

"For two days now, this Eddie fella has been switching back between being a meek little lamb to a bull madder than hell. I can't wait to get him out of my jail. When he's quieted down, he swears his other half should be charged with the murder. Have you heard of such? Says *the stranger*, as he calls him, makes him commit acts against his will . . . that ain't part of his genuine nature." Fat Jack shook his head in amazement and ordered another drink.

Doctor Kent's brown eyes were alive with interest. "Now isn't that something?"

"He got worse day before yesterday. He was in the middle of a nightmare, twisting around and hollering. I just meant to wake him up by banging on the door, but he jumped up ready to choke me. Maybe tear me to pieces. Now it's like having two different men in the cell at different times. He's Eddie for a few hours, then that *stranger* all of a sudden. They's something wrong with that boy, that's for damn sure. You got any idea what it might be?"

"That is truly puzzling," said Doctor Kent, rubbing his chin, then running a finger around the rim of the beer glass.

"It does remind me . . . well, have you ever heard of Doctor Benedict Morel, Sheriff?"

"Nope. Was he an Englishman, like you?"

"French, actually. I read some of his papers while I was studying medicine. Morel observed patients in asylums who exhibited similar behaviors."

"Well, maybe Eddie was one of 'em."

"It's doubtful. His findings were from studies conducted over twenty years ago."

"Hmm. Before Eddie was born. And what did this Morel fella make of it?"

The doctor pressed a finger to his temple, conjuring a memory. "Blast it, what was that term? Morel had observed declining mental capacity in older patients but this was a phenomenon he saw in younger ones. Dem . . . ah! *Démence précoce*! That's it!"

"Oh, well, I could have told you that." Fat Jack laughed at his own joke. He was fast losing interest in the discussion and waved at someone across the room.

"At any rate, it means *precocious dementia*. Not terribly specific but at least he understood that it was a unique disease of the mind. Sheriff, would it be all right if I observed Mister. . .what did you say his name is?"

"Luken. Edarto Luken. Known as Eddie . . . or the stranger. Depending on the time of day, I reckon."

Doctor Kent shook the sheriff's hand. "I'll drop by in the morning. Thank you for tonight's invitation."

As the doctor left the saloon, Fat Jack realized the man hadn't even touched his beer. "Well, no use in it going to waste." He slid the glass over and raised it to his lips.

At Doctor Kent's request, the sheriff again awakened the fitfully sleeping Eddie. However, he only called out his name rather than using the poker to arouse him. He wasn't sure his heart was up to another confrontation, even if he knew it might be coming. Eddie tumbled out of the bunk, irritated, but at least not bent on murder.

He curled his lip and said, "What do you want with me?"

Fat Jack whispered to Doctor Kent, "Yeah, be careful, Doc. This here is the stranger we're talking to. I can tell by his eyes."

After fifteen minutes of interrogation, Eddie said, "I've had enough of your questions, limey." So far, he'd given mostly rude responses.

"One more, if you'll allow me. Your mother and father . . . did they have any . . . peculiarities? Unusual moods?"

The stranger that was Eddie looked suddenly stricken. Fat Jack thought the man was about to break down and cry.

"Mother . . ." he mumbled. "My mother." His lower lip trembled and, sure enough, tears welled up. Before Fat Jack and Doctor Kent's eyes, his demeanor changed. His hands slid down the bars and he seemed to melt into a frail child crouched on the floor. When he looked up, he wore the same expression as when he'd been arrested—sorrowful, crushed.

"I am so terribly sorry, sheriff. And you . . . are you a doctor? You look like one."

Hiram Newkirk stopped outside the sheriff's office to adjust his collar and flatten his hair on top for the tenth time. His wiry strawberry hair was a constant bother. Suits never hung well on his gangly frame and, no matter how he fiddled, his tie and Adam's apple were always at odds. At least, no one judged his fashion sense harshly here in the west. If anyone looked askance, it was solely because he was wearing a suit in the first place. He collected his thoughts and opened the door.

"Sheriff Jennings? I'm the lawyer you sent for. Well, not the one you sent for precisely but . . . Mister Hodge is away in California. I'm Hiram Newkirk."

Fat Jack sized up the tall, awkward young man. "Obliged," he said, shaking hands. "You, uh, new in town?"

"I am, sir. Not so new. I've been here for three months. From Indiana."

"Might've seen you at the courthouse then. Well, three months. You're a regular old-timer, by mining town standards anyhow. You're taking some heat off of Hodge, are you? There's lawsuits flying around this town like locusts."

"I am aware of that. I've handled a dozen claim disputes already. Mister Hodge has kept me busy. But you wanted to speak to me about representing someone in a murder case?"

"Yes, murder. It would be a simple thing, what with having several witnesses. But, well, it's taken a peculiar turn. Ah! Doc Kent just rode up. Maybe he'd better explain it."

"So you're really going to court today and arguing that Eddie can't be held responsible for the actions of another part of who he is? This is making my head hurt." Fat Jack plucked the key ring off the hook and turned to Hiram Newkirk and Doctor Kent, who both looked as excited as school boys.

"Yes, sheriff. It sounds preposterous but if you think of it logically, it makes perfect sense," said the doctor. Mister Luken has a distinct and separate entity within himself who seems to surface when he is under strain. I have interviewed both of these 'persons,' if you will, and found them to have remarkably opposite values and character traits."

"All right, Doc. Save it for court. And you think you can pull this off, Newkirk?"

The lawyer nodded. "I'm looking forward to making the case. Why, there's never been such an argument presented in court. We could very well set a precedent. In fact, we shall do so simply by bringing it before a judge, whether we win or lose."

"Well, winning or losing when you're the same person doesn't sound like good odds to me. What are they gonna do? Hang half of him?" Fat Jack puffed out his chest, sure that he'd made a valid point.

Newkirk frowned. "No, sheriff, that's not my strategy. I hope to convince the judge to absolve Mister Luken from the crime and commit him to a doctor's care. This, per the M'Naghton Rule of 1843, which states *'at the time of the committing of the act, the party accused was laboring under such a defect of reason, from disease of the mind, as not to know the nature and quality of the act he was doing; or if he did know it, that he did not know he was doing what was wrong.'"*

Fat Jack rolled his eyes. "You lawyers. Spence! Go get Eddie and take him to the courthouse. The three of us will be there in a few minutes."

Spence fetched Eddie and fastened a manacle onto the prisoner's narrow wrists, which were crossed behind his back. The heavy iron bands were made for much bigger men, and the weight of them made Eddie straighten as they pulled down on his arms. The deputy herded Eddie out of the sheriff's office and through the door. The miner looked exhausted. He had intentionally kept himself awake to avoid slipping into the stranger's terrifying grasp.

Spence didn't hold out much hope for the prisoner's chances in court. The judge was an irritable man, and generally ruled on the harsher side of the book. Spence felt a pang of pity.

"We're just walking to the courthouse and going in the front door, Eddie. Looky here what a beautiful day we got." He usually transported prisoners through the back entrance that led directly to the courthouse, but the door and frame were being painted. Somehow the job required two boys, each with a bucket and brush. It was nearly eight thirty, and the morning ore train whistle drifted down the street, three short blasts as it backed up to receive a dozen cars of raw ore. After chugging twenty miles to Bullionville, it would return to Pioche at the end of the day.

Spence held open the front door. Eddie trudged ahead, shoulders drooped. They passed a fence with a scraggly rose bush entwined in its pickets. Eddie stopped and bent over to sniff one of the forlorn blossoms, then smiled. Spence cleared his throat. "Let's move on."

A crowd had gathered in front of the courthouse, waiting for admittance. News of Eddie's trial had attracted a lot of local interest. Spence motioned for the onlookers to step back and let them pass.

Later, the deputy would say the movement was like that of a rabbit bursting from under a bush. With one quick shrug, Eddie pulled one of his hands free from the too-large manacle, and broke into a sudden, blurred flight, skirting the crowd of people and bolting across the street. He vanished between two buildings and Spence took off in pursuit just as the ore train blasted twice and its wheels began moving forward. Fat Jack's voice boomed from behind. "He's headed for the train! Catch him, Spence! Shoot him!"

The deputy caught glimpses of Eddie as he darted low and fast from one block to the next. He angled toward the edge of town, as if he meant to intercept the train as it gained momentum and left Pioche. When Spence ran past the livery at the end of the street, he saw Eddie in the clear. He had shaken loose of the other iron cuff and slung the manacle aside. The engine was picking up speed, its pistons chugging faster and faster. Soon, it would be in the open and Eddie would be up-track to meet it with time to spare.

"Eddie!" Spence, still running, yelled over the sound of the approaching train. He was sure the miner couldn't hear him but he didn't want to shoot him in the back without a warning. Eddie reached the edge of the railroad bed and turned around. He looked directly at Spence, who was only fifty feet away, holding a Colt at arm's length. They stared at each other for several seconds as the engine rounded the building and approached, steam billowing from its stack. The deputy had a clear shot and they both knew it.

Spence aimed high on the torso and thumbed the hammer. Another second passed, and another. Fat Jack would be catching up soon. Eddie didn't move even a finger—just kept staring. Spence began lowering the revolver, inch by inch, and slowly uncocked the gun. Standing ten feet from the tracks, Eddie held up a hand in solemn thanks.

The space between Eddie and the train narrowed. Spence still held the Colt straight down at his side, waiting for the miner to crouch and jump onto a passing ore car when the time came. Instead, Eddie scrambled up onto the tracks just before the engine got there. He slowly laid himself down and stretched his body along the top of the rail farthest away, face up, hands and arms spread wide. The engineer sounded the steam whistle frantically.

"No! Eddie, no!" Spence shouted, and began running toward the tracks, knowing he couldn't reach Eddie before the engine did. The ore train's brakes screamed against the rails, but too late to make any difference. A wall of hot air and dust pushed Spence back as the the train thundered by.

Doctor Kent joined Fat Jack at a corner table in the Capitol Saloon. It was midafternoon and the place was quiet. "Well, Sheriff. So ends the remarkable story of Edarto Luken."

"Yep. Didn't end the way anybody figured. Crazy son of a gun. Knew I shoulda shot him first off. Might've spared him some misery."

Both men stared at the table, coming to grips with the aftermath of Eddie's last act. They would not soon forget the horrendous image. The ore train had accomplished what Eddie intended–rendering him, more or less, in half. For the first and final time, he had separated himself from the stranger.

"I hope he finds peace in the afterworld," said Doctor Kent. "Poor chap deserves it."

Fat Jack nodded. "I reckon he does at that. Say, I bought you a beer. You gonna drink it this time?"

The doctor smiled sadly. "Yes, I believe I shall. To Eddie. . ."

Fat Jack clinked his beer against the doctor's. "Yeah. To Eddie."

Fire Mountain

Michael Zimmer

Chapter One

Pineview was bustling.

Halting his mount at the head of the town's broad main street, Buck McCready eyed the scurrying townspeople with the same kind of wonder he'd once held for circus sideshows, where bearded women and tattooed men invited the guileless to step closer and not be afraid. He recalled that the paintings on the sideshow tent's wall had promised even more exciting oddities and frightening displays inside.

There wasn't much mystery about what had the citizens of Pineview worked up. If the smell of smoke and the gray pall mantling the valley weren't enough to convince a person there was something evil on the prowl, then surely the swirling bits of floating ash would. Destruction was on its way, and it was coming with a vengeance.

The last time Buck had ridden through Pineview, the place had been little more than a raw settlement scratched out along the bank of a swift-flowing stream of the same unimaginative name. Back then, Pineview Creek, with its lush spring grass, brilliant wildflowers, and towering ponderosa pines darkening the mountain slopes to either side, had seemed like a little chunk of paradise broken off and fallen to earth.

He'd been heading north then, bound for Oregon and Washington Territory. Now he was on his way back south, with no inclination to tarry longer than it would take to buy a few supplies to see him down the trail. After that, he'd be gone. Or at least that was his intention.

Sitting his mule at the head of the street, Buck contemplated the changes that had taken place since he'd last been through here. The street had lost its creekside meander and now ran in a straight shot south to north, and there was what looked like a thriving business district at its southern terminus. Buildings that had once been cramped and dark—solid log walls with sod roofs and dirt floors—had been replaced with more welcoming structures of planed lumber, glass windows, and roofs of tin and tar, while brightly colored signs advertised everything from beer to boots, cigars and stoves. Several of the larger establishments had second floors, and a few that didn't sported false fronts to perpetuate an appearance of size and prosperity.

There was a residential district now, too, with a scattering of flower beds, picket fences, and neat front porches. A few of those were also two-storied.

But of all the difference that had sprung up in Pineview since Buck's last visit, none stood out more prominently than what lay at the far end of the street, where a line of passenger cars and boxcars were queued up behind a panting locomotive that was adding its own black coil of smoke to an already badly smudged sky. The train's depot seemed to be the hub of most of the activity, although Buck couldn't tell whether the chaos there stemmed from arrivals or departures.

Beyond the depot and the mouth of Pineview Canyon, the broad Snake River Plain stretched like a tan blanket in the arid heat of late September, its sky the same leaden color as the town's.

Tapping heels to the ribs of the black mule he called Zeke, Buck rode into town. He dismounted at a mercantile on the west side of the street and looped his reins over the rail. The store's double front doors were propped open, and men and women were hustling through them in a near frenetic confusion. Some, upon exiting, headed for the depot with their purchases clutched tightly in their arms. Others tossed their goods into the backs of carriages, traps, and buckboards assembled in the street. One enterprising fellow left the store pushing a wheelbarrow piled high with merchandise and immediately turned south to make his wobbly trek toward the waiting train.

Catching the eye of a burly man in a corduroy cap leaving the store with a forty-pound sack of flour balanced over one shoulder, Buck said, "What's all the commotion about, friend?"

The guy stopped with an impatient scowl and looked him up and down, as if gauging his worth in time. Buck had a fair idea of the image he presented—a lean, weathered stranger in his early thirties, wearing wool trousers, low-heeled boots, and a faded blue shirt. Buck's hat was wide-brimmed and round-crowned, his revolver a converted Army Colt in .44; he carried a heavy-bladed hunting knife on his left hip, and had a well-oiled bullwhip tied to his saddle. The coiled whip marked him as a muleskinner; the worn-down heels of his boots and sweat-stained hat spoke of a drifter. But drifting didn't stifle a man's curiosity. Motioning toward the mass of people clogging the boardwalk and spilling into the street, Buck repeated his question.

"What's it about?" the man in the cap echoed incredulously. "What do you think it's about?" He flung an arm behind him, toward the store, although Buck understood he meant what lay beyond the building, to the west. "Ain't you got eyes?"

"That fire is still a long ways off."

"The hell it is," the burly man retorted, and brushed past Buck to join the exodus in the street.

Standing next to the mercantile's door, a bald man wearing sleeve garters and a cotton apron reaching from shoulder to shinbone lowered a clipboard. "It's not as far away as you might think," he said, then cocked his head quizzically. "Don't I know you from somewhere?"

"I came through here a few years ago."

"No, it wouldn't have been that. I didn't show up myself until a year ago last spring, just before they opened the Crown."

"The Crown?"

The storekeeper pointed past him, and Buck followed the line of his finger to the mountain range that dominated the east side of the valley. Its slopes were dark with pines, its craggy peaks nearly lost in the smoky haze.

"The Crown Mine, up over the top of those mountains," the storekeeper elaborated, then shrugged and added, "You do remind me of someone, though. But what Fred said about the fire is true enough."

"Fred? That the guy with the sack of flour on his shoulder."

"It is. The town's been in an uproar ever since the telegraph from Boise went dead last night, likely from the fire. Then the OSL . . ." he tipped his head toward the chuffing locomotive, the markings of the Oregon Short Line Railroad prominently displayed on the tender ". . . barely made it through from the west this morning. The engineer said the fire's already scorched the bridge over Breakwater Canyon. The conductor says there won't be any more rail traffic until it's repaired."

"That could take a while."

"A couple of weeks," the storekeeper agreed. "Meanwhile, with the telegraph down and the last train leaving at sundown, folks have caught themselves a serious case of herd fever. It's like when a cow spooks at its own shadow, and the rest of the bunch takes off without knowing why they're running."

"I've seen it," Buck said.

"Folks want a seat on that train, especially those who don't own a business or have livestock to take care of. A lot of them are buying what they think they'll need to wait out the flames."

"Must be good for business."

"It is. I've got two clerks and my wife trying to keep up. If this continues, I'll be cleaned out of by sundown."

"Are you planning on leaving with the others then?"

"No, although I bought tickets for my wife and kids to leave." He shrugged. "I might regret it, but I intend to stay and keep an eye on the store. Some folks are claiming all of western Idaho is burning, which isn't all that hard to believe with the amount of smoke that's been pouring through here the past week, but if the Breakwater Bridge is already torched, that means the fire could be moving well to the north of us."

"It's a gamble," Buck said, turning his face to the southerly breeze.

"So is opening a store in a mining town," the merchant replied. Then he turned away when someone from inside called: *Felix*. "I need to see what this is about," he said, and disappeared into the mercantile.

Buck followed more slowly, strolling through the market's narrow aisles to find what he thought he'd need to see him down the trail. He suffered only a single elbow to his ribs from an impatient shopper—a woman with gray hair and poorly fitted dentures—when they both reached for the last box of baking soda on a nearly empty shelf. Allowing her the purchase, he settled for some dried apples, two pounds of flour, another of coffee, and a quarter of a sugar-cured ham. He took his supplies to the counter, and while waiting for a clerk, noticed a jar of peppermint candy sitting on the counter. Succumbing to impulse, he added a pair of red and white sticks to his selection.

In time a sandy-haired clerk with a sullen curl to his lip arrived to accept Buck's money, then loosely wrap his purchases in a piece of brown butcher's paper that he tied off with a cord and shoved back across the counter before moving on to the next customer. Buck put the kid's rudeness down to the tight press of demanding shoppers and took his package outside. He stowed everything except the peppermint in his saddlebags, then stuck one of the sticks in a corner of his mouth like a slim, colorful cigar, and broke the other into two pieces that he offered, one at a time, to his mule. Being a longtime fan of anything sweet, Zeke accepted the confectionery without hesitation. Buck was watching him chew the second piece when a voice rang out behind him.

"By damn, now I know who you are."

He turned to find the storekeeper—Felix—standing on the boardwalk with his clipboard still in hand. He came over with an expansive grin.

"Still riding that black mule, too."

"You say you know me?"

"Sure, I know you. Buck McCready, right?"

"That's what I've been told."

"I'm Felix Payne. I used to run a little grocery on Montana Street, down in Corinne."

Buck nodded and relaxed. Felix was talking about Corinne, Utah Territory, where freight used to be offloaded from the Transcontinental Railroad and shipped north into Montana by wagon. "Yeah, I remember your place. Payne's Groceries."

"And you worked for Jock Kavanaugh's Box-K. You were a wagon master, if I remember right."

"Toward the end," Buck acknowledged.

"They said you were one of the best mule men in the mountains."

"Well, I wouldn't believe everything I heard from that pack of horse thieves in Corinne. They were notorious truth stretchers, especially after a couple of beers."

"And if they're in town . . . ."

". . . they've had a couple of beers," Buck finished for him, and they both laughed at the memory. Then Felix's expression sobered.

"What brings you to Pineview, Buck?"

"Just passing through."

"You wouldn't be looking for a job, would you?"

Buck's gaze shifted briefly to the store, then away. "I reckon not."

"I don't mean inside. The fact is, I need a good mule man, and they're scarce in these parts."

"What's the job?" Buck asked, interested now that Payne had mentioned working with mules.

"Come on inside. This isn't something I want the whole town to hear."

Intrigued, Buck bit off the end of his peppermint and handed what was left to Zeke. Then he followed Felix inside. They skirted the line of customers waiting at the counter and walked to the rear of the store. Buck ignored the surly clerk's puzzled stare as they passed. Felix led him to a small office with a desk and a couple of chairs, then on through that to a large storeroom. A heavy loading dock door on their left had been rolled open to allow some light inside, but save for a small mountain of oilcloth-covered goods stacked against the rear wall, the cavernous warehouse looked almost empty. An older man sat in a chair next to the supplies, a stubby clay pipe jutting from his nest of whiskers like a tobacco-stained hatchling. Felix's face darkened when he saw the pipe.

"Damnation, Wallis, get that pipe out of here!"

The older man eyed Felix for a moment, then stood and ambled outside.

Felix glanced at Buck and shook his head. "Damn fool," he muttered.

"Was that Cam Wallis?"

"You know him?"

"Used to. He was a good muleskinner in his day, until a wagon slipped off its jack while he was greasing the hub and pinned him against the side of a barn. I guess it busted him up pretty bad."

"That's more or less what he told me," Felix said. "He's handy around livestock, but a poor watchman."

"I haven't seen him in years. Last I heard, he was using whiskey to dull the pain."

"It's addled his thinking, if you ask me. He should know better than to smoke in a warehouse, especially one that's been used to store wheat and oats. It doesn't take but a spark to start a fire in grain dust."

Buck nodded, but his attention had already returned to the piles of merchandise Wallis had been guarding. "Is that why you brought me here?"

"It is." Felix walked over to the stacks and peeled back a ten-foot square of oilcloth. Underneath were several hundred pounds of flour and corn meal in stenciled forty-pound sacks. "These are supplies I've contracted to deliver to the Crown Mine."

Recalling the storekeeper's earlier description, Buck hooked a thumb over his shoulder, in the direction of the mountains east of town.

Felix nodded. "They call it the Crown Range now, named after the mine."

"How far away is it?"

"Not too far as the crow flies."

"And with a pack mule?"

"Three days with normal loads and a full crew. It'll probably take you four, if you're interested."

Bucked eyed the rows of supplies. "How much of this goes?"

"All of it. Right at two and a half tons."

"That's more than a one-man job, Mr. Payne."

"I can get you a couple of men, but I need a lead packer, someone who knows freight and mules, and how to get a job done. No one in Corinne has forgotten how you took Jock's freight wagons through to Virginia City, and won the old man his contract, too."

Buck was silent a moment, reliving the incident. His old mentor, Mason Campbell—the man who had rescued Buck from the Sioux, then raised him as his own—was supposed to lead that wagon train. But someone had gunned Mase down on a deserted Utah street just days before the outfit was scheduled to pull out for the Montana gold fields. With a lucrative freight-hauling contract riding on the Kavanaugh train reaching the rowdy mining camp of Virginia City before its competitor, Jock offered the position of wagon master to Buck. He'd almost turned it down in his determination to find Mase's killer. But he'd also made a commitment to Jock's Box-K, and in Mase's honor, he'd accepted the challenge. It wasn't until they were underway that Buck learned there was a saboteur among his crew, and that a gunman had been hired to stop him—the same gunman who had killed Mase in Corinne.*

"What about it, Buck?" Felix asked, pulling him out of his thoughts. "Are you interested?"

After a pause, Buck said, "What's the pay?"

[*_The Long Hitch_, by Michael Zimmer]

"Two hundred dollars." Felix smiled at Buck's reaction. "It's a lot of money, I'll grant you, but there's a lot riding on it, too. The fact is, I've got a situation similar to what Jock had in Utah, although this isn't a race so much as a commitment."

"What kind of a commitment?"

"I guaranteed the Crown Mine that I could deliver their goods on a monthly basis. There were a couple of other outfits that wanted the contract, but I got it. So far, I've been able to fulfill my end of the agreement, but with that damned wildfire burning so close, people are panicking. The men I'd normally use to haul these supplies to the Crown have left town. They said they didn't want to get caught up there if the fire burns that far."

"I can't say that I blame them."

"That may be, but it's my tail caught in a trap if I can't deliver these goods when promised."

"When are they due?"

"October first . . . six days from now."

"It puts you in a tight spot," Buck acknowledged.

"That's why it's worth two hundred dollars to me. It's not just these supplies that are at stake, but my contract with the Crown for next year if I don't meet my obligations this year. Sooner or later, if the mine keeps producing, they'll build a road up there, and then I'll be out of the picture. Like they say, Buck, you've got to make hay while the sun is shining."

"And they wouldn't care if the fire caught your mules and men on the trail."

It wasn't a question. Felix didn't take it as one. "All that matters to men like that is that their supplies are delivered on time."

"What about you, Mr. Payne?" Buck asked. "Would it matter to you?"

"Of course it'd matter. I wouldn't send men out if I didn't think they could make it. But if that fire has already burned along the Breakwater, then it could easily swing miles north of here."

"Or not?"

"Or not," he agreed. "If there weren't risks involved, Buck, I wouldn't be offering you two hundred dollars for half a week's labor."

"You said you could get me a couple of men?"

"I can get you two more."

"Then I'll be leading a string myself. Six thousand pounds of cargo . . ." He did the calculations in his mind, then whistled softly. "Thirty mules, meaning ten pack animals apiece. That'd be a tough job in open country, let alone over mountain passes and through thick forests." He glanced to the loading dock, where a tendril of blue smoke from Cam Wallis's pipe curled past the door. "Is he one of the men you had in mind?"

"He is, and I'm afraid you won't have thirty head, either. Right now I've got twenty-two mules under contract, plus a couple of Indian ponies for my packers to ride. I might find a few more head from people wanting to leave on the evening train, but I wouldn't count on thirty."

"I know Cam's reputation. What about the other man? How much experience does he have?"

Felix seemed relieved by the question. "He's a good man. You won't have any trouble there." He paused for only a second. "Will you do it?"

"No, not for two hundred, but I'll do it for five."

"Five hun—!" Felix's head rocked back as if he'd been punched in the nose. "Damnation, Buck, that's . . . ." His words trailed off. "Hell, I guess you've got my back to the wall. All right, five hundred dollars."

"And two hundred for each man."

Felix's lips thinned. For a moment, Buck thought he was going to refuse. He wasn't sure that wouldn't be the smarter move, all things considered. But Felix had pretty well summed up his situation when he acknowledged his back was to a wall. Besides, they both knew the money he'd spend on packers this trip would be more than offset by a new contract next summer.

"All right, it's a deal," he grated.

Buck nodded, but he didn't smile. Neither did Felix Payne. The two men shook hands solemnly, and Felix said, "Come into my office. I'll show you a map to the Crown."

Chapter Two

Tentative knocking irritated Anton Luce. In his opinion, it reflected a timid character, and the distinct likelihood of unsatisfactory results. Unfortunately, Anton didn't always have the option of picking the best men for a job.

He gazed curiously at the door separating his office from the saloon's upstairs hallway, then resolutely went back to filling out his order for the upcoming winter. What he'd need most was whiskey and beer, but a couple of cases of cheap cigars and a few more of pickled eggs and jellied pig's feet would help keep his customers salted down and thirsty once the deep snows of central Idaho put a stop to their restless search for gold.

Unlike most of the sheep fleeing town, Anton Luce had no intention of abandoning his livelihood. Basing his decision on what the engineer from the Oregon Short Line had reported earlier, he judged the odds were in favor of the forest fire going well to the north of Pineview, maybe even skirting the valley altogether.

His pen ceased its brittle scratching as a taut smile curled his lips upward. Although he was counting on the fire missing the town, he was equally certain there would be a few exceptions—little flare-ups here and there to conveniently eliminate some of the competition.

Leaning back in his chair, Anton had to marvel at the good luck some errant lightning strike or careless campfire had dropped in his lap. Pineview had four saloons. Taking out three of them would put his own High Dollar Emporium in the enviable position of supplying the alcohol and gambling needs for a sizable swath of Central Idaho for the rest of the winter. And on top of that, he'd made sure Felix Payne wouldn't find enough men to fulfill his obligation to the Crown Mine—which was going to leave Luce's Fast Freight and Express next in line for the following season's contract.

Just thinking about the possibilities made Anton want to laugh, but when the knock came again, even more diffident than before, his smile vanished. He'd forgotten for a moment that only fools placed their trust in luck, and that sooner or later good fortune always found a way to spin around and bite a man on the ass.

He eyed the closed door speculatively for a moment, then slid the top drawer of his desk partially open to expose the butt of a four-barreled Sharps pistol. Resting his hand on top of the drawer, fingers resting lightly the pistol's walnut grips, he barked, "Come in, goddamnit!"

The door creaked open and a hank of sandy hair tipped into view. "Mr. Luce?"

Anton slapped the drawer closed with a curse. "Get in here, Foster, before someone sees you."

"Yes, sir," the kid replied, slipping sideways through the door and closing it behind him. He stopped, as he always did, to glance timidly around the office, then shuffled forward.

"What is it?" Anton demanded. He'd promised the churlish youth money for information—the amount dependent upon the value of the news—but didn't consider courtesy a part of their arrangement.

Foster had removed his hat upon entering. He held it in front of him now in an obvious gesture of servitude, clutched in both hands, knuckles pale against the darker fabric of the bowler. "You said you wanted to know if Mr. Payne found a muleskinner."

Anton scowled. "That's right. Are you telling me he did?"

"Yes, sir, it appears that way."

"Who?"

"I don't know his full name. I heard Mr. Payne call him Buck."

"Buck? That doesn't tell me a damn thing," he replied. Then his brows furrowed at some distant memory, but the kid went on before he could sort it out.

"He just rode into town," Foster continued. "I think Mr. Payne must've known him from before, the way he acted."

Anton's scowl deepened. Some years back, both he and Felix Payne had operated businesses out of Corinne. In those days, before the ever-spreading tentacles of the railroad had diminished Utah's grip on the mining communities of Montana and Idaho, the big freight outfits—his own among them—had ruled the northwestern mountains. Although the two men had never been friends, their shared history was something Anton kept tucked away in the back of his mind.

"What does this new man look like?"

"I'd say he's around thirty, maybe six foot, brown hair." Foster shrugged. "That's about it."

"That's about nothing," Anton snarled, and the kid swayed back from the hot rush of the saloon owner's anger. "Brown hair? How's he wear it?"

"Kind of long in back, over his collar."

Anton's gaze narrowed. "What's he riding?"

"A mule."

"A black mule?"

"Yes, sir." Foster looked startled. "Do you know him?"

Anton nodded, more to himself than to the kid. "Go find Tom Burrows. Tell him I want to see him."

"I gotta get back to the store," Foster objected. "I told Mr. Payne I was going to the privy, but he'll start to wonder if I ain't back pretty quick."

"You find Burrows first, then go back to Payne's and start nosing around about this new man. Find out what you can, and as soon as you've got something I can actually use, haul your ass back here and tell me what it is."

Foster nodded and swallowed audibly, and Anton shook his head in disgust. He waited until the kid had left, then stood and walked to the window. He couldn't see Payne's store from here, it being on the same side of the street as the High Dollar, but the crowd in front of it looked as chaotic as it had ever since the OSL's conductor had announced his would be the last train from Pineview until the fires were out.

Staring into the street, Anton's view dissolved into an image of Buck McCready as he remembered him from Corinne. It was McCready who had been the cause of the Crowley and Luce Freight outfit going bankrupt, ruining him and sending Herb Crowley into the gutter with a bottle of cheap whiskey. A slow heat spread across the back of Anton's neck as the memory of the match between two of Utah's largest freight outfits played across his mind. McCready had not returned from Montana after the race, leaving any chance for retribution out of Anton's reach. But it appeared now that he was back, and once again sticking his nose into issues that were of no concern to him, but that could cost Anton Luce another fortune.

Well, by damn, he wasn't going to allow it to happen. Not again. The first time Buck McCready had stepped in his way, it had been a matter of chance and bad luck. This time it would be different. This time, it was personal.

Chapter Three

"We're here," Felix Payne said, placing a finger on the lower portion of the map spread across the desk in his office. "This is Pineview, and this," he moved his finger a couple of inches, "is Pineview Creek. Half a day's ride upstream from here is a side canyon that comes in from the east."

"I saw it this morning," Buck confirmed. "Nice-sized stream with a big grove of cottonwood at its mouth."

"That's what I've heard, although I've never seen it personally. It's called Owl Creek Canyon, but don't ask me why."

"Who drew the map?"

"One of the Crown's managers. He gave me a copy after I signed their supply contract last spring."

"Then he knows the trail?"

"He'd probably been over it twenty times before he sketched the map." Felix's finger shifted sideways. "Another half day up the Owl will bring you to a narrow canyon called North Fork. Unless you have trouble along the way, you should reach it by the end of your first day. Just past it, but still on the Owl, is a decent place to camp with plenty of water, grass, and wood. That'll probably be your best bet for the night.

"Up to here, you'll have had it fairly easy, but once you start up North Fork it's going to get ornery. From everything I've heard, the trail is as crooked as a tin horn. There'll also be rock slides and fallen trees you'll have to get your pack strings around. Then, toward the head of the canyon, it gets even worse." He traced a wiggling line that reminded Buck of a snake on hot sand. "This'll be the hardest part for the mules, sharp switchbacks and slick rock that'll make it difficult for them to keep their footing." He moved his finger once more. "After North Fork, you'll be above timberline. There's a glacier lake along the trail where they say the grass is good, although there probably won't be much wood for a fire. Chances are, you'll spend your second night there. It's not far in miles, but by the time you reach it, you'll be ready to stop. So will your mules."

Buck nodded that he understood, and Felix went on.

"After you leave the lake, you'll cross over to the eastern slope and drop down into some heavy timber, but the trail through here will be fairly straight, and there won't be any more steep grades. It'll still be another full day's travel to the mine, though." He looked up. "Any questions?"

Buck shook his head. It sounded like an arduous journey, but not an especially challenging one to follow. "What about the men?" he asked. "I already know Cam Wallis. Who's the second packer?"

"You've probably heard of him. China Jake."

"China Jake? Why are you asking me to lead your crew if you've got him?"

"Because no one will follow a Chinaman," Felix replied bluntly.

"Not even a man with his . . . ." Buck's words trailed off, recognizing the truth of Felix's words. It might not be smart, and it sure as hell wasn't fair, but it was the way it was in that part of the world.

"China Jake will be your ace in the hole if you let him," Felix continued. "You're as solid a muleskinner as ever came down the pike, Buck, but your experience is mostly in hauling freight with wagons. Jake has been dragging pack mules through these mountains, hauling goods into camps too remote to reach by wheeled traffic, since the first big strikes in the Boise Basin in '62. And he knows the trail to the Crown."

"Where is he now?"

"Jake is watching my mules. I send them out to graze during the day, then he'll bring them in at night. Jake and Cam have already sorted the packs, so that's done. All you'll have to do tomorrow is saddle up and pull out."

Buck glanced out the small window above Felix's desk. The day was waning, the afternoon light grown dim behind the smoke. Picking his hat up off the chair at his side, he said, "I'm going to go take care of Zeke, then have a look around town."

"You can stable Zeke here," Felix offered. "I've got corrals for the pack mules, but there are a couple of individual stalls you can use, and some shelled corn in a grain bin next to the tack room."

"Obliged," Buck said. "I'll probably sleep out there with him, too, if you've no objection."

"You'll have company. Jake and Cam are both bunking down next to the stables where they can keep an eye on things."

Buck hesitated, recalling how Wallis had been guarding the Crown's supplies. Now he found out they were both staying close to the mules at night. He wondered if Payne was expecting trouble, then recalled the precautions Jock Kavanaugh used to take with his wagons and dismissed the concern. With a brief farewell, he put on his hat and left the office. As he walked back through the store, he spotted the sandy-haired clerk with the sullen expression ducking in through the front door. The clerk lurched to a halt when he saw Buck, then moved swiftly behind the counter, keeping his gaze averted. Buck's brow creased in puzzlement at the kid's odd behavior. Then he dismissed that, as well. He had 5,000 pounds of supplies to deliver to a remote, high-country mine, and an uneasy feeling that there wasn't going to be a lot of time to accomplish it.

Chapter Four

Buck liked China Jake from the start. He was a small man, slimly built but wiry and strong. Unlike most of the Chinese immigrants Buck had worked with over the years, Jake had been born in the

United States. Orphaned before his second birthday, he had been raised by an orchardist near Stockton, California.

Jake had long ago shrugged off the tenets of a culture he no longer felt a part of. He kept his hair trimmed close, without the traditional queue of his countrymen, and wore the sturdy range clothes of his trade—canvas trousers, hobnail boots, a wool shirt under a dark vest, and a narrow-brimmed hat of a style once called a beehive, which made it easier for him to navigate the dense pine forests of central Idaho without having to worry about losing his headgear every time he passed under a low-hanging bough.

And he knew mules. That much was evident within the first twenty minutes of working together that evening. In a voice soft, eloquent, and devoid of accent, Jake informed Buck that the pack train was ready to pull out at first light.

Although Buck didn't doubt him, as head packer it was his responsibility to make sure the string was up to the task ahead. It was also important that he meet the stock. Mules had a different temperament from horses, and generally required a more personal touch. As Buck moved among them, talking to the individual animals, inspecting hooves and backs and leg muscles, he knew the long-eared mountain canaries were judging him—his skill, confidence, and authority—with the same critical eye he had for them. Experience had taught him that if the mules trusted and respected him, they would be more tractable in the days ahead. And Buck sensed that was going to be important. Felix Payne seemed certain the fire would burn well to the north of them. Cam and Jake weren't as confident.

"'Sides, even if it do go north, ain't that the direction we're goin' in?" Cam had demanded, after Payne returned to his store following introductions. "Hell, we're liable to ride straight into the blasted thing, we ain't keerful!"

They ate supper together afterward, a simple meal of beans and side pork, eased down the throat by swallows of iron-strong coffee. It was Cam who prepared the rough feast, squatted over a small cook fire behind the store with his pipe cocked from his mouth at a jaunty angle, his eyes squinted against its smoke. Now and again a harsh, racking cough would tear through the man's slender frame, and his breath would catch, then wheeze dangerously before he pulled himself together again.

"It ain't nothin' for either of you two hounds to fret over," the older man had snapped the first time he went into a hacking fit. Worried, Buck had hurried over from inspecting the mules to make sure he was all right, but Cam waved him off.

"It's his lungs," China Jake confided after Buck returned to the corral. Having already been scolded by the old man, Jake had stayed with the mules. "He claims they were damaged when a wagon fell against him, but I don't believe it."

"What do you think it is?"

"I couldn't say for sure, but from the way it sounds, I'd guess his lungs are beginning to fail."

Buck studied the elderly man from between the corral rails. Felix had claimed Cam was in his mid-forties, but he looked at least twenty years older than that. He was as skinny as a starved rabbit, with straggly gray hair poking out from under a wilted Stetson and clothes that were threadbare in spots.

It was obvious the smoke from the fires was playing havoc with the older man's lungs. During the meal and in the hour or so afterward, before they retired to their blankets, Cam acknowledged that a doctor at the time of the accident had suspected a punctured lung.

"It gives me fits, time to time," Cam admitted, stifling a cough.

"You figure you can make it to the Crown?" Buck asked. It was a blunt question, but an important one. They were already short-handed. If Cam couldn't keep up or pull his share of the load, they'd have to find someone to replace him or call off the trip.

"I'll be there right behind you, boy," Cam growled, and Buck nodded his approval for the man's adamancy. Then a fresh fit of coughing tore through the old man's chest, and Buck's doubts returned. It seemed a long time before Cam finally leaned to one side and spat into the weeds against the store's foundation. After wiping his lips with the back of his hand, he added hoarsely, "This damn smoke's as bothersome as a nit fly."

"That pipe that's always stuck in your mouth doesn't help," Jake said. "Why don't you give it up, at least until the fires are out?"

"You just mind your own damned string," Cam replied. "I ain't yet taken advice from a heathen. I don't aim to start tonight."

Jake's gaze narrowed and Buck stiffened, determined to step between them if he had to. But Cam lowered his eyes to the coals at the base of their coffee pot and kept them there, and after a minute Jake shoved to his feet and walked to the corral. Leaning forward, Cam casually pulled a twig from the fire and relit his pipe. Buck stared, waiting for him to speak or look up, to offer some kind of explanation, but the older man's expression remained inscrutable, and after a couple of minutes Buck stood and stalked into the darkness.

Chapter Five

The evening light was fading rapidly now. From behind the window in his dusky office above the High Dollar Emporium, Anton Luce scowled down at Pineview's single thoroughfare. The OSL had pulled out just before sundown, its twin passenger cars packed like ammunition crates, the boxcars trailing behind them bristling with citizens too broke or too late to purchase tickets for a coach seat. Now, in the deepening twilight, the town looked almost deserted, its wide street empty of traffic, the boardwalk a plank highway leading nowhere.

Anton stood with his right hand held rigidly in front of the middle button of his brocaded red vest, a cigar clenched firmly between his fingers. On the desk behind him, the order he had been composing for winter supplies sat unfinished, the ink in the pen's nib dried to a black clog. He was staring south into the smoke-hazed distance, but it wasn't the vast grasslands of the Snake River Plain that filled his view. It was the look on his old partner's face when they learned of McCready's victory in securing the Montana mining contract for the Box-K.

Herb Crowley had known immediately what the loss meant for the company he and Anton had cobbled together through hard work and some less-than-honest business dealings. Anton had been a little slower to put all the pieces together, but when he did, his throat had turned instantly to dust. Buck McCready had ruined them both; maybe he hadn't meant to, but motive didn't change the outcome.

A heavy knock rattled the office door. Anton turned as it swung inward without invitation. A large man entered with a swagger that brought Anton a grim sense of satisfaction. Nobody had ever accused Tom Burrows of timidity.

"You're late," Anton said brusquely.

Burrows hesitated, and his expression momentarily darkened. Then, with a guffaw, he elbowed the door shut and crossed the room to Anton's desk. "There's maybe half a dozen people in this world I'd let talk to me that way," he said pleasantly; then his voice turned to stone. "After today, you ain't one of 'em."

"I'm paying you handsomely," Anton replied. "One of my requirements is that you show up when summoned."

"Luce, I don't summon worth a damn, and I ain't much concerned for other people's requirements, either." Halting in front of the desk, Burrows poured a shot of bourbon from a decanter sitting on one corner into a glass. Then he looked up with a taunting grin. "I'll tell you something else, anybody who does ain't fit for the kind of work you want done."

Anton bit off the retort that nearly slipped from his tongue. Burrows was right about the kind of men he'd need for a job like this. But there was a second truth to his hesitation, one that galled him deeper than he'd ever admit. The fact was, Burrows frightened him. The man's reputation as a killer was well-known throughout the Northwest, and his volatility was a part of his legend.

Changing the subject, Anton said, "Have you talked to Foster?"

"That the little runt who works for Felix Payne?"

"You know who he is."

Burrows shrugged. "Yeah, I talked to him."

"Then you know about the new man Payne hired. What have you found out about him?"

"I ain't found out nothing. The runt says his name is Buck McCready. Some of the boys I talked to in the Little Ace says he used to work for a freighting company out of Corinne."

His lips settling into a hard line, Anton leaned forward to snuff his cigar in an iron ashtray. Noticing his impatience, Burrows grinned and took a long swallow of bourbon.

"And did any of those boys from the Little Ace Saloon say what McCready was doing in Pineview?" Anton asked.

"They didn't, although one of 'em mentioned he's been up Oregon way the last few years, skinning mules for an outfit out of The Dalles. They reckoned he was heading back to Utah. At least he was until Felix Payne offered him a job." His brows ridged in curiosity. "Just what is it you want done, Luce?"

"I want you to kill him."

Burrows had raised his glass for another drink. At Anton's words, he nearly choked on the liquor in his throat. "Payne?" he asked throatily.

"No, of course not," Anton replied, just barely refraining from adding: *you idiot.* "I want McCready dead." He paused, then clarified, "But not in town. Do it somewhere along the trail to the Crown."

"That makes more sense," Burrows allowed. "What about the others, the old man and the chink?"

Anton tapped a finger thoughtfully on top of his desk. In his single-minded fixation on McCready, he'd failed to consider the other two packers. After a moment's reflection, he shrugged. "That will be up to you. I want the pack train stopped and its supplies destroyed. And I want Buck McCready dead. Beyond that, just make sure nothing finds its way back to my door."

Burrows shrugged and set his empty glass down on the desk. "It's your money, Luce. If that's what you want, you'll have it."

Chapter Six

They were up before dawn the next morning. Cam brought the mules in two at a time and saddled them, while China Jake and Buck hoisted the loads into place by lantern light. True to his word, Felix had rounded up two more mules, bringing the total to twenty-four. That was still less than then the thirty animals Buck would have preferred, but it was nothing they couldn't work around.

In addition to the pack animals, they had Buck's mule Zeke and a trio of horses. Two of those were saddle mounts for Jake and Cam. The third was a zebra dun mare, too old to carry more than some basic camp supplies—skillet and coffee pot, some rice, hardtack, and side pork, plus their bedrolls. According to Jake, the zebra dun had been a member of Payne's pack string since the animals were purchased last winter, and had quickly assumed the position of bell mare.

For some reason Buck had never fully understood, mules would often develop a fondness bordering on devotion for a certain animal. In his experience, it was usually a mare, and more often than not a horse rather than one of its own kind. Smart muleskinners had learned to take advantage of that kinship, and would loop a bell over the horse's neck to allow its steady jingle to be heard by the rest of the string. No matter the situation or terrain, the sound of the mare's bell always seemed to reassure a long line of pack animals that she was still somewhere up front, and that there was nothing to fear as long as the older animal remained calm.

"A good bell mare is worth her weight in gold," Jake claimed as he buckled the leather strap around the dun's neck. Then he looked at Buck and grinned. "Well, maybe not gold, but we'll be glad we have her before we reach the Crown."

It didn't take long to get everything lined out. Although Cam Wallis was older than the others, and slower due to his injuries, he was a still good hand, and Buck had spent most of his life around mules, handling the big freight wagons and, more recently, packing into the mountainous country southwest of The Dalles. But it was China Jake who put them both in the dust with his skill and efficiency, lifting his packs effortlessly into place, then cinching them tight. In the lantern's yellow light, his diamond hitches looked as if they had been drawn onto the rough canvas covers, so perfectly were they aligned and knotted.

Felix Payne showed up just as Cam extinguished the lantern. He looked surprised to find them so far along. "I thought I'd come down and help, but it looks like you don't need it."

"I wanted to get an early start," Buck said. He tipped his head toward the western horizon, where twisted clouds of pale smoke snaked into the sky, their bellies tinged crimson from the inferno below. "I'm not sure that fire is going to go as far north as you'd hoped," he added.

Felix nodded solemnly. The southerly breeze from the past few days had died overnight, leaving the air still and heavy.

Stepping into the saddle, Buck took a loose hitch around his horn with the lead pack mule's rope and rode over to where Felix was unlatching the corral gate. Leaning down to shake the storekeeper's hand, he said, "We should be back by the end of the week if we don't run into any trouble."

"Let's hope you don't," Felix replied, but his grip lingered as if there was more he wanted to say. Finally, dropping Buck's hand, he got to it. "I had a man quit on me last night, one of my clerks. Do you remember Foster? I think he waited on you."

"The kid with the chip on his shoulder?"

"That's him. I figured he'd scooted to catch the Oregon Short Line out of the valley, like half the damn town did, but then I saw him this morning going into the High Dollar."

Buck recalled the saloon from his ride through town yesterday, a two-storied structure a block up the street from Payne's mercantile. "Maybe he wanted a drink," Buck said. "I know my throat feels about half raw from all the smoke I've swallowed the past couple of days."

"That's possible, but the first chance you get, ask Jake or Cam what they think about the High Dollar."

Buck hesitated. "That's an interesting suggestion, Mr. Payne. Any particular reason you're making it?"

Felix stared at him a moment, indecision like a flickering light in his eyes. Then he shook his head. "Just ask them," he said, and walked the gate open. "You might want to keep an eye on your back trail, too."

Buck didn't reply. It troubled him that there might be more to the job than Felix had originally let on, especially since he didn't want to share it. But with the light growing steadily, illuminating the towering columns of smoke in the west, Buck felt an urgency to get underway. He nodded for Jake to take the lead, the bell mare first in line, the rest of his mules strung out behind her tied tail-to-halter. Cam fell in on the heels of Jake's string with his own, and Buck brought up the rear where he could keep an eye on the entire outfit. Felix nodded a somber goodbye to each of them as they passed through the gate, but spoke to no one. Buck thought he looked worried, and that bothered him, too.

They followed the old road out of Pineview, hugging the creek's edge and avoiding the town's main thoroughfare, although Buck hadn't heard a wagon's rumble or a horse's whinny all morning. If they hadn't been in such a hurry, he probably would have opted to loose-herd the stock and keep just the dun bell mare on a lead while he and Cam brought up the rear, but there was no doubt, as the day brightened, that the smoke had grown heavier overnight, the fire drawn closer.

North of town they swung back onto what passed for a road in this direction, and by the time the sun pulled free of the mountains, they'd put a good five miles behind them. From time to time Buck would glance back the way they'd come, but Pineview was lost from sight in the haze, and above the eastern peaks the sun looked more like a small, faded peach than anything of significance.

They reached Owl Creek at midday. The leaves on the tall cottonwoods growing along its banks were already fading into brown after the hot, dry summer. In another couple of weeks they would begin their gentle drift to the ground—assuming they weren't turned to ash beforehand.

China Jake led them away from the main road, toward the mouth of Owl Canyon still a quarter of a mile away. As he did, he turned to casually look behind them. Even from the rear of the train, Buck could see the sudden alarm that flitted across the man's face. Twisting in his saddle, Buck stared back the way they'd come. Earlier, there had been nothing there except autumn grass and a gray pall of smoke. Now he spotted a trio of horsemen sitting their mounts atop a low rise near the valley's eastern rim, staring toward them.

Jake slowed his string crossing the valley; Buck hurried his, and they met at the canyon's mouth. Cam rode up to join them, the mules splayed out to the rear like strands of unraveled yarn.

"Who are they?" Cam demanded hoarsely, staring back to where the horsemen still calmly sat their mounts, watching and waiting.

Buck glanced at Jake, but the younger man shook his head.

"Well, whoever they be, you can bet they're bound for mischief," Cam declared.

"That sounds about right," Jake agreed softly.

"Just before we pulled out this morning, Felix told me to ask you two about the High Dollar Emporium," Buck said.

Jake darted a look at Cam, who rubbed thoughtfully at his lower lip with a knuckle. "That might could be," the older man allowed.

"What do you mean?" Buck asked.

"The guy who owns the Dollar also owns a small freight outfit," Jake explained. "He promised the Crown he'd build a wagon road from Pineview to the mine if they gave him the contract, but the Crown's owners didn't want to wait. They gave it to Payne, instead. Luce didn't take it well."

"Luce!" Buck's head came up. "Anton Luce?"

"You know him?"

"Yeah, I know him. Or I did back in Corinne."

"He came to Pineview after his Utah company went bankrupt."

"Bankrupt? I hadn't heard about that."

"Luce showed up here a few years back," Cam said. "Started hisself a saloon, but once they made that big strike at the Crown, he quick put together some wagons and harness stock and called it a freight company. It weren't much from the beginning and ain't gone far since, but I've heard ol' Anton can carry a grudge farther than any two mules put together."

"He was that way in Utah, too," Buck said. "Unless he's changed, he wouldn't be above trying to stop us."

"He hasn't changed," Jake replied, and Cam nodded sober confirmation.

"Anton has got hisself a streak of mean that runs from heel to topknot," the older man added.

"Then we're going to have to watch our backs from here on," Buck said.

He kept his tone even, but inside, he was seething. Now he knew what Felix hadn't wanted to tell him that morning at the corral. Payne had to realize how Luce would react if he found out Buck was leading his pack outfit, yet he'd deliberately withheld that information. Even though it was infuriating, Buck thought he understood the store owner's motives. Time was running out for Felix; he couldn't afford to lose his contract with the Crown, or risk having Buck back out of his commitment to haul his supplies to the mine. Freighting, no matter what the method used to transfer goods from one location to another, had always been a cutthroat business, and whether Buck agreed with him or not, Felix had only been playing the odds as he saw them—never mind that he'd been wagering Buck's life and the success of the haul on his bet.

Exhaling loudly, Buck looked at Cam, then Jake, and said, "Let's keep 'em moving."

Chapter Seven

Owl Creek was narrow and fast, but with a gentle flex that made it easy to follow. The trail clung to the left bank, well-marked and solidly packed from who knew how many others that had tramped this way before. The canyon's north-facing slope was steep and densely pined, but the other side of the gulch was more moderately sloped, with little groves of shimmying aspens scattered like discarded coins along the canyon floor.

Normally Buck would have ordered a noon break to rest the stock, but with the approaching maelstrom out of the west and a trio of men suspiciously dogging them from the south, he opted to keep the long string of mules moving forward at a brisk walk. As the afternoon waned, the Owl's walls began to pinch in on either side, and the trail became more sinuous. China Jake was lost from sight much of the time, and Cam's presence was marked largely by the increasing volume of his hacking coughs as the smoke intensified. Although Buck kept a close watch to the rear, he saw no sign of pursuit, but his gut told him the three horsemen were still following . . . biding their time.

An early dusk was closing in around them by the time they reached North Fork Canyon. They paused only briefly at its mouth to discuss their choices. Earlier that afternoon Buck had weighed the advantages of pushing on into the evening, but as he eyed the twisting creek-side path disappearing into the canyon's interior, he realized they'd have to wait until morning if they didn't want to risk injuring the stock.

Jake led them to a long clearing another hundred yards up the Owl, where they dropped stiffly from their saddles and began off-loading the packs. They hobbled the mules but picketed their saddle stock and the bell mare, knowing that as long as the zebra dun was close, the rest of the herd wouldn't stray far.

With darkness closing in, Buck ordered Cam to start a fire and fix a meal, while Jake rubbed down the stock and checked for fresh cuts or sores. Meanwhile, he took his rifle and hiked back down the trail on foot. He probably covered a mile or so, taking his time and watching sharp for an ambush, before nightfall forced him to turn back. Although he hadn't spotted anything alarming, the uneasiness he'd felt all afternoon refused to lessen. They were out there. Damnit, he could *feel* them.

Cam had a meal waiting by the time he got back. Looking up as Buck stepped into the light of his small cook fire, he said, "Figured for a bit there you'd got yourself lost."

"No," Buck replied stoically, leaning his rifle against a nearby pack.

"Did you see anything?" Jake asked.

"Not a thing." He dug a plate and spoon from his saddlebags and scooped up a mess of rice and raisins—spotted pup, they called it— and some slices of beef cooked on a flat rock set close to the flame.

"Maybe they weren't following us, after all," Jake mused.

"That ain't likely," Cam replied dourly.

Recalling the hawk-eyed manner in which the horsemen had watched the pack string enter the canyon, Buck was inclined to agree with Cam. He took a bite of meat and chewed it down, and said, "I figure they'll jump us tonight, after we're bedded down. That wildfire's getting too close for them to want to stay out here any longer than they have to."

"What we oughter do is take the fight to 'em," Cam said.

"We don't know where they are," Buck replied. "And we'd have to leave the mules and packs unguarded to look for them. I won't do that."

"We could bundle some pine boughs in our blankets, then slip off and wait for them," Jake suggested.

"Oldest trick in the book," Cam said. "They'd never swallow it."

"Simple is best," Jake argued.

Cam snorted dismissively. "Chinaman's logic."

Jake's eyes narrowed. "There's a limit," he said quietly, "to how much bullshit I'll take from you."

"That's enough," Buck said, shooting Cam a warning look. "Besides, you're both right. We'll just change it up a little. We'll let the fire die to coals and rig a couple of bedrolls to look like some of us are asleep, then have a third one leaning against one of the packs so that they'll think there's a man keeping watch. We'll wrap that in a blanket, too, and I'll put my coat around it and my hat on top, but tipped forward so that it looks like I've dozed off. I can lay my rifle across what they'll think is my lap. Without a fire, they'll have to come in close enough for me to use my Colt."

"That sounds about right," Jake agreed after a moment's consideration.

"You damn right it's right," Cam added. "Long as they ain't out there now with their peepers peepin' on us."

"I doubt it," Buck said, then stood and dumped what was left of his coffee over the flames. "But let's kill the fire and get set up, anyway."

It took less than twenty minutes to set their trap. When they were finished, Buck sent Jake and Cam into the trees upstream, while he took a downstream position, the direction from which their ambushers would likely appear. He found a pine not too far away and scooted back under its low hanging branches. From here the coals of their cook fire seemed to pulsate like a slowly beating heart, its faint glow the Owl's only illumination that evening.

Buck settled in cross-legged with his revolver in his right hand, its long barrel cradled in the crook of his left elbow. He didn't know if he was surprised or relieved when he heard a soft voice between him and the creek—close enough to make him flinch—whisper: "There they are."

Another replied in equally hushed tones: "Shut up, you damn fool."

Then the muzzle blast from a rifle speared the night, and Buck jumped and swore. The man who had breathed *Shut up, you damn fool* cursed loudly and shouted, "Lay into 'em, boys!"

Gunfire crackled from two sides, yellow lances splitting the darkness. Buck threw himself flat and thrust the Colt before him. Jake and Cam were returning fire, but they were farther away, and their shots were being deflected by the web of trees limbs separating them from their attackers.

Buck's view was less impeded. Targeting a muzzle flare barely ten yards away, he adjusted his aim and squeezed the trigger. He heard the man's grunt even above the report of his own weapon, but fired a second time for good measure, before rolling out from under the pine boughs. A frightened shout echoed from downstream. Buck rose and started in that direction but hadn't covered more than a few paces when a hulking figure appeared out of the shadows on his right.

"Tom!" the man called, and Buck said, "No," and pulled the trigger.

The man cried out and fell backward, and Buck resumed his downstream pursuit. He heard the shout again, though from farther away this time, and broke into an awkward run. But with the canyon's floor like pitch, he kept stumbling over the uneven ground, careening off pine boughs that tried to shove him first one way, then the other, until he finally gave up for fear he'd break a leg or knock himself senseless on a stout limb if he didn't.

Gasping in the smoky air, Buck dropped to one knee and waited with his revolver cocked, his finger taut on the trigger, but after several minutes with no sound other than the swift beating of his own heart, he stood and made his way back to the camp.

Pausing in the shadows outside the pale glow of their fire, he quietly hailed the camp. Jake and Cam answered immediately, and the three men stepped cautiously into the light. A couple of quick questions assured Buck that neither of them had been injured; other than for some pine-needle scratches across one cheek, he'd also escaped unhurt.

"I got one of 'em," Cam claimed excitedly, but Jake quickly refuted the claim.

"The only thing we shot were trees, although I think Buck might have hit one of them."

"I think I hit two of them," Buck corrected. "We'll have to wait until morning to know for sure, though." Glancing around the exposed campsite, he added, "At least one man got away, so we can't stay here."

"I know a place near the mules where we can hole up until dawn," Jake said, and Buck nodded stiffly.

"Lead the way."

Chapter Eight

The first gray blush of dawn had barely reached the canyon's floor when Buck and Jake walked out to examine the previous night's battleground. As Buck had feared, they found two men, both of them dead.

"It was either you or them," Jake said, noticing the expression on Buck's face.

"I know," Buck replied. He stood from where he'd knelt next to the larger-framed man. "Do you know them?"

"That's Tom Burrows at your feet."

The name jarred a recollection from Buck's years in Oregon. Burrows had killed a man for refusing to give up his seat in a poker game. It hadn't been a fair fight; Burrows had simply drawn and fired into the player's chest, killing him instantly. There had been no trial afterward because no one wanted to attempt to arrest him, least of all the town marshal.

The other man was a local tough called Salmon River Kelly. According to Jake, Kelly was a part-time horse thief who liked to ride with Burrows, as if hoping some of the gunman's reputation might rub off on him. Kelly had been shot in the side, and Burrows had taken a slug through his neck. Judging from the unbloodied ground around them, both men had died quickly. Buck was grateful for that.

They found the trail of a third man ending where the ambushers had left their horses. One mount was gone. The other two remained hitched to saplings along the trail. They freed both animals, dumping their tack on the ground, then walked back to where Burrows and Kelly lay. Buck wanted to bury them, but Jake pointed out that there wasn't time.

"That fire's getting closer, Buck. Besides, if it was Luce who sent these men, he'll send out even more as soon as he finds out what happened."

Grudgingly, Buck led the way back to camp, where they found Cam slumped against one of the packs, chin tucked to his chest.

"Hey," Jake cried in alarm, and hurried to the older man's side. "Are you all right?"

"'Course I'm all right," Cam snarled, jerking his head up, but the words sounded phlegm-smothered, and there was a shine of spittle at the corners of his mouth.

"You don't look all right," Jake told him. "You don't sound like it, either. Fact is, you sound kind of wind-broke to me."

"That's 'cause your ears are filled with smoke," Cam replied. He struggled to his feet, swaying briefly until he caught his balance, then spat into the ashes of last night's supper fire. "Hell," he added indignantly, wiping his chin with the back of his hand, "I'll likely be carryin' you two hounds before we reach the top, puny as you both look."

"I'd rather we didn't have to carry anyone," Buck said, stepping forward to peer into Cam's eyes.

"You just worry about yourself, boy," Cam replied stonily. "I'll be there the same time you are, if not five minutes before."

Buck glanced at Jake, but the younger man refused to return the look. His expression was stoic, like a chunk of seasoned oak. "Don't worry about him," he said harshly. "He's just a stubborn old fool."

"That's right," Cam retorted. "And mule-headed enough to see a job through to its finish, too."

Buck had had enough. "Let's get this outfit moving," he said curtly. "Before Luce shows up with an army."

Chapter Nine

Leaning back in his chair, Anton regarded the battered figure standing before him. He wasn't sure how to take Foster's assertion that Buck McCready had killed two of his best men—including the gunman Tom Burrows. It didn't seem possible. Yet what other explanation could there be for the kid showing up with such a tale?

Nor could Anton dismiss the memory of McCready's intractable pertinacity in leading Jock Kavanaugh's wagon train of freight north from Corinne. Anton knew in his heart that the firm of Crowley and Luce should have won that race—they'd had the lead nearly the whole way, damnit, and a hired gun to stop the Box-K if the elements didn't—but Buck had kept his outfit in an unrelenting pursuit that had ultimately proved successful.

It had also impressed upon Anton that McCready wasn't a man to give up easily. Or to be dismissed.

His gaze came back to Foster. The kid stood shivering as if chilled. He was hatless and bloodied, and claimed he'd been shot in the cheek, although the angle of the wound spoke more of a heedless flight through the night and a stout branch than it did a bullet. But the youth's claim . . . .

"You're sure they're dead?" he repeated.

Foster's head bobbed in accord. "Yes, sir, both of them."

Anton looked away, considering his options. He saw two immediately. One was to just let them go, lick his wounds and count his losses, then tip his hat to that son of a bitch Felix Payne the next time he saw the wretched little shopkeeper. Hell, if it had been anyone other than McCready, he might have done it. But not again. Not when there was a second option.

Standing, he strode to an accordion rack nailed to the wall next to the door. His hat and coat hung there, along with a nickel-plated Merwin Hulbert revolver in a belt of tooled leather. He strapped the gun belt on first.

"W . . . what are you doing?" Foster asked, looking as confused as he sounded.

Anton's reply was terse. "Go find Cunningham and Harlow and tell them to meet me downstairs at the bar, now. Then swing past the livery and saddle my horse." He slid the Merwin Hulbert from its holster, but paused before opening the gate to check its loads. "Get yourself a fresh mount, too. You're coming with us."

Chapter Ten

There had been no moon to light their trail the night before, and there was no hint of the sun that morning, despite its pearly suffusion by midday. They'd left the Owl shortly after dawn to start up the North Fork in the same order as the previous day, Jake leading with the bell mare, the rest of them strung out to the rear.

The trail proved as difficult as Felix had promised, with boulders from the cliffs above strewn everywhere, and downed timber that had to be jumped over or threaded past. They reached the head of the canyon just past noon and halted to check their loads—tightening where it was needed, making sure the packs were still evenly balanced. The trail left the creek soon after to begin its final ascent to the top, a narrow ribbon of switchbacks rising toward where eagles nested and vultures waited and watched.

It was here, too, not long after starting, that the mules began to grow restive, yanking back on their lead ropes and snorting at shadows and sticks like they were mountain lions and rattlesnakes. Buck knew it was the ever-thickening smoke that bothered them more than the steepening grade. That and the ash husks swirling past them like gray snowflakes. Even the zebra dun was becoming fractious, and from time to time as they climbed, Buck would glance above to see Jake struggling to keep the horse calm, his own pack string moving forward.

They were probably halfway up the worst stretch of it, Zeke's hooves clattering on hardpan and granite as he struggled to keep his footing, when Buck heard a roaring like a runaway train slamming through the canyon behind them. The flesh across the back of his neck crawled as he swiveled around to stare back the way they'd come. He wouldn't have been surprised to see a sloth of angry grizzlies charging up the trail after them, but the path was empty as far as he could see. Then the sound came again, and at the bottom of the canyon the tops of the pines began to whip back and forth as if writhing in pain. The smoke bucked and churned, and the bits of blackened twigs and fine ash that had so recently fallen past them now reversed direction to barrel up the canyon's wall on a powerful gust of wind.

The sound grew to a shriek, and the mules brayed and kicked and laid their ears back. From above, the bell mare's terrified whinny added to the chaos. Then the tempest struck them with a force Buck could hardly credit as natural. Like a giant hand, it shoved him back in his saddle, and he had to grab his hat to keep it from taking flight. Zeke snorted his displeasure, but otherwise held steady; so did the rest of Buck's string, the wind being a more familiar phenomenon than the screaming of an unseen assailant they'd imagined coming up behind them.

Squinting against dust and ash, Buck watched a piece of oilcloth off one of the packs from above soar past. Then Cam's battered old hat sailed after it, as if to round up the stray canvas and hie it back into the herd.

The pummeling blasts lasted only a few minutes, before the air grew calm again. Using his thumb and forefinger, Buck scraped the worst of the grit from the corners of his eyes before raising his head and looking around. At first everything appeared normal.

The wildfire's detritus was floating down again, in a direction that made sense, and the pines along the canyon floor had ceased their frantic gyrations. It was when he glanced overhead that Buck felt a sinking in his breast. A heavy coil of black smoke was spilling over the canyon's rim and falling rapidly toward them. He shouted a warning to the others, but couldn't tell if they heard him. Then it no longer mattered as the smoke curled around them in a choking embrace.

Buck lowered his head and closed his eyes, and after a couple of minutes he raised his left arm to cover his face. Zeke hawed in protest, dancing near the edge of the drop-off, hooves clattering atop the hardpan. Behind them, the line of mules shifted restlessly, making a guttural braying sound Buck had heard only rarely in his life, and then only in moments of extreme peril. His pulse quickened at the thought of the whole string slipping off the narrow trail and plummeting to their deaths. After a moment's adjustment to the roiling fog, Buck lowered his arm and raised a bandanna over his mouth and nose. Then he resolutely tapped Zeke's ribs with his heels, the pack string buckling down and compliantly following.

It was another hour before they cleared the switchbacks. Although the trail continued its upward climb, it was no longer so narrow and dangerous. Jake brought his string to a stop about a hundred yards past the canyon's rim, and the others rode up to join him. Buck looked at Jake, but Jake was staring wordlessly past him. It didn't take long to figure out why. Dropping from his saddle, Buck walked over to place a hand gently on Cam's knee.

"You still with us?" he asked.

Glowering at him from reddened eyes, Cam croaked, "Where the hell else'd I be?" Then he leaned from his saddle and spat. Straightening with effort, he pushed a lank of greasy gray hair back off his forehead. "It ain't bad enough . . . the fire's taken away my breath, now the wind's . . . stole my hat."

"I saw it on its way back down the canyon," Buck confirmed. "I think it might have waved at me as it sailed past."

Cam gave him a condemning look, then shrugged indifferently. "Well, the damn thing never . . . waved to me, so I reckon it's better off on its own somewhere."

"The way it was flying, it's probably back in Pineview by now."

"You can buy another hat," Jake said impatiently, then turned to Buck, before Cam could respond. "The trail between here and the Crown is fairly open. We could probably loose-herd the mules the rest of the way if you wanted to." He glanced at Cam, then away.

"Don't you do me no favors, boy," Cam growled hoarsely. He looked at Buck. "You, neither.

"How much farther is it to the mine?" Buck asked Jake.

"Most of another day, I'd guess."

Buck looked west to where the glow of the approaching flames lit the horizon. From here it appeared as if the entire range west of Pineview Valley might be ablaze. Although he wasn't surprised that Felix had guessed wrong about the fire's direction, its speed was worrisome. In the canyons it had been impossible to tell from which direction the wind was coming, but there was no question of it now. It had changed course while they were climbing the switchbacks, and was sweeping in from the northwest with a chilled bite that had been absent earlier.

"It's going to blow in a storm," he predicted.

"Them's about the truest words I've heard all week," Cam said throatily. "But you'd best hope it blows in fast, else we're all gonna be as crisp as ma's biscuits before the next sunrise."

Facing the older man, Buck said, "You figure you've got enough sand to make it to the Crown if we kept riding?"

"Now, that there is probably the dumbest thing I've heard all week," Cam replied. Then he got a panicky look on his face as his lungs closed off in a rattling cough that nearly tumbled him from his seat. When it passed, he dragged a sleeve weakly across his lips; it came away streaked with blood and mucus. He stared numbly at his cuff for several seconds, then raised his eyes to Buck's. "Keep your trap shut, boy."

Nodding stiffly, Buck walked back to Zeke, gathered his reins, and stepped into the saddle. "Let's go," he told Jake. "We'll keep the mules on their leads for now and try to ride straight through." His gaze slewed west to where the mountain peaks glowed like stacks of rose-tinted gold on the horizon. "I figure we'll have enough light to see the trail," he added bleakly.

Chapter Eleven

Anton pushed his men hard, using quirt and spur to keep his bay gelding alternating between a lope and a jog for most of the day, and savagely rebuking anyone who started to fall behind. Without a cavvy of headstrong mules to slow them down, they were making good time, yet he chafed at every small delay.

The wind caught them shortly after entering North Fork Canyon. What had been calm only moments before turned suddenly as wild as a trapped catamount as it swept first one way, then the other. The unexpectedness of its gale-like force startled them all. Anton's bay was especially unnerved by its shrill arrival, switching ends to face the wind, then crow-hopping through a maze of boulders, brush, and scattered trees, while Anton cursed and sawed at the reins.

Most of the others—Burt and Chad McLaughlin, who tended bar evenings at the High Dollar; Sid Cunningham, Anton's last remaining hired hand at the now all-but-defunct Luce Fast Freight and Express; and Bob Harlow, who did odd jobs around the saloon and freight yard as needed—were having similar problems. Only the kid, Foster, managed to keep his horse under control, guiding it off the trail and turning his back to the black smoke pouring down canyon like a chimney unscrewed from the bottom. It wasn't until those first rapid blasts of steadily colder air calmed to a hard blow that Anton was able to force his horse back onto the trail. The others joined him there. As the last man rode up, Anton snarled, "If you boys can't control your horses, then maybe you'd better get down and lead 'em."

Only Cunningham had enough backbone to stand up the saloon owner's abuse. "It didn't look like you were faring a whole lot better than the rest of us."

"I'm here, ain't I? Here and waiting for you jokers when we should be riding." He darted a quick glance at Foster, but the youth knew better than to pipe in with an opinion, and kept his gaze averted. "Let's go," Anton snapped, yanking the bay around and giving it another quick dig with his spurs.

They started up North Fork at a trot, but the horses soon turned balky in the stifling smoke, tossing their heads and fighting the bit. With Anton's own mount the worst of the bunch, he had to swallow the razor-sharp barbs he wanted to fling at the others.

Anton knew his foul mood was the result of Burrows's and Kelly's failure to stop the muleskinners. It had deteriorated even further with his discovery of the two men along the trail, each of them killed by a single, well-placed shot—shootings that had taken place in near pitch darkness, if Foster was to be believed. Although someone had taken time to wrap the bodies in oilcloth to keep the weather off them and scavengers away, they hadn't buried them. Nor would Anton allow his men to scratch out even a shallow grave. Buck McCready and his crew had too much of a lead as it was; he'd be damned if he'd allow them even more.

The down canyon wind held steady. Although not as strong as those earlier gusts, it was constant, worming through their clothing like icy fingers. Buttoning his brown herringbone jacket as high as it would go, Anton wished he'd thought to bring along something heavier. But who could have predicted the temperature would turn so frosty when the whole damn country seemed to be aflame?

No one spoke as they made their way miserably up canyon. The only sounds were the moaning of the wind and the protesting creak of the tall pines, shoved back and forth like bullied kids. Even the clopping of their horses' hooves against the rocky trail seemed muted. There was a spookiness to the day, Anton thought, and an ominousness to the narrow canyon that chipped at his nerves until his whole body pringled with tension. Part of the trouble was that he couldn't get the vision of Burrows and Kelly out of his mind. They had both been tough men, neither fools nor reckless in their habits. Yet they both lay dead by McCready's hand. It made Anton question how he could expect to fare any better with only a pair of bartenders, a hard-nosed freighter, a hostler, and a fool kid to back him when they finally caught up with the mule train.

Anton was still lost in these musings when, coming past a bend in the trail, he saw a man standing half-hidden in the alders across the creek. With his heart slamming into his throat, he jerked his horse to a stop and palmed his revolver, firing two quick rounds through the man's chest. Then the wind brushed the gun smoke out of his line of sight and he saw the figure standing as before, immobile. As he watched, it gradually transformed itself into a sapling, a tattered old hat caught near its peak.

Slowly, Anton lowered his pistol. He was aware of the others halted behind him, watching . . . judging. After a minute, he took a deep breath and reined back to face his men. Thumbing the Merwin Hulbert's hammer to full cock, he raised it in a straight-armed aim to cover the silent crew, and said in a voice he barely recognized, "The first one of you sons of bitches says anything about this . . . ever, I'll put a bullet through your skull and cut your tongue out after you're dead. Anyone here doubt that?"

He waited, giving them time to mull it over, but no one spoke, and there was no dubiety in their eyes. Nodding, he returned the revolver to its holster. Then he pulled his horse around and started back up the trail.

Chapter Twelve

Even after leaving the narrow switchbacks above North Fork, it was another two hours across a low, grassy saddle between the head of the canyon and the glacier lake Felix's map had indicated they would find there. The lake lay at the center of a shallow basin on the edge of timberline, a deep blue oval surrounded by boulders and freeze-stunted evergreens. Old fire pits along its near shore spoke of past camps, as did the close-cropped grass encircling it. The trail to the Crown spun off on their left, still climbing.

It was coming onto sundown as they led their mules to the lake and let them fan out to drink. Looping Zeke's reins around his saddle horn to keep them out of the water, Buck dismounted and walked over to where Cam Wallis was barely clinging to his seat. Cam's eyes had taken on a watery glaze, and his thin chest and ruined lungs heaved erratically. Gently prying the lead rope from the older man's hand, Buck tossed it over the mule's neck, then helped him dismount and led him to a cluster of boulders where there was some protection from the wind. Flecks of blood stippled the front of his shirt, and there was a bluish tinge to his lower lip.

Pulling his bandanna down, Buck said, "It's consumption, isn't it?"

Cam nodded weakly. " 'Pears like."

"How long have you known?"

"Knowed certain-sure, or just wondered? 'Cause, certain-sure, it was just today, when the blood started comin'." He gave Buck a plaintive look. "Lordy, boy, I can't get no wind in me. It's like tryin' to breathe underwater."

"It's the smoke making it worse," Buck said. "That and the thin air."

Cam slumped back against a boulder. "I ain't gonna ask for my pay, Buck."

"Nobody's talking—"

"Hush now, and listen," Cam interrupted thickly. "I don't curry favor from no man, and I pull my own weight or step outta the way of them that do. Only . . . ." His gaze swept the basin. "They ain't no place up here to step to, is there?"

"We'll get you to the Crown. You'll feel better after you've rested a spell. It'll be easier after this smoke clears out, too."

"It'd better be, 'cause if it ain't, I don't think I'm gonna be leavin' these mountains."

Buck didn't have a reply for that. Not if he didn't want to lie. Rising, he said, "Stay here and rest. I'm going to help Jake with the mules."

"You ain't stoppin', are you?" Cam got a kind of stricken look to his face. "Not on my account."

"No, we aren't stopping." Buck raised his gaze to the eerie red glow climbing the mountain toward them, and thought that if they weren't careful, and maybe a little lucky, it was possible none of them would leave this mountain range alive.

Chapter Thirteen

The trail opened up after they left the lake. Although still a clearly defined path, there was enough room to either side that the mules were no longer forced to travel single-file. China Jake continued up front with the zebra dun, but they turned the rest of the pack string loose—lead ropes hitched to their sawbucks—while Buck brought up the rear and watched for stragglers.

There weren't any, not really. The mules were staying close to the mare and the reassuring jingle of her bell, while the flames, quartering in from the northwest, kept the herd moving at a brisk, anxious walk. Hanging on gamely, Cam fell in behind Buck.

The sun went down and took its light with it, but the land remained bathed in a quivering, apricot radiance. Flitting embers drifted overhead. Now and again one of them would float down into the tree-line scrub, but very few caught, and then only briefly. Farther down the mountain they likely would have ignited instantly, but spring came late to the high country, and summers were usually cool and damp.

It was after midnight when Jake called another halt. The mules immediately crowded up around the bell mare, like frightened children seeking the protection of their mother. Buck forced Zeke through the mob, Cam close behind. They were among the highest peaks of the Crown Range here. The boulders were spotted with lichen, and the few spindly trees they'd passed had appeared wind-twisted and vaguely grotesque in the wildfire's light. But when Buck reined in at Jake's side, he saw that, going forward, the trail dropped swiftly back into heavy timber—close-growth forests of towering Ponderosa pine. They were on its southern fringe here. The fire was pushing in from the west, and for the first time, its flames were clearly visible to the weary muleskinners.

"That's our destination," Jake said, pointing northward.

Buck followed the line of his arm to a solitary mountain peak, probably another four or five hours away. From here its highest point looked like a—he smiled. From here it looked like a crown, the kind he'd seen in books and newspapers, worn by kings and queens.

"The mine is at its base," Jake added.

"What's the trail like?"

"It runs more or less in a straight line. I don't think we'll have to put our mules back on their lead ropes, not as long as they can hear the mare's bell."

Buck eyed the ragged line of flames gnawing into the belly of the forest from the west. Fueled by resin-heavy pines and fanned by strong winds, the fire was burning hotter and faster than he would have anticipated. Watching, he estimated it was moving at about the same rate of speed as a man walking over level ground. Every time a new tree caught, it did so with an explosive blast that sent pillars of flame into the sky, and spewed a fresh crop of cherry-red cinders forward. Buck could feel its heat even from here, tamping down the high-country chill, promising even worse to come.

A voice at his side wheezed, "It's too far, boy."

Buck turned angrily. Cam had pulled the bandanna down off his face. He was peering intently into Buck's eyes, his own gleaming unnaturally in the throbbing light.

"It's too far, and you know it. Same as Jake—" He broke off in a rattling cough, grasping his saddle horn with both hands.

Buck bit back the denial he wanted to throw in the old man's face. Turning to Jake, he demanded, "Is he right?"

"If he is, we'll all die," Jake replied simply. "It's too late to go back, and too far even if we tried. And if we got down in there," he tipped his head to the east, where the forest seemed to run on forever, "we'd never come out."

"You got any ideas?"

"If we can reach the Crown before the fire cuts us off, they'll have room for us and our stock inside the main shaft. I'm guessing that's where the miners are holed up now."

Buck looked north, although without much hope. Without much option, either, he reminded himself, and lifted Zeke's reins. "Move 'em out," he told Jake. "As soon as we get into the trees, put your horse into a hard trot. I'll keep the mules close behind you."

Cam hacked and spat, then lifted his ruddled gaze. "Leave the mules, boy. They'll only slow us down."

"No!" Buck shook his head. "I won't do it, not yet." He motioned Jake forward, then guided Zeke out of the way. Mumbling under his breath, Cam followed. "You can go your own way, if that's what you want," Buck told him as the pack mules flowed past. "You'd probably be smart if you did."

"Jus' shut your yapper, boy," the old man growled. "If you two hounds're too dumb to know when you're licked, then I reckon I'll have to hang on 'til you do."

Chapter Fourteen

It was after sundown when they reached the glacier lake. Despite his desire to push on, Anton allowed Sid Cunningham to talk him into stopping long enough to rest the horses.

"We've been pushing 'em hard all day," Cunningham warned. "If we keep on like this, they'll start to cave on us."

Anton had to grit his teeth to keep from spitting out that he didn't give a damn if he killed every last one of them, as long as McCready and his mules were brought to bay. But Cunningham wouldn't understand that—none of them would—so Anton kept his mouth shut and reluctantly conceded to a thirty-minute halt.

Dismounting, he slipped the bit from his horse' mouth, then made his way to the shelter of some rocks bordering the lake. The others moved off in the opposite direction, standing close and lighting their cigars and pipes as they saw fit; Bob Harlow used a jackknife to slice a thumb-sized piece of tobacco from a plug he kept in his shirt pocket, and stowed it in a rear corner of his mouth to soften. Anton considered lighting a cigar of his own— he'd brought a couple of them along—but decided against it. He didn't want anyone thinking his resolve to catch up with the pack train might be weakening.

Anton knew he was being a jackass. He supposed there were a lot of people around Pineview who'd say he always was. But in the past he'd tried to treat the men who worked for him, the competent ones anyway, with at least a degree of deference. It was a concession he'd learned to make years before, when a crew of muleskinners had quit *en masse* to protest his haranguing them to move faster. It galled him to do so—he paid his help well, damnit—but he'd discovered to his chagrin that there were things in life even money couldn't supply.

Anton anticipated a similar mutiny tonight. He'd been listening to his men grumbling ever since they topped out above the switchbacks and spotted the approaching flames, so much nearer than even the most pessimistic among them had expected. The McLaughlin brothers were doing most of the complaining, but he'd also heard Cunningham and Harlow chiming in from time to time. Only Foster seemed to hold his tongue, either that or he was keeping his voice low so that he wouldn't be overheard.

Despite his impatience with the men, Anton could understand their fear. Rising and stepping clear of the shoreline boulders, he gravely eyed the no-longer-distant inferno. The whole damn horizon seemed caught in the throes of its own *Danse Macabre*, a frighteningly primitive gambol that gave even his own determination pause.

Separating himself from the others, Sid Cunningham came over. "Looks like the fire's going to do the job for us, boss."

Bracing himself mentally, Anton turned to face his crew. "I figured it would've been one of the McLaughlins," he said.

"They're more talk than gumption. Fact is, if not for that—" Cunningham nodded toward the wildfire— "I'd be inclined to see it through. But it ain't worth risking our necks for."

"I hired you to do a job."

"You hired me to run a freight outfit, which I've tried to do to the best of my ability. This ain't part of that."

Anton studied the others a moment, then said loudly, "Sid isn't quitting. None of you are, not until I'm sure those mules are stopped and Buck McCready is dead. It's as simple as that, boys, and any man doubts me had best draw his piece now."

"No," Cunningham replied firmly, hooking his thumbs behind his gunbelt. "I'm sorry Mr. Luce, but we're—"

The sound of Anton's revolver cleaved the smoky air between them. The men jumped, and Harlow choked as if he'd swallowed some of his wad. Sid Cunningham stumbled backward with a look of surprise on his face. Then his knees buckled and he crumpled to the ground.

"You boys listen up, now," Anton said, his voice shaky but resolute. "We're going forward, and we ain't stopping until I'm certain those mules are stopped. I asked before if any of you had doubts about my word. Nobody did then, and you'd damn well better not now."

No one spoke or moved, and after a moment Anton nodded and returned the Merwin Hulbert to its holster.

"All right, let's mount up and ride."

Chapter Fifteen

They did their best. China Jake kept his horse and the zebra dun moving at a swift trot, and the trail was wide enough that the mules could follow without losing sight or sound of the mare, or snagging their packs on trees.

But the fire was too quick. It caught them a couple of hours into the final leg of their journey, although in a way Buck hadn't expected. From a distance the blaze had looked like a solid wall of flames; up close, its front was more ragged than he'd expected, flaring up along both sides of the trail and burning wide swaths of timber, but bypassing others. Eventually, he knew, the fire would consume everything in its path, but for now the fluctuating winds were offering them a slim reprieve.

Although they kept their bandannas over their faces, the smoke wasn't as bad here as it had been farther back. As they passed through the spinning colonnade of flames, it rose above them in a writhing mantle that reflected the light back onto the land in what

Buck imagined hell must look like. Embers darted like maddened hornets, and his sleeves and trousers were soon pocked with tiny, charred holes, the flesh underneath blistered red.

The stock suffered similarly, the mules braying and whinnying at the fiery prods, sometimes kicking out blindly to drive the hot coals away. Buck did what he could for Zeke, trying to swat the embers aside before they landed, or as soon as he saw them, but he couldn't reach them all, and there was nothing he could do for the pack animals.

Cam suffered in silence, but there was a spark in his eyes now that had been absent earlier, a rock-like resolve to see the job through to its finish. Buck didn't ask how he was faring; that was also visible in the older man's red, tearing eyes . . . along with the acceptance that his will was no guarantee he'd realize his goal.

Neither Felix nor his map had mentioned any kind of clearing, so Buck was surprised when they came to a long meadow with green grass and a creek running through its center. They stopped at its ford and the mules spread out eagerly to dip their heads to the purling water, but when they raised them again, their muzzles were dry; the stream looked almost syrupy from soot and half-burned debris.

Buck splashed Zeke across the fetlock-deep creek to where Jake waited on the other side. "How much farther?" he shouted above the crackling wail of the fire.

Jake pulled down his bandanna. "Maybe another hour."

Buck's gritted his teeth. It was too far. But they couldn't stop here, either. Eventually the flames would advance into the meadow. Or else the smoke would drop back down and engulf them. Either meant an agonizing death.

Looking west, past the sporadic flames to where the fire burned hottest, sending its sable plumes into the sky, Buck felt a sudden hopelessness.

"The worst of it isn't here yet," Jake shouted, as if reading his mind.

"It will be soon enough." He looked around as Cam rode up beside them. Cam didn't speak, but Buck recalled his earlier advice to abandon the mules. For a moment he actually considered it. Then he shook his head. It wasn't the supplies he refused to leave behind, but the livestock. "We're going to have to make a run for it," he told them. "We won't leave the mules, but we can't stop if we lose one or two of them, either. They'll have to keep up as best they can."

"At a hard run, we should reach the Crown in thirty minutes or less," Jake said, but his expression implied he wasn't sure if even that would be enough.

"We'll have to do the best—" Buck stopped talking when he noticed Jake's attention had shifted. He looked over his shoulder, following the direction of the younger man's gaze. About the last thing he would have expected to see at that moment was a group of horsemen emerging from the flame-lined southern trail. "Who the devil . . . ?"

"It's Anton Luce," Jake said tautly.

"Him and others that work for—" Cam's voice was severed by a restrained cough.

Jake took up the dropped thread of his explanation. "It's Luce and the McLaughlin brothers, and that's Bob Harlow behind them."

Luce and his men were still at least a hundred yards away. They were huddled close just inside the meadow, talking among themselves. Buck thought they appeared as surprised to see the pack train as he was to see them. Then he noticed a fifth rider, hanging back behind the others.

"Who's the kid?" he asked. "The one in the bowler hat?"

"That's Foster. He works for Felix Payne."

"Looks like he's working for Luce now."

Cam pulled his bandanna down and spat a wad of bloody phlegm into the grass. "Has been all along, I figure, the damn fool," he croaked.

"That sounds about right," Jake agreed grimly. "Luce is a son of a bitch, but he pays good wages . . . if you can stomach working for him. He offered me a job last spring, but I turned him down."

Buck didn't ask why. He knew Luce's reputation from Utah. Nor did he have any doubts about what had prompted the saloon owner to follow them into this hellish morass of flames. There could be only one answer to that, and Buck's hand moved instinctively to the rifle booted under his right leg.

"Get 'em moving, Jake," he said tersely. "Keep the bell mare with you if you can, but keep her in a high lope and don't stop for anything until you reach the mine. Cam, you go with Jake."

"Like hell," the older man protested.

"You can't fight all of them," Jake added.

"I don't intend to fight them. I just want to slow 'em down a little."

"They'll kill you, boy," Cam rumbled.

"I figure Anton Luce has wanted to kill me for a long time," Buck replied. "He hasn't done it yet." He looked at Jake, then Cam. "Go on, you two. Get out of here."

Jake glanced at Cam, who jerked his head toward where the trail plunged back into the forest to the north. "Lead on, heathen," he said, drawing his revolver.

There was no animosity in Jake's reply. "Are you coming with me?"

"Just 'till we get 'em started, then I'll come back'n help Buck."

Jake cast an anxious glance toward Luce and his men, edging their horses deeper into the meadow. He nodded curtly. "All right, just don't get yourself shot, old man." Then he pulled his horse around and gave the zebra dun's rope a tug.

"Go on," Buck told Cam. "Stay with the mules. That's an order."

Jake kicked his horse into a lope, the pack mules automatically following the bell mare. Cam swung behind the loose stock, hazing the slower ones into a quicker gait. Buck drew his rifle and settled it across his saddlebows. Cam's return within a couple of minutes startled him.

"I told you to stay with the mules."

"Them mules don't need my help," Cam replied. Then he noticed Buck's rifle, and snorted with derision. "A damn single-shot Remington? Hell, boy, we ain't huntin' buffalo."

Buck glanced over his shoulder to where the last of the pack animals were funneling into the north trail. "Goddamnit, go help Jake."

"No, sir, I ain't. You can't—" He broke off in a wet, sputtering cough that bent him nearly double. The revolver slipped from his fingers, and one of his reins fell. His horse danced back a couple of paces and might have bolted if Buck hadn't grabbed the dangling rein and pulled the animal back.

Wheezing, Cam reached out clumsily for the rein. Buck placed it in his searching hand, then leaned from his saddle to pluck the fallen revolver out of the grass. He wedged it back in its holster, then circled Cam's horse and smacked it on the rump with his hat.

"Go on," he said kindly as the horse trotted off. "Help Jake with the mules. I'll be along directly."

Cam hung onto the saddle horn with both hands, his head bobbing. Buck waited until he was certain the horse would follow after the pack mules, then brought Zeke back around to face the southern side of the meadow. Luce and his men had advanced nearly a third of the way into the clearing while he was dealing with Cam, and Anton had drawn his own rifle. Buck's throat constricted when he realized Anton was already leveling his sights on him. He snapped the Remington to his shoulder and quickly pulled the trigger. With such a hurried shot, he wasn't expecting to hit anything. He only meant to give the saloon owner pause. So he was surprised when Luce tumbled from his saddle.

The others hauled up uncertainly, exchanging glances. Then the two brothers Jake had identified as the McLaughlins wheeled their mounts and raced back the way they'd come. Buck would have preferred it if they all fled, but Harlow and Foster stayed. Foster dropped to the ground and rushed over to where Anton was rolling back and forth in the grass at his mount's side, while Harlow slid his own long gun from its scabbard.

Buck swiftly rolled his hammer to full cock and thumbed the block open to eject the spent cartridge. He dug a fresh round from his belt and inserted it into the chamber. Familiarity with the old weapon gave him speed, but not enough to beat a lever gun. Harlow's first bullet screamed past Buck's ear with an angry hiss; his second peeled a layer of flesh from the side of Buck's neck even as he closed the Remington's breech. He sucked his breath in at the bullet's sharp bite, but couldn't afford the time to even reach up and explore the wound's depth. He tried to shoulder the Remington, but Zeke was shifting nervously under him, more spooked by the gunfire than by the encircling flames.

Buck kept trying to steady the rifle against his shoulder, but the sights were jumping all over. Finally he swung down and dropped to one knee. Harlow fired his third round, the bullet burrowing into the dirt at Buck's side, peppering his thigh with clumps of sod. He raised his rifle and squeezed the trigger in a single fluid motion. The Remington's big .50 slug pushed back solidly against his shoulder. Across the clearing, Harlow cartwheeled off the back of his horse.

Buck lowered his weapon to reload. Luce was already back on his feet, one hand planted firmly to his side. He gripped his revolver in the other. Foster stood behind him, looking more confused than scared. Bellowing a curse that seemed to rival the roar of the flames, Luce started forward, and despite the distance between them, despite the eerily pulsating light, his bullets were coming alarmingly close. The first tugged at Buck's jacket; the second hit the ground less than a foot in front of him. Tight-lipped, he closed the Remington's breech and threw the rifle to his shoulder just as Luce fired his third round.

The Remington jerked violently upward, and Buck cried out at the snap of bones in his right hand as the rifle was torn from his grasp. It flipped to the side, its forearm shattered by Luce's bullet. Pain lanced through Buck's arm from fingertip to shoulder as he instinctively cradled his right hand to his chest. Luce continued to stagger toward him, a demonic grin splitting his soot-darkened face, his ribs glistening with blood.

Buck reached for his revolver with his left hand, but the Colt was holstered too far back on his right hip. He tried sliding the belt around, but it snagged on something and refused to budge. He looked up. Luce had closed the gap between them to less than twenty yards, and still had half a cylinder of live rounds left in his revolver. He stopped and raised the gun, and Buck muttered a quiet, "Aw, hell."

Then a ragged howl echoed across the clearing. Buck twisted partway around to see what he thought at first might be a phantom. In the next second he recognized Cam Wallis, spurring his horse across the meadow.

Luce paused and his grin slipped; his eyes widened in alarm. Cam was firing rapidly, his pistol thrust before him like a saber. Luce jerked and half spun, then came back around to return the older man's fire. Both were shooting as fast as they could thumb their hammers and pull the triggers. Buck couldn't have said who hit whom first, but it was Anton Luce who took a clumsy step backward, then abruptly collapsed.

Half a second later, Cam toppled from his mount, pitching face-first into the knee-high grass at the stream's edge.

Chapter Sixteen

Standing at the mouth of the Crown's main adit, Buck stared at a sparkling landscape that, only a couple of days before, he hadn't been sure he would ever see again. Half a foot of snow had fallen overnight, smothering whatever buried embers might have remained after yesterday's icy rains. The gusting winds that had kept the wildfire burning so hot and wicked were calm now, the sky a deep, brilliant blue.

At Buck's side was China Jake; around them nearly forty others, the miners and outside laborers who had taken refuge inside the mine's broad main entrance to escape the flames, gazed in wonder at the drifted snowbanks.

It was an unusually early storm according to the Crown's manager, a stumpy man with bushy side whiskers named Burdett, but he insisted he wasn't worried about its effect on the mine's operation.

"This won't last," he predicted, his breath creating a thin fog in the chilled air. "Even at this altitude, we won't have to shut down for another month at least."

Buck didn't know, nor did he care. It was enough for him that the fire was out. Still, the conflagration had left its mark on the land, a stark transformation of blackened tree trunks, scorched bushes, and an acidic odor that not even rain and snow had been able to erase. The Crown's buildings—storage sheds, bunkhouse, kitchen and mess hall, stables, and office—had all suffered to some degree from the fiery hell that had passed through the high-mountain valley less than forty-eight hours before.

Glancing at Jake, Buck said, "I think I'm about ready to pull out."

"What about Foster?"

Buck turned quiet as he considered the youth and what to do with him. There had been no fight left in the kid after Luce's death, and Buck was beginning to think there never had been. It had been Foster who helped get Cam's body loaded onto his horse, then rounded up Zeke and brought him back for Buck. Foster was somewhere behind him now, hanging back in the mine's wide drift as he had in the meadow, as if wanting only to fade into the shadows.

"Foster can do what he wants," Buck decided. "I'm not going to worry about him."

"If we leave now, we'll have to come back later to haul out the ore they've busted up for the panniers."

"Someone else can do that. My job was to get the supplies up here. As soon as I collect my money from Payne, I'm heading south again."

After a moment's reflection, Jake said, "I think I'll stay. Felix will need a packer."

"He'll need several packers."

"I'll find them."

The miners were shuffling past them now, into the light and snow to pick up where the fires had forced them to leave off. As if nothing had changed, Buck reflected, but he knew it had.

Staring at the small miners' cemetery behind the Crown's bunkhouse where he and Jake had buried Cam yesterday in a hard rain just shy of sleet, Buck said softly, "He was a son of a bitch, wasn't he?"

"Cam?"

"Yeah."

A wistful smile crossed Jake's face. "You didn't know him very well."

"I know he rode you pretty hard a time or two."

"How? By calling me a heathen? He called you a boy more than once, and he called both of us hounds. I'll tell you something

I'll bet you haven't heard about Cam Wallis. Last spring a bunch of prospectors cornered me in a livery in Pineview. They were determined to pound some sense into my chink head, as they put it, and convince me to go back to China. They were doing a pretty fair job of it, too. Then Cam showed up with a singletree and laid into them like he was chopping firewood. If he didn't save my life that day, he sure saved me from a bad beating."

"I wondered why you put up with him."

"I put up with him because there was solid wood under that rough bark, and because he was a man to stand by your side, no matter the odds." He looked at Buck. "Like he did for you with Anton Luce."

"He saved my life, that's for damn certain."

"Don't ask me to explain it, but that's why I'm going to stay here and wait until the panniers are filled," Jake said quietly. "It shouldn't take more than a day or two, and that way I won't have to make a second trip."

"You're going to stand by Felix Payne's side the way Cam stood by yours that day in the livery, is that it?"

"More or less. Like I said, don't ask me to explain it, because I can't. It's just something I want to do."

"Even after Felix sent us up here knowing Luce would likely follow?"

"Even then," Jake replied.

Buck turned his gaze back to the snowy mountain range to the south. After a pause, he said, "And you figure you can handle twenty-four head of mules by yourself?"

"I can if I take my time. They should follow the dun without giving me any trouble."

"That's a lot of packs for one man to handle. Heavy ones, too."

"Maybe I can get Foster to help me."

Buck worked his shoulder experimentally. Harlow's bullet hadn't cut too deep of a trough through the flesh, but it was still sore, the muscles in that whole area as stiff as dried rawhide. Worse was the damage to his hand, when Luce's bullet had struck his rifle. The force of his bullet and the way the Remington had been twisted out of his grasp had broken three of his fingers and cut a deep gash in his wrist.

Jake said mildly, but with the hint of a smile, "The bigger question might be, can you saddle Zeke with only one hand and a bum shoulder?"

"Zeke won't be a problem, but maybe I'll hang around a few days, after all. That way I can follow you and Foster back to Pineview and help with the mules."

"I'd welcome it," Jake said.

"I'll want to take a shovel along, find those I couldn't bring out with me and give them a proper burial."

"Luce and Harlow?"

"And anyone else who didn't make it."

Jake nodded, and after a pause, he said, "That sounds about right."

The Hanging Tree Committee

Michael Knost

The census had taken Caleb Truitt farther west than prudence advised, past the last marked roads and into a country that seemed to wear no name. The wind there bore scents unknown to him—odors he would as soon not seek the origin of. He urged his horse along a dry creek bed, its banks thick with cottonwoods that offered scant defense against the pressing weight of the sun.

He came upon the town in a bend of the land, sudden and quiet. It was not on any ledger nor spoken of in the prairie hamlets he'd passed through. No sign named it. No mile marker pointed the way. Just a slatted fence leaning under the burden of years and a narrow road drawn straight between two rows of buildings, each shaded by overhanging eaves, their dark undersides hiding the windows.

There was no rail line, no saloon doors swinging. The hush of the place settled over him. It was not yet noon, but the town lay in a silence he'd come to associate with Sundays or funerals. The buildings stood weathered and gray, their timbers bleached by long years of wind, yet in the records of past counts there was no mark of this place. By all appearances it had been here for decades, though the government had never put it down on paper.

He tied his mare to a weathered hitching post and studied the structures.

The federal government had hired him to count heads and mark down the details of lives: names, origins, trades, and kin. The great machine of a nation turned on such reckonings. A name in the ledger was a man acknowledged, seen by the country that claimed to govern him. A name unwritten was a soul left to drift in the dark, unclaimed and neglected.

He had taken the post for the pay, plain enough. A man could live on little if he had to, but he could not start a life on it, not the kind he'd hoped to give Claire. She was waiting back in Kansas, her answer given if he could make the means. Counting heads in far-off places was the quickest way he knew to put a roof over them and bread on their table. Every mile west was another toward that life, though it was carrying him farther from her.

He began at the nearest dwelling, a low-built place with a sod roof bowed beneath its own weight. A woman in a brown kerchief stood in the doorway, her eyes fixed upon him.

"Morning, ma'am," he said, presenting his document with its government seal. "Name's Caleb Truitt, enumerator for the Ninth Census of the United States."

"Already been counted."

"Happens every ten years, ma'am." He removed his hat and wiped his brow. "This here is the one of 1870."

She ignored his document, simply pointing him toward the sheriff's office.

He found the place boarded up, its sign faded and peeling. The door hung loose and grass pushed up through cracks in the foundation. If a sheriff had ever kept office there, he hadn't worn the badge in years.

"There's no lawman here," said a voice behind him.

A man approached with a long-legged gait. He was tall, maybe six foot and some inches, with a beard the color of old lumber and a shirt so white it marked him as no farmer. His hands were clean, the nails neatly kept. A man who worked, yes, but not with a spade or bridle.

He introduced himself as Elias Tamm and offered a hand that was as smooth as it was clean. "Enumerator, you say?"

"How did you—?"

"Word gets around in these parts," he said with a smile. "You aim to find lodging while you carry out your count?"

Truitt peered down the street. "I saw no hotel, nor any place of such when I came through."

"Ain't none to be had. You're welcome to stay with us. My wife's a fine cook, and you can commence your enumeratin' there."

"Much obliged." Truitt glanced again at the empty building. "No lawman in town?"

"None needed."

On the way toward the Tamm place, Truitt caught movement farther down the row of houses. A thin old man sitting in the shadow of a porch. The man wasn't rocking, wasn't shelling beans, just watching. His face stayed in shade. When their eyes met, the old man rose without hurry and stepped inside, closing the door in a single, even motion, his gaze fixed until the gap was gone.

They had corn cakes that night, and potatoes boiled to softness, dressed with pork drippings scraped from a saved tin. No meat. Elias made no mention of it, and Truitt didn't press. Over the meal, his mind drifted to Claire. She would have made a face at the lack of meat, but she'd have eaten her share without complaint, the way she had on those lean years after her father died. It was her steadiness in such times that had fixed him on her. He had sworn that when he came back to Kansas, it would be with means enough that they'd never again scrape at the bottom of the pan.

After supper, he and Elias sat on the porch listening to frogs sing as the wind moved through the trees in a low and hollow sound.

Elias smoking his pipe and Truitt whittling at a slat of pine with no aim to shape it, only to pass the time.

A rising pitch of voices came from within the house across the way—first a man's, hard-edged and booming, then a woman's, softer, tangled in either fear or defiance. Her words were harder to catch, but he heard the break in them. It was a sound that stuck in the chest.

Truitt rose from the chair, meaning to cross the road and make himself seen. Sometimes the appearance of a witness was enough to pause a hand raised in anger.

"You don't want to go over there," Elias said, his voice low and fixed.

"He's beating her."

Elias nodded once.

Heat moved into Truitt's neck and ears. "Then someone ought to stop it."

Elias nodded again. "It'll be taken care of." His voice did not rise. There was no anger in it, no fire. Just that same plainness, that certainty that struck colder than the shouting across the road.

Ada stood in the doorway twisting a dishrag. Her gaze met Truitt's only for a moment.

"What do you mean, *taken care of?*"

It was the girl who answered. Sarah, crouched near the woodpile, her small hands curled around a kindling stick. "The Hanging Tree Committee sees to it," she said without looking up.

Elias turned toward her, his eyes narrowing just a fraction. That was all it took. She returned to her task as if nothing had been said.

"We don't speak of things we do not understand," Elias finally said.

The shouting had gone quiet by then. No final scream. No whimpering or sobs. Just a silence that fell too quickly.

Truitt didn't sleep easy that night. The quiet of the place was more than he could bear. He stared at the sky through the window, wondering if Claire lay awake beneath the same moon, and whether she would take his word in letters should he tell her of this place.

The next morning, Ada asked if he'd fetch water, and Truitt

took the pail to the pump where the handle squealed and groaned. On his return, he saw her—the woman from the house across the way—crouched by her garden row, sleeves rolled, fingers moving through the dirt.

She stood when she saw him and turned in a manner that revealed the purpling bruise on her right eye. Her mouth fell slightly open, and for an instant he thought she was about to speak. But whatever words had risen withered before reaching air. She turned and walked stiffly back to her house.

After supper, Truitt joined Elias on the porch. The two sat without speaking for what seemed hours. Ada had gone in to lay the children down, and the faint light from the windows brought a flurry of moths and millers. Truitt's thoughts traveled back east with the small porch at Claire's family home and how she would sit in the evenings, watching the road for him. He had told her the work might run long, but it would be worth the wait.

A stir in the street pulled him from his thoughts. A man was crossing toward the porch across the way, bearing a long, narrow parcel swaddled in canvas and bound with twine. He laid it down before the door with care. No knock came, nor any word. He lingered but a moment before heading back the way he'd come.

Truitt rose to his feet. "Who was that?"

"I wouldn't trouble yourself with it."

Truitt was already off the porch, crossing the road in long strides.

The bundle lay on the porch boards. About two feet in length. The canvas was stiff in places, darkened with something that might've been water or blood. The seam had pulled slightly open at one end. Inside were sticks. Thin, clean-cut switches—caning wood, smooth and straight, trimmed at both ends. The kind of thing a man might use to set a wayward soul straight.

He had near reached the Tamms' porch when the door of the neighboring home creaked open.

The man of the house stood fixed, his eyes on the bundle at his feet. For a moment it seemed he might give way to tears. Then, without a word, he stepped back into the house.

In little time, he came around the side leading a saddled gelding and mounted with a hurried, uneven motion. The animal shied at first but soon settled into its stride.

The man rode hard, head down, out past the last fence post, his shape dwindling into the darkness without once looking back.

"That bundle. Was it a warning?"

Elias's voice came quiet and unbothered. "Of a kind."

"From who?"

Elias looked at him then. His eyes were steady, not cold but emptied of anything resembling surprise. "You ought to mind your census work. Leave off what don't belong in it."

Behind the screen door, Ada had returned. She stood with both hands on the handle, as though steadying it. Or herself.

Elias leaned forward, forearms on his knees. "You're a guest here. We've shown you kindness. Don't go chasing things that don't concern you."

Truitt took a breath, and the air caught like splinters in his throat. "That man beat his wife. Surely that concerns everyone."

"And it's been handled," Elias said. Not with harshness. Not even weariness. Just fact.

Long after Elias and Ada retired, Truitt sat on the porch alone. He listened for the hoofbeats to return, for a scream carried on wind, for anything at all. But nothing came. He thought of Claire again, and how he had meant to bring her west once he had the means. Tonight he wondered if this was a place a woman could live without fear.

On his way to the general store that morning to purchase flour for Ada, Truitt had passed a man standing alone in the street. The man faced a shuttered house, his hands in his pockets.

He kept his stance the whole time Truitt passed, never once meeting his eye. When Truitt looked back a minute later, the street lay empty.

The store stood square at the corner of what passed for the town's lone crossroad. Its false front rose plain above the dust, the clapboards bleached to the hue of old ash. Over the door, a sign hung a little askew, its paint worn near to nothing. It read: GOODS & PROVISIONS in red paint flaked by sun and wind. No name beneath it.

The man behind the counter was broad through the shoulders, built solid, not yet bent by age though it had left its mark on him. He looked to be in his fifties, his beard kept short, the gray showing strongest at the chin.

He introduced himself as Barrow and began giving names when Truitt told him his business. Listing his wife, now passed. A daughter married out east to a man who repaired rail clocks. No other family under his roof.

"You've been stayin' with Elias," Barrow said.

Truitt nodded.

"Good people."

"They've been generous."

Barrow turned to scoop flour from a barrel, the tin pail ringing once against the metal lip. Truitt watched the slow pour of white into a cloth sack. His thoughts went to Claire, and the way she would smile at the sound of coin laid out for something that might be made into bread. She had often said a house was nearer to home when the air carried the scent of baking.

"That business the other night," Truitt said, watching Barrow's face. "The man across from them. Gone now."

Barrow didn't look up. He tied the sack off with a practiced twist and slide. "He left."

"On account of the bundle?"

Barrow set the flour down and met Truitt's gaze for the first time. "Folks here take care of their own. We don't let poison settle in. If a man can't govern himself, the town will see to it."

"That's not law. That's vengeance."

Barrow shook his head. "It ain't vengeance if there's no hate behind it. It's justice. Quiet and proper."

The light through the windows had grown brighter, sharp with morning, and bringing a stifling warmth.

"Is there no judge? No sheriff? No hearing of any kind?"

Barrow gave him a long look. "We've got eyes, son. And ears. And we remember. That's more than most men can say about their judges." He turned away to stack tins behind the counter, letting it be known the discussion was finished.

Truitt left the store and walked to the restaurant, passing a saddle repairer's shop with its door half-closed and dust gathered thick on the windowsills. No one had gone in or out all morning.

The restaurant was modest with its walls bleached and worn by years of sun and dust. The smells of simmering beans and seared pork set his mouth to watering.

"I hope you're hungry," the woman behind the counter said.

"I'm actually here on business, ma'am."

"Business can wait," she said with a laugh. "Find you a table and I'll be right back."

"Would you be the proprietor, ma'am?"

"Guilty as charged," she said, returning with a plate of pork steak, beans, and cornbread. "People call me Mrs. Cutter, though my husband's been gone fifteen years now."

"I'm sorry to hear that."

"I ain't," she said with a wheeze of laughter. "Not nary a bit."

The meat was browned at the edges, tender to the bite, and seasoned with something that reached the back of the throat like warmth from a hearth.

"Ma'am," Truitt said after a few bites, "this may be the finest pork I've ever tasted."

She gave a thin smile and sat across from him. "Old recipe."

"My name is Caleb Truitt, and I'm here enumerating for the census." He put down his fork. "I've done this job a while. Traveled far. Most people aren't eager to speak to a government man. They worry we're here to collect taxes or conscript their sons. But the census does good. Representation. Aid. Supply fair shares. It strengthens a place."

Her eyes did not leave his. "We've no need for outsiders telling us what's fair." The words came out clean, not sharp. Like scripture read from memory.

"You don't seem the kind to fear a ledger."

"I don't," she answered. "But I've lived long enough to know some knowledge sours as soon as it's spoken."

The next evening the dust hung low in the street, undisturbed. The general store had closed its shutters. The restaurant's curtains were drawn. The saddle repairer still hadn't opened his door.

As he passed the house across from the Tamms', he noticed the porch stood bare now. He meant only to pass by, but movement caught his eye.

The wife stood in her garden among rows of wilting greens with a basket hooked over her arm. Her fingers picked over bean stalks and limp chard, harvesting what remained, head bowed low. The bruise on her face had reached its final bloom, fading at the edges now into that sickly green. Her eye had gone hollow, but the skin around it was tight with healing.

Truitt stepped off the road and approached with open hands. "Ma'am, can I lend you a hand with that?"

She gave a start at his voice and near let the basket fall. Her fingers tightened on the handle until the knuckles showed white. She glanced quickly—first to the Tamms' home, then down the road toward the buildings. At last, she held the basket out to him.

"The horse came back," she said.

It took a moment for the meaning to settle.

"Your husband's horse?"

She nodded, eyes down. "The gelding. I found him tied out back. Saddle twisted. Bag still on."

She turned and led him to the stable where the horse stood content, its mouth working slowly at a half-empty trough. The saddlebag still hung on its flank. Stiff with dust.

"I told him," the woman said. "Told him not to ignore it. Told him to mind himself. But he wouldn't listen."

"What did you mean to warn him of?"

She carried the bag into the house, her hands shaking as she laid it on the table and untied the flap. "It's not right, the way it's done. But I ain't strong enough to change it none."

She didn't open the bag. Her hands moved to her face instead, pressing into her eyes until her palms grew slick. When she lowered them, her expression had shifted. Her mouth was set, her gaze sharpened—not into defiance, but into warning. "He thought he could strike me, sit down to supper like nothing passed. But you can't hide from the Committee. They see."

"Did they . . ." He paused. "Did they hang him?"

She didn't speak for a long moment. Then she leaned forward and whispered, "There's the tree, and then there's the pen."

Truitt sat back slowly. "The pen?"

Her eyes went to the window. "I should not have said that. I let my feelings run away with me. You must put it from your mind. Let it rest."

He gazed down at the saddlebag. Part of him wanted to open it. Part of him wanted to flee the house and ride until the sky changed color. But another part thought of Claire, and the promise he'd made to come back to her with a future worth having. If he turned away from the truth here, what kind of man would she be taking as her husband? "I can't forget what I've seen."

"You best mind your place," she said. "Mind your purpose. Or you'll find the switches on your doorstep, same as him."

He opened his mouth to answer, but she raised her hand. "You don't ask about the tree. You don't ask about the pen. You don't ask about them that went missing. You keep to your numbers and your little book. Or you'll end up among the ones we don't speak of."

❧

Truitt saddled his mare at first light and rode past the last row of houses, past fence lines where corn stalks stood bowed and sunburnt. The land beyond rolled gently at first—grassy knuckles of prairie rising into the hills, the soil turning stony and the wind sharper.

He rode on without set purpose until coming upon a trail that climbed into higher ground where the cottonwoods yielded to black locust and juniper.

At the crest of a low ridge stood a single tree.

It leaned a little to the east from years of hard weather, yet its roots held fast, the bark cut deep with heavy furrows. Its crown spread wide and lean, and from one thick limb—low, broad, and bare where bark should have been—he saw the wear. A rope had been there. Not once, not twice, but many times. The bark was worn smooth, the limb hardened to its labor.

He did not speak. The silence here was not empty, it was full. Full of what had happened, of what might still.

He turned in his saddle when he heard the hoofbeats.

Barrow rode closer on a red-coated gelding. His posture was relaxed, his face unreadable.

Truitt straightened. "I was just—"

"Documenting landmarks?" Barrow offered.

"Yes. For the record. Terrain. Notable fixtures."

Barrow nodded, as if humoring a child caught near a locked box. "Then you've found one."

Truitt dusted his hands. "This tree—"

"Has stood here longer than any living man remembers," Barrow said. "And it remembers things best left buried."

"The man who beat his wife. Did he end up here?"

Barrow shifted in the saddle. "Don't rightly know. When a man's warned, he chooses his road. Either the trail, or the rope."

"And the pen?"

The man's jaw moved slightly, the only sign of discomfort he'd seen in him.

When the man didn't speak, Truitt said, "I've heard talk."

"We thrive here because we keep each other right. There's no fires set by drunkards. No thieving hands. No screams behind walls. We remember what the world was before men forgot how to behave."

"That's not law," Truitt said. "That's fear."

"You're damn right it is."

Elias was waiting at the gate when Truitt returned. His arms rested at his sides, hands loose. He did not look angry, only resolved. "You ought to move along."

"I suppose I've worn out my welcome."

Elias shook his head. "It ain't that. It's the shadow you've kicked up. We try to keep it off our families."

"I never meant harm."

"You brought questions. That's the seed of harm."

"I didn't come here to stir trouble," Truitt said. "I came for the wage. There's a woman waiting on me back in Kansas—Claire. I mean to marry her come spring. This job was the fastest way I knew to make enough for a roof and a start."

Elias's eyes softened, but not enough to change his meaning. "Then you ought to keep to the work and ride on when it's done."

"It falls to someone to tell the law."

Truitt gathered his things. There wasn't much—a bedroll, a coat, the census ledger. He mounted and rode out beyond the town's last breath, to where an old lean-to sat among wind-scoured cottonwoods. Elias had mentioned it once. Said it belonged to a tinker who'd gone quiet some time back.

The shack was empty now. The door hung from a rawhide hinge, the floor swept clean but dry with dust. He laid his bedroll out and placed the ledger beside him. He sat in silence, taking in the room. The floorboards near the hearth caught his attention as one of the boards was slightly raised, the edge warped.

He worked it loose with the back of his knife and reached beneath. What he found was a journal bound in oilskin, brittle at the edges but intact. The pages inside smelled of mildew.

The entries began plain. Notes on repairs, trade, seed orders. But the tone changed.

The tinker had grown uneasy. He wrote of voices at night. Of bundles left on doorsteps. Of men and women who vanished without word, whose names were quietly erased. He wrote of Barrow, Mrs. Cutter, and others.

A chill took hold in his gut as he read how the writer had kept to the shadows by the pens one night, intent on seeing the Committee's doings. He told of three men hauling a fourth—bound, gagged, and wailing—toward the gate. The charge was theft of sugar and dried meat. No trial. No scripture. Only a gate unlatched. Hogs loosed. Screams that ended quickly.

Truitt stood, lightheaded. The room seemed to move around him. He went to the door and stepped outside to draw a breath against the thud of his heart. He meant to ride, to be gone from there—and to get back to Claire while he still could.

That's when he saw it. Laid neat at the threshold. A bundle of caning switches, bound with twine. No note. No sound.

He stepped back, mouth dry and something struck the back of his head—hard.

The world buckled and everything fell to black.

Truitt woke in the dark with a throb in his skull that would not settle. Dirt and iron sat on his tongue. His arms were drawn behind a rough post, the rope burning at his wrists. One boot had slipped, heel lodged against the slats. Cloth was jammed in his mouth so he could scarce draw breath.

The pen breathed around him. Warm mud held the day's heat. Hogs shifted and worked their jaws behind the slats in front of him. The air was close and heavy with them.

"You got up," Barrow said at the fence. "Good. I hoped you would be up for it. Men ought to meet the thing awake."

The hogs stilled when Barrow spoke, then went back to their rooting, the small sounds of them carrying steady.

Barrow kept his eyes on him. "You were a guest. Elias told me you kept to yourself at first. You ate what was put in front of you. You kept your questions to the weather and the road. If it had stayed there, you would have gone on with a mark beside our name and no harm done. You were not run out for being a government man. We have carried worse."

A hog pressed its flank against the post and the wood answered with a low grind.

"We had a man who beat his wife and a boy who took stock that was not his and men who drank until their hands shook and then put those hands on others. We sent for help from the last county seat that still answered mail. A deputy came two months after the letter went. He walked around in the daylight and told us he would make it right. Then he left in the evening and never returned. The man kept his fists and the boy kept his habit and the men kept their drink. That was the year we buried two who had done nothing but live in the wrong house."

Barrow did not raise his voice. "So we made a rule that a man could understand without reading. You keep your own house and the door stays on its hinges. You do not keep it and we will remind you that a door can be taken off. First there is a talk. If a talk will not do, there is a warning. If a warning will not do, there is the tree. A few years of that and we did not need the talk or rope as often. This is the work that brought quiet back."

He looked to his left where Ada stood next to Elias and the children. They kept their eyes on him, not on Truitt. "We do not hold meetings under lanterns and we do not put men on benches and pretend a show at law. We say what needs saying and then we do the part that is hard to look at. It costs us something every time. Do not mistake the set of a face for ease. The payment is made inside, and it does not pass."

He glanced at Elias's children. "We bring them so they learn that peace is not free. They must see what holds it. If we send them away they will grow to think that quiet falls from the sky. Then the first time it does not, they will have nothing to push against."

He turned back to Truitt. "You think there is law waiting beyond the ridge to judge this. There is no law that comes here in time to keep a woman from going black in the eye again and again or a boy from taking a knife to a man's gut by the lantern at closing. There is only what we do before things break. We have lived by it long enough to know the price and we keep paying it."

Barrow moved along the fence toward the shadowed gate. "I would have let you ride this morning. You had your bedroll in hand and your ledger under your arm. But you were set on bringing others here to pry into it, and that would have brought disorder, crime, and misery."

He reached the gate and rested his palm on the latch. "You will say this is no trial," he said. "You are right. We handled the trial each day we watched you ask another question and weigh another household and turn another plate over in your mind. I do not need to hear you plead. You spoke already when you would not stop. Your words were what you did."

He raised the latch. It clicked and settled back against the post. The line of hogs shifted and pressed forward a step, then another. Mud worked under their hooves. Barrow stood aside and the gate eased open against its hinges. The hogs came through without hurry. They did not crowd.

Truitt pulled at the rope until his shoulders burned, and the post took the strain and gave nothing. Cloth swallowed what little sound he pushed from his chest. Coldness gathered around his legs as the hogs moved closer. In that moment, Claire came to him in memory as plain as the morning he had parted from her—sunlight in her hair, gaze fixed steady on him. That's when the real pain came, long before the hogs reached him. It was then he realized his name would never be written with hers in a ledger.

Contention

Johnny D. Boggs

I didn't know the Widow Kieberger from Adam's off ox, but she came up to me inside a Yuma grog shop, sat down, introduced herself, and told me her hardships, which were plentiful. Though she wasn't hard to look at, I had pretty much stopped listening and started cogitating a polite way to get away from her, maybe suggest that she find a deputy U.S. marshal, contact the Pinkerton National Detective Agency, or perhaps I'd mention a couple of buckets of blood where she could find men who killed cheap. Having just gotten out of the Hellhole, I had little desire to go back behind those walls. Or hang. That's when I happened to catch a few words she whispered.

Setting my glass on the table, I cleared my throat, and she stopped talking.

"Did you say . . . baseball bats?"

Her face paled, and she stared at squashed scorpions on the floor. "Yes." I barely heard her.

I killed my bourbon. "Let me get this straight. This major, he breaks into your house, with eight other ballists, and they proceed to beat your husband to death?"

She didn't look up.

"With baseball bats?" I added.

"Forty inches," she whispered. "White ash. One was flat."

I nodded. "For bunting."

"Or pounding a sleeping man's head to mush."

"Baseball bats." I waved at the barkeep, who sent a strumpet over with more Chicken Cock and another glass. Once the barmaid left, the widow added, without looking up, "Then he ran me out of Contention City as a . . ." Her eyes lifted toward me. I understood.

"Baseball bats," I repeated, then killed half of my fresh bourbon and felt that heat rising, turning my ears red, like they were prone to color when some umpire made a bad call or Hank Fuller swung at a pitch a mile over his head.

"That ain't right," I said.

She had to tell me the story again, but this time I listened. When she finished, I asked, "Isn't there any law in Contention?"

"The town marshal is the right fielder. He came with them that night."

My head shook, trying to comprehend this outrage. "Folks in town let this go on?"

"When's the last time you've been to Contention City?" she asked.

I shrugged. "Haven't been anywhere, ma'am, for three and a half years."

"They love their baseball," she explained. "And Major Perry has never lost a game."

I pondered. This Major Perry fielded one of the best baseball clubs in Arizona Territory. Undefeated in six years. Throttled teams from Tombstone and Tucson. Even beat the boys from Bisbee, which had some mighty fine ballists. But when they weren't dominating a baseball diamond, Contention's First Nine kept the workers under control. So, when some revolutionary like Mr. Kieberger started talking about improving conditions at the stamp mills, Major Perry and his ballists, including the town's law dog, would bust into a darkened bedroom and bludgeon the man to death for being an anarchist—with forty-inch bat-sticks.

Gives ballists like me a bad name.

"So . . ." I hesitated. "What do you want of me?"

When she told me, I sighed. "I haven't played in years, ma'am."

"You played with the prison guards," she said. "I saw you in a couple of games. I found out about you. That's what gave me the idea."

My head shook. "The guards needed a catcher. It got me out of shoveling caliche or getting tossed into the Snake Den. And we lost plenty of games, even to those velocipede riders on that train to California."

Her green eyes hardened. "I said, I *found out* about you. *You* could get a team. *You* could beat Major Perry's murderers."

That gave me pause. I squinted. "What exactly is it you want me to do?"

She told me.

"And . . ." I put this kind of delicate. "What's in it for me?"

She told me that, too.

The next eastbound Southern Pacific took me to Lordsburg, New Mexico Territory, where I caught a stage to Silver City and met Hank Fuller in the Copper Tarnish Saloon. Last time I saw Hank, he was a hundred and seventy-seven pounds of baseball prime and on his way to sign with the Louisville Colonels. Now, he topped two-fifty and played for the Fat Fellows. The bib front of his uniform shirt pictured a foaming mug of beer. His meaty right hand held an empty mug, which was getting refilled, again. The Fat Fellows were celebrating their 20-to-6 victory over the Slim Jims. That's how far Hank Fuller had fallen. He'd gone from playing professional ball to playing for kegs of beer.

Since the Fat Fellows had won, the Slim Jims bought the beers— and all were drunk—I didn't have to spend any of the Widow Kieberger's greenbacks. After the crowd thinned out, or passed out, Hank asked what I wanted. I told him. He asked how much it paid. I told him that, too, which sobered him up right quick.

"What do you want from me?" he asked.

"To lay off any pitches a mile over your head," I said.

We traveled to Tombstone and sat high up in the grandstands, watching the Contention Millers wallop the home Tigers.

"Who's the big guy?" Hank asked.

I swallowed my peanut. A first baseman who tops two hundred and fifty pounds was asking about a "big guy." That ought to tell you something about Contention's baseball team. Only none of Contention's First Nine carried his weight in his belly. Those boys packed solid muscle, and every time their bat-stick crushed a ball, I envisioned the Widow Kieberger's unfortunate late husband.

"That's Major Perry," I answered. I knew him because the Widow Kieberger said he played center field. He played it pretty good, too.

"The third baseman is Caleb Cartwright," Hank said.

"You know him?"

"I played against him when he was with the Pittsburgh Alleghenys. He played last season for that Kansas City club in the National League."

"The team the National League kicked out?"

"Yep. For hooliganism."

The Contention Millers didn't need to resort to hooliganism or beating men to death on this Saturday. Tombstone was awful. The Tigers lost, 35-to-1, but this Major Perry wasn't the nicest fellow I'd ever seen on a diamond. I mean, the jackass berated his fellow ballists when the third baseman made an error in the eighth inning, allowing Tombstone to score its only run.

They taunted the poor Tombstone ballists. Major Perry screamed insults at his opponents. His teammates laughed when the Tigers made poor plays. Considering how bruised and bloodied Tombstone's players looked after the game, you would've thought Contention's First Nine used brass knuckles or billy clubs on the players in the field—and maybe they had.

After the slaughter mercifully ended, the Millers tore apart the visiting team's bench, laughed, and headed for the depot. The Tigers of Tombstone just stared. Nobody protested. Hank drained his beer. "We've got to beat *this* team?"

Me? I sat there fuming at what I had just witnessed, and I had taken part in some inappropriate behavior on baseball fields. I told Hank, "The Contention Millers have forgotten A.G. Spalding's prime rule for our sport: 'To make baseball playing respectable and honorable.'"

Hank shook his head. "They forgot another rule, too, Skip: 'Thou shalt not kill.'"

Rounding up ballists in the Southwest isn't hard. It's not even tough to find baseball players who lack ethics. But finding exceptional ballists willing to risk a stay in prison or having their faces pounded to jelly by forty-inch timbers of white ash proved about as taxing as trying to tag out King Kelly when he's sliding into home. I had to meet up with the Widow Kieberger in Tucson to get more money, but she didn't put up any fuss. Her husband had been dead pushing two years now, and she was eager to exact her revenge on Major Perry and his murdering thugs.

I didn't ask where she came by such money.

Finding a *Spalding's Base Ball Guide* proved a mite difficult, but that only set me back ten cents in Phoenix, and I needed to bone up on the rules since I had been out of circulation for three and a half years. Prison guards, you see, made up rules they thought appropriate, and didn't give a fig how the National League or American Association played the game.

Once I had hired all my accessories—I mean *ballists*—we practiced just across the border, away from prying eyes. We probably could have swept a three-game series against the territorial prison's guards, and maybe even whipped those California velocipede riders. But we certainly were not undefeated after four barnstorming seasons.

Yet that's what the *Tucson Enterprise* reported, of course, since I paid the inkslinger one of the Widow Kieberger's double eagles to print exactly that: that we were undefeated. It's also what the posters the Widow Kieberger paid to have printed announced, too. I made sure Contention City got some of those posters.

Sure enough, when the American Zephyrs—Hank came up with that handle for us—played the Tucson Base Ball Team (there's an original name for a club) on a Friday afternoon, Major Perry arrived by train to see us play.

"Congratulations," the major said after our 20-to-nothing victory. He held out his massive right hand.

"You'll forgive me if I don't accept your hand, sir." I kept shaking to get the feeling back into my stinging hands. "Masterson wasn't at his best today, but even his worst hurts like blazes after nine innings." (Kent Masterson wasn't at his worst, either, but nigh his best, and my hands remained swollen and numb after catching him.)

"You don't wear a mitt, sir?"

Some catchers did—so did infielders and outfielders who could take the heckling—even in the professional leagues. But you try wearing a mitt playing for and against prison guards. They'd have thrown me in the Snake Den. I shook my head.

Major Perry praised our pitcher, and lauded Hank's hitting—Hank hadn't swung at one bad pitch the whole game—and then the major got down to business. Why, his team down in Contention City was undefeated, too, and he thought a game against us would bring in quite the crowd.

"We don't play for beer, sir," I told him. "We get half the gate and an appearance fee."

"What's the fee?" the major asked.

I told him.

He wasn't smiling, but he said that could be arranged. Had I known that a baseball team could charge that kind of money to play a game, I might've avoided forty-two months in the Hellhole.

Then I got greedy. "And it's customary for a little wager between the teams."

"What do you propose?" he said.

I grinned. "How about your bat-sticks and all your equipment? We put up the same."

He paled, but nodded. A man like him, with an undefeated team, can't back down from a wager. I was pleased. After we clobbered his team, the major wouldn't have any bat-sticks to make another anarchist's wife a widow.

"How about next Friday?" Major Perry asked.

My head shook. "Sir, we have to be in Los Angeles in a few days." I excused myself, found my grip on the bench, opened it, and pulled out a book, which I opened and stared at a blank page. "I'm sorry to say that we're booked for all this month," I lied. "Let's see. We're playing the White Stockings on Saturday the twenty-third before going to Detroit the next Monday."

Major Perry's eyes widened. "The White Stockings?" His words come out like a gasp. "In Chicago?"

"Yes, sir," I said. "Cap Anson's a real nice man. And a fine ballist." The last sentence was the only truthful one I spoke.

"And Detroit?" Perry asked.

"The Wolverines," I said.

"You . . . play . . .?"

My chuckle silenced him. "Sir," I said, "those are just exhibition games. The National League, you must be aware, doesn't start its season till later that week. We Zephyrs are just a traveling team of ballists—like the Red Stockings of '69." I smiled. "They went undefeated, too, you know."

"And you've beaten the White Stockings . . .?"

Closing my book, I waved my hand. "Oh, I'm sure if we played Cap's boys in a full series, we wouldn't still be undefeated. In fact, Detroit played us close last year. If Hank had not homered in the last inning, well, our record might be a hundred twenty-three and one."

I opened the book to another empty page. "I guess, though, if you really want to risk your perfect season, we could squeeze you in . . . would Friday the thirteenth of May work?"

"Sure," Major Perry said weakly.

I closed the book. "We do require half of our appearance fee in advance, sir."

He paid that, too—by check, but the bank cashed it without argument—and walked, a mite unsteady, out of the baseball park.

Inside the nearest saloon, Hank said, "Maybe we should just take that money and skedaddle while we're ahead."

"What about the Widow Kieberger?" I asked, and when Hank just sipped his beer, I added: "Is that what you want to do?"

"No," he said. "I'd like to beat those Contention killers."

"So would I," said Masterson, who had pitched for the Boston Beaneaters till the National League found out about his relationship with gamblers.

"Then we better start practicing," I said. "And find us a southpaw hitter."

Naturally, we did not take the train to Los Angeles. Nor did we travel to Chicago and Detroit. I did go to Denver, where I signed up Skyrocket McSorely, who played right field with a center fielder's speed and batted left-handed. By the end of the month, we were back across the border, practicing every day for our date with the Contention Millers.

While celebrating a real fine practice on the third of May, we all got knocked off our feet. The earth shook. Hank lost six pounds. Masterson lost his breakfast. Skyrocket McSorely confessed all his sins, which sounded considerable. I cried out for my ma.

The rumble didn't last that long, and the Almighty did not open up the earth and drop us down to Hades. The next morning, another little shake rattled our nerves, and after we found our scattered horses, I rode to Bisbee to see what had just happened.

What had happened, of course, was an earthquake. The telegraph lines were all down, so I spent some of the Widow Kieberger's money on a stagecoach ride to Contention City.

Not that I was drunk, but what I saw and heard sobered me.

Roofs had collapsed, the whistles at the mine and mills kept blaring, and the baseball diamond lay in utter ruins. Somehow, amid all this commotion, I managed to find Major Perry. Seeing me, he shook his head, and waved at the mess behind him.

"We cannot play," he told me. "Not on this."

Ever seen photographs of Atlanta taken after Sherman's boys marched through? That's what the Contention City Base Ball Field resembled. It's what a lot of Contention looked like. I quickly thought of this: "But you do understand that there is no refund on the deposit of our appearance fee."

"I don't give a whit about that, sir!" he snapped.

That earthquake was a godsend—for me.

"Why don't we reschedule our game?" I suggested.

"Next month?" Major Perry said.

"Next year," I said.

Yep, that was a gamble. But I had seen Contention play and my boys practice. We couldn't beat the Millers, not with the ballists I had lined up. I also saw just what a boomtown Contention City was, and figured once she got fixed up, there might be more money to earn. I am greedy. Which, along with my temper, had cost me forty-two months in Yuma. And was why even the Beer and Whiskey League wouldn't let me play on their teams anymore.

"You'd do that?" Major Perry asked.

This was no lie: "Major, it'll take you a year to get this diamond, and your city, back in shape."

I can't call the Widow Kieberger understanding. When I met her up in Benson, she did not sound like the meek, frightened, revengeful woman I had talked to in Yuma. But eventually, reason prevailed. If we were to beat the Millers, if she was to get what she wanted, then patience, and practice, came first. She also conceded, after a second brandy, that she had yet to find a man suitable for her purposes. Turned out, I knew a fellow who would be out of Yuma in November.

After paying off my middle infielders, two outfielders, and a backup hurler, I let the rest of the boys find baseball clubs for the upcoming season whilst Hank and I took off to Galveston . . . New Orleans . . . St. Louis . . . Cincinnati . . . and even Laramie, where a couple of ballists I knew were getting out early on good behavior. From those towns and a handful of others, I sent telegraphs to newspapers in southern Arizona, letting their readers know that the American Zephyrs had won another game, making up a few details and a final score, and hoping no editor would ask for confirmation from another source.

By late October, the mercenaries that made up the American Zephyrs reconvened in Bisbee, and we crossed the border again. In early March, I sent a telegraph to Major Perry, suggesting a date to make up our ball game. He happily agreed to the date and our original terms.

Even the Widow Kieberger looked happy. I had rounded up a pretty good bunch of ballists, and that fellow I'd told her about proved mighty handy at cracking safes.

The game pitting two undefeated teams would be played on Monday, April 30. The payrolls would arrive in Contention City on the evening train on April 28. Contention's miners and millers would not be paid until May 1.

I didn't think another earthquake would postpone our game this time. As long as it didn't rain . . .

We arrived on the same train as the payrolls, and the armed guards, including Contention's right fielder/marshal, greeted us at the depot. Turns out, some of Major Perry's ballists—when not beating town teams or clubbing some anarchist to death in his bedroom—also protected Contention's money on its way to the bank for safekeeping till payday.

Caleb Cartwright, Contention City's third baseman, grinned a broken-tooth smile and directed us to Mason's Western Hotel.

That rundown adobe structure wasn't much to look at before the earthquake, but a year ago, the windowpanes had glass, the adobe walls didn't show straw, and the roof covered the entire hotel.

"Criminy," Skyrocket McSorely whispered as we walked down the deserted street. "I thought you said Contention City was a boomtown."

"The key word in that sentence," our shortstop, Professor Anderson, said, "is *was*."

The Contention Millers had won all twenty-two games last year, but every contest had been played on the road after the earthquake had destroyed their field. Though I had briefly seen the town after the earthquake, I never really appreciated the extensiveness of the damage.

After settling into our hotel rooms, we walked to the Contention City Base Ball Field to practice. On our way, a little waif sprinted out of a ramshackle *jacal*. He didn't wear shoes, and I doubt if the urchin had seen a washcloth in months. "Are you the famous Zephyrs?" The boy held out a baseball.

Silent Cobb, our third baseman who hated everything and everybody, took the ball and stared at it. "Uh," he said, "yeah"—more words than he'd spoken in two weeks of practicing.

"Gosh." The boy snatched back the ball. "A Zephyrs ballist touched my baseball. Nobody but me will ever touch it again. Even if you beat my team Monday."

"Your team?" Cobb just doubled his dialogue.

An old man arrived over from the other side of the street. "About all we have left in this town now," he said, shaking all of our hands, "is our baseball team." He said it was a pleasure to have us here, that a team with the national reputation of the American Zephyrs would be a great test for the Millers.

"We'll see if we can compete against something other than other town teams," said a woman in a parasol who stepped off the boardwalk to welcome us to Contention City.

"At least you're honorable players," said a gent in sleeve garters. "Unlike the Tigers of Tombstone."

"They burned our bench the year before last," the urchin informed us.

"And abused our womenfolk," said the old man.

"We hate Tombstone," said one of the bunch of folks greeting us.

Hank Fuller shot me a glance, and I knew he was wondering if maybe Tombstone had deserved that abuse and beating we witnessed last year.

I didn't dwell on that, however, because a woman brought us cookies. Another resident, bless his soul, carried buckets of bottled beer. But that was nothing compared to what we saw at the Contention City Base Ball Field.

Our practice, I realized, was the first time we had played in front of spectators, excepting, just before we left Mexico, the Widow Kieberger and her safecracker and a few other rogues she'd hired. I'd played real games before smaller crowds.

"Wait till tomorrow," one man said. "The whole city will be here. Everyone in town!"

Which is what the Widow Kieberger had said when I first met her in Yuma.

Even though we were just practicing, everyone cheered us. They whistled. It felt great, like it used to feel when I was playing years ago. A long time had passed since anyone had hollered encouraging words for me at a baseball field. I sure never heard anything like that whilst catching for Yuma's guards.

Then I remembered what brought us to Contention.

Just nine years back, this city had boomed after the discovery of silver. Miners found pay dirt in the hills around the town, but Contention thrived because of the stamp mills—hence their baseball team's nickname, the Millers. The San Pedro River provided water, which most of the mining towns—including Tombstone—didn't have. Two stamp mills had been established, the railroad arrived, the team kept winning, and life looked fine in Contention City.

We learned all this as those poor folks treated us to supper and beers after our practice.

Of course, nothing lasts forever, someone pointed out, to which Kent Masterson leaned toward me and whispered, "Like the Millers' undefeated streak," and grinned.

Folks, we learned, found a way to get water to Tombstone. The mines around Contention got flooded. So did the two mills, especially after that earthquake. One mill had already closed this week, and its miners were waiting to collect their last pay before moving on. Everybody knew the other mill's days were numbered, too. The railroad had reached Fairbank a few miles south, meaning fewer folks needed to travel to Contention. The Bisbee stage line had already stopped running to Contention. Since the earthquake, folks had been leaving for better jobs, or any jobs. Once, you could hardly find an empty spot at the Contention City Base Ball Field when the Millers played. These days, the grandstands could seat twice the town's current population.

The team had struggled, as well. Once, the Millers had an outstanding First Nine, a Second Nine that could beat most town teams easily, and even a Muffin Nine that played solid baseball. Now, they had ten players total, and last year they won their twenty-two games by an average of one-point-nine runs. Four of the games went extra innings. One game they won by forfeit. Such things never happened in the glorious days before the earthquake.

When we got back to the hotel, I had to remind the boys, even Cobb, why we came to Contention, what those thugs did to the widow's husband, and what we could take home after beating the Millers to a pulp.

The last day of April dawned bright and sunny with no wind. We had the Millers whipped before the umpire, an Army chaplain from

Fort Huachuca, called us out to flip a coin. The Millers won the toss and elected to be the home team. Masterson snickered, "That's all they will win today."

Indeed, it looked that way. Masterson struck out the first six batsmen he faced. We scored two runs in the first inning, and three in the second. The crowd looked like they were attending a funeral.

But, by grab, how they cheered in the bottom of the third. That's when Caleb Cartwright singled up the middle. He didn't get past first base.

We led 9-to-2 in the sixth inning. I could hear sobs coming from the little waif whose baseball Silent Cobb had briefly held. Major Perry hit a little grounder to third, and Silent Cobb's throw had that brute out by a mile—till Hank Fuller dropped the ball.

"Safe," the chaplain said.

Masterson then hit the next batsman with a pitch.

"Take your base," the chaplain said, and I muttered an oath. Giving a batsman first base when he got hit had just become a rule in '87. The soldier boys at Fort Huachuca knew their baseball.

The next Miller got hit, too, loading the bases, and sending me out to calm down Kent Masterson. Hank Fuller waddled over, too.

"Relax," I told my pitcher, who wasn't throwing as hard as he could. "Your arm hurting?"

"No."

"Well, Hank muffed a play. It happens. Forget it."

"I didn't muff that ball, Skip," Hank told me.

Masterson said: "And I know what I'm doing."

I pulled off my cap to scratch my head.

"We can't beat this team," said Silent Cobb, who trotted over to take part in our discussion.

"We can beat the tar out of them," I said. "Which we've been doing."

The chaplain hollered: "Hurry up!"

Seeing my teammates' faces, I put my cap back on. "You can't throw this game, boys." I felt sick.

"You did," Silent Cobb said, and I wished he would turn mute again. "With the Brown Stockings in '82."

"And the Buffalo Bisons in '79," Hank recollected.

My ears reddened, and Hank hadn't swung at a ball over his head this afternoon. "You . . ." I jabbed my swollen finger at Hank's fancy lace-up shirt that the Widow Kieberger had paid for. "You remember how these Millers played ball that time we saw them. Played like hooligans."

"You heard what the Tigers did here," Hank pointed out.

I countered: "I *heard*. But I *saw* how this team played. Like hooligans."

"Just like I played with the Maroons in '86," the professor said. He had walked over, too.

"And ain't that why you got sent to Yuma?" Masterson said. "Beat up the umpire with your bat-stick in Prescott for calling you out on strikes?"

"Fool deserved it," I said. "Ball was a foot outside, and low."

"Do you want to gossip?" the chaplain yelled. "Or play baseball?"

"They beat a man's head in," I told my Zephyrs. "With bat-sticks. That's why we're playing them."

"We're playing them," Hank said, too honest for his own cheating good, "for what the Widow Kieberger, that safecracker you knew in Yuma, and those gunmen she hired are doing right now."

"Because," I argued right back, "of what Major Perry, the town marshal, and the rest of these murdering ballists did to her husband."

"The Millers aren't the point," Masterson said. "I can't beat them . . . for their sakes." He nodded at the practically empty stands, filled with the last of Contention City's lovers of baseball, pretty much everybody in town.

I made the mistake and looked. I saw the little urchin, the old man, the lady with the parasol, and that redheaded strumpet who brought us all the beers we could drink at the cantina we had been frequenting. I saw their faces. The chaplain yelled again, but what struck me was the crowd. Any other city, any other team, and the spectators would be shouting louder than the umpire for us to quit chattering and play ball. They just sat, respectful, patient.

"Don't be suckers, boys. We're professional ballists, or once were. Let's get out of this inning," I said. Then I slapped the ball into Masterson's hand and trotted off to my spot.

Caleb Cartwright hit the next pitch over McSorely's head, and all four runners scored. It was 9-to-6.

It stayed that way till the bottom of the ninth inning. With two outs, and the Contention City faithful resigned to their fate, Major Perry singled. The professor let Contention's marshal/right fielder's hard roller go between his legs, and Major Perry wound up on third. Masterson then threw five consecutive balls to the Millers' second baseman, who ran down to first base.

"It takes seven balls before he can take first," I pointed out.

"That was in '86, Skip," the chaplain said. "And it was four strikes instead of three last year, and they counted walks as hits. Who knows what the rules will say next year?"

Course, I figured if the umpire knew the rule about hitting a batsman, he'd know how many balls it took to send a player to first. It was worth a chance, though. Sometimes, you get umpires who don't know a thing. Not in Contention City, though. They used smart umpires.

I asked for time and went out to talk to Masterson. When my infielders started to join us, I yelled at them to stay put. I didn't need my boys teaming up against me.

"Walk Cartwright," I told Masterson.

He blinked and beamed. "You're with us!"

"No. I want to win."

Confusion masked Masterson's face. "You want to put the tying run on second base, Skip?"

"Yeah, because Cartwright has power. Their shortstop hasn't hit all game. All we need is one out."

Masterson grinned. He thought he could outsmart me. "All they need is four runs. I could walk or hit Cartwright, the shortstop, and everyone else."

"You can try to walk that shortstop, and he'll still strike out. You can try to hit him, and he'll dive out the way like the coward he . . ."

I stopped. It sort of struck me curious that a member of the Millers could be such a coward on the baseball field and a rapscallion who beat men to death in bedrooms. But Contention wasn't the same Contention anymore.

Something else, something better came to mind.

"You can walk in all the runs, let Contention win," I said. "And you'd not only be a sucker, you'd be a heel. You'd be cheating all these folks here. You'd crush them. Kill them. They want to see the Millers win. Not the Zephyrs blow it. You let those boys win with walks and hit batsmen, and you'll just disappoint everyone left in Contention City. So go ahead. Do it your way. Shame these poor folks. Walk Cartwright. If that shortstop after him can tie the score, good for him. That's baseball."

Knowing I had Masterson—because I'd just, for once, told the truth—I walked back, squatted, and waited for Masterson's pitch.

It came, faster than he had thrown since the first inning. Straight across at Cartwright's belt. Cartwright swung. I cussed. The ball once again sailed over McSorely's head, but this one went even farther. Three runners crossed the plate, and Cartwright was coming home. The crowd stood, screaming, cheering, but the chaplain started yelling something, too. I kept waiting for McSorely to get the ball, but he just stood at the fence. I didn't think Cartwright had knocked the ball over the fence. It couldn't be a home run. Could it?

"Double!" I heard the chaplain. "That is a ground-rule double. Back to second, Cartwright. You —" Our umpire pointed at Contention's second baseman. "You must return to third base."

Now, Contention's faithful in the stands booed the Army chaplain. Major Perry came from the bench to argue.

"Sir," the ump said, "there is a new rule this year that states if a fair ball bounces over the fence, and that the fence is not more than two hundred and ten feet from home plate, then the hitter must remain at second base."

That Army man knew everything. The crowd stopped booing. The old man said, "The umpire is correct."

"So," I said, just to make sure I understood everything. "The score is now 9-to-8, with two outs?"

"Yes."

I grinned. The chaplain let McSorely climb over the fence and fetch the ball, and I got ready as Millers shortstop Rotten Willie took his place inside the batter's lines.

Again, I trotted to talk to my hurler. "Hey," I argued. "They gave us a good game. Those folks won't be disappointed now. This'll be a game they'll remember, and there won't be no shame in the Millers losing. So don't be a softhearted sucker."

Masterson nodded. I went back to catch him.

The crowd roared. Masterson threw a pitch at the waist that the chaplain called a strike. I had to dive to snag Masterson's next pitch—that's how bad it was—and heard the ump yell, "Strike two."

I dusted myself off. Rotten Willie had swung at that pitch? It made me laugh.

Masterson bounced the next one in front of the plate, but Rotten Willie did not swing. The crowd fell silent. Sweat poured down Rotten Willie's cheeks. Masterson began his windup and fired another pitch. This was a ball, too, way off the plate. Rotten Willie swung. And somehow, his bat connected and sent the ball over Silent Cobb's outstretched hands as he leaped toward his left. But the professor was running on contact, backing up Cobb, and he snagged the ball in shallow left field on the second bounce.

Contention's man on third touched home, turned, and waited. That tied the score, but we could win in extra innings. All I had to do was catch the professor's throw and tag Cartwright out. Winning meant a lot to me. So did the money the Widow Kieberger was stealing.

I saw the baseball clearly. Then, out of the corner of my eye, I spied that little urchin, who still didn't have shoes, still looked dirty, and still clutched that ball he had let Silent Cobb hold the day we got in. I caught the professor's throw. The Contention player behind me yelled for Cartwright to slide. Cartwright slid. I saw the face of the woman with the parasol. I heard the kid yell, "Slide, Cartwright, slide!" I glimpsed the old man. And I imagined seeing a woman and some men leaving the alley that ran alongside Contention City's bank. I had real good eyesight and imagination. You need that when you play catcher. I brought the ball down.

"Safe!" the chaplain yelled. "Safe! The runner is safe. The Millers win!"

The place turned into bedlam. Major Perry and his boys exploded off the bench and poured beer on Rotten Willie's head. The folks in the grandstands cheered and sang and sang and cheered. And they cried.

I couldn't argue. Cartwright's toe touched the plate just before I tagged his knee. I made certain of that.

As we shook hands with our valiant opponents, those folks in the stands cheered us, too. A few of us cried, as well.

Even when Major Perry collected our bats, balls, and equipment, my Zephyrs just smiled. A wager's a wager. We weren't welshers. I handed Major Perry a hundred-dollar note, too.

"What's this for?" the major asked.

"Well, some of the folks in this town look like they could use it."

Tears welled in his eyes. "Our citizens will need this money far more than we shall need your bat-sticks and baseballs, sir, for our future . . ."

That's when somebody shouted about something going on at the bank.

So, there we sat, waiting for the train to take us up to Benson, sipping hot beer and trying to keep the dirt sifting down from the roof from turning our drinks to mud. Caleb Cartwright came inside, nodded at us, downed a tequila at the bar, and said that the robbers had made off with twenty-three-thousand dollars.

"That'll finish Contention City," the barkeep said.

"I've already found a job in Globe," Cartwright said. "Baseball team's not that good, but it's baseball." When Cartwright pulled out a coin, the barkeep said, "No, it's on me. Loved watching you play these past few years. Maybe I'll get a job in Globe, too."

As he walked outside, Cartwright told us we played a fine game, said he thought he was out for sure when he had started his slide.

Twenty-three-thousand dollars. The professor ciphered in his head. "Ninety-two-hundred dollars for us. That takes the sting out of losing."

"When do we meet the Widow Kieberger?" Hank asked. He spoke too loud 'cause the barmaid was bringing us another round.

"Joyce got married?" Her face beamed.

"Joyce?" I said.

"Joyce Kieberger. Is that who you was talkin' 'bout. I used to work with her. She got married?" The rest of what she heard saddened her. "And her new husband up and died?"

I needed that bourbon. "The Widow . . . Joyce . . . Missus Kieberger. She wasn't married . . . while she was . . . working . . . here?"

Hank drank his beer and Skyrocket McSorely's, too. Both looked as sick as I must've.

The barmaid lowered her voice. "Goodness. Girls in our line don't get married. Not in the towns where we ply our trade." She started to leave, turned, and said, "If you see Joyce, tell her Dixie says congratulations—and more congratulations if her late husband was real rich."

When she stood back at the bar, I muttered something that the professor told me was anatomically impossible.

The urchin stuck his head in what once was a doorway to the saloon. "Train's coming in," he said. The whistle affirmed his statement.

"You think that widow will pay us?" McSorely asked.

I gave him the look I give Hank when he swings at pitches a mile over his head.

"You think," the professor asked, "that she might somehow let word out that we were in on this heist?"

"A few telegraphs," Hank said, "and they'll figure it out themselves."

We made a beeline for the depot, passing the Contention City Base Ball Field. Hank, McSorely, Masterson, and I took a detour, but we got on the train all right, and soon were steaming as far away as we could from Major Perry's ballists, especially Contention's right fielder.

As we tried to relax in the smoking car, Masterson sighed. "The thing is, we could have beaten those boys. Had them beaten."

I shook my head disgustedly. Masterson had been among the first to go soft.

"Won't get another chance now," Hank lamented. "Contention City's done for. That team will always be remembered as going undefeated in seven seasons and one game."

Cobb leaned toward me. "And you owe us our dough. You said we'd be paid win or lose." That silent third baseman never shut up.

Hank pointed this out: "The deal was we'd get paid when the Widow Kieberger paid Skip."

"When we get to Tucson . . ." I began, the idea coming over me and making me feel as good as that urchin and those other Contention City folks must have felt after watching their team win that game. "Why don't we try to play Tucson's town team?"

"With what?" the professor said. "Thanks to your bet, we lost our bat-sticks, balls, and all our equipment to the Millers."

Hank chuckled. So did I.

"No," I said. "The marshal and major led that posse off as soon as they heard about the bank being looted. Most of the Millers rode out with him."

Hank added: "Left their equipment and ours, too, at the field. We picked it up. All of it. Put it in the baggage car."

"Major Perry won't be using those bat-sticks to club anyone to death ever again," Kent Masterson said.

"Like that ever happened," Skyrocket McSorely said. "I'd like to use my bat-stick on that widow's noggin."

"Now, now," I said. "You don't want to wind up in Yuma. And I'm serious. Let's play Tucson's team when we get there."

"Hey," Masterson said. "Maybe Benson has a team, too."

"Most towns do," Silent Cobb said. "We could also play Tombstone."

I pointed out: "After we beat Tucson, we should leave the territory. Unless you want to play prison baseball."

"I bet," Hank said, "we could play the Fat Fellows in Silver City."

McSorely said: "And there are plenty of town teams in Colorado."

Cobb and the professor didn't look so angry now. Cobb even admitted, "We do have a good team."

"We might even best the Millers' record," McSorely said.

Masterson grinned. "The American Zephyrs. For real, this time."

"No," I said. "We use that handle, the major and marshal would undoubtedly find us, and even if those boys didn't beat anarchists to death with bat-sticks, they surely would stove in our heads."

We thought.

Long before the train pulled into Benson, we had our name.

The American Suckers had a nice ring to it.

Headwaters

Vonn McKee

Lex Tucker knelt on the high mountain slope beside three fallen rocks wedged into a pyramid. He'd found it, at last. A rivulet gurgled from beneath the stones, straight from the mountain's heart. Lex stuck his hand in the icy flow and jerked it back from the shock. Cupping both hands, he scooped up the clear water for a drink. His horse stepped into the shallows where they widened to an arm's breadth, eased his thirst and splashed across the stream to feast on a patch of sedge grass.

Riding over Stony Pass earlier in the day, Lex caught silvery glimpses of the Rio Grande—only a humble stream here in the San Juans. It threaded through alpine meadows to join other meandering trickles before dropping into the valley. Downriver, it would broaden and tumble and flatten and snake itself to south Texas, where the great Gulf of Mexico would receive its muddied waters.

Lex had left the trail to trace the stream to its beginning farther up the mountain. He had no reason for the detour, except perhaps to put off reaching his destination. Although, according to his father's letter that somehow found him in Silverton, time was not something he ought to waste.

Everything begins somewhere, he thought, and usually not without a fight. Pure, cold water, clear as a diamond, pushed up from a dark unknown source and squeezed through hidden cracks in the mountain until it gushed into the open. Now, it was no longer an underground spring but a river, albeit it a young one with no notion of its journey ahead.

Young and wild, bound for adventure. Lex smiled, remembering how he'd once felt the same.

Rubbing chilled hands on his pant legs, he went to fetch his horse, crossing the Rio Grande in one step.

"Oh, Lex. When are you going to stop crossing rivers and mountains to see what's on the other side?"

Sarah stood barefoot, with arms crossed. She was almost as tall as he, and he met her dark sapphire stare, noting the cocked eyebrow. In the blue silk dressing gown he bought her in San Francisco, she looked like the lady her mother had raised her to be. But Sarah only acted like a lady when she chose to, and Lex happened to admire that about her.

"You haven't answered me," Sarah said. They stood inside her front door.

Lex reached for his hat and gun belt hanging on the hall tree. Before he put on the pinch-crown Stetson, he stepped forward and kissed Sarah soundly. "I'll stop when I run out of rivers and mountains to cross, I reckon."

Sarah frowned, and he caressed the crease between her eyebrows with his thumb. "If it means anything . . . I take you with me . . . always," he said.

"It means something." She closed her eyes. "It could mean you would rather hold on to a memory than the genuine article. Memories don't ask for much, do they, Lex?"

He kissed her again and walked out. The closing door slammed with a finality that echoed in Lex's thoughts all the way out of Durango.

Jimmy Bowes had handed Lex the wrinkled, stained envelope with his good arm. He took a tumble down a mine shaft in the bowels of King Solomon Mountain, crippling his shoulder and, being no longer of value to the Las Animas Mining District, Jimmy found work in Silverton at the mercantile and post office. He was apt to lose this job as soon as a New Yorker named Thomson finished building a massive brick and granite hotel on the corner of Greene Street, which would also house the new post office, a store, bank and city offices.

"Why, I never knew your name was Lexington," said Jimmy. "Mister Lexington J. Tucker. Sounds right dignified."

Lex grimaced. His pa had stuck the name of his west Tennessee birthplace on his firstborn son. That meant Lex could never completely escape his father's reach, in memory, in scars—visible and otherwise—and even when he signed his name.

With a quick nod to Jimmy, Lex left the store with a folded blue flannel shirt tucked under his arm and a new plug of tobacco in his back pocket. He'd open the letter when he got to his matchbox of a rented room.

So the old man was in La Veta. Lots of freighters and treasure seekers traversed the high pass between Silverton and Del Norte, and La Veta lay a hundred miles beyond there. Someone must have seen Lex, had a drink with him, maybe bested him at cards, which was unlikely. Lex had learned to let others grub for money or gold and silver nuggets. It was easy enough to win them off the poor fools, slow and easy, with whiskey and a decent cigar at hand. One way or another, word that Lex was in Silverton traveled over the mountains to Pop.

If the unsteady scrawl was to be believed, the old man didn't expect to be around for long. Wanted to have a word with his sons.

Lex tried to remember the last time the three of them had been in one room. Guess it would've been that shack up north by the Rabbit Ears, close to where a couple of creeks formed the North Platte. It seemed the Tuckers were drawn to places where rivers begin.

Lex put the letter out of his mind for a day. But then, after washing his face in the dry sink wedged beside his bed, he looked up at the streaked mirror that hung askew on a rusty nail. His brown curly hair, past his shoulders, was shot with gray, though he was six months shy of thirty. Dark eyes, near black, were among the few reminders he had of his New Orleans-born mother, who died two days after his younger brother was born. Lex had only a few fleeting memories of her. But the thin face with its square, clefted chin, the fierce eyebrows—one split by a scar from an encounter with a fire poker—the full lips set in a line . . . Lex Tucker took a step back from the mirror's truth—his mother's eyes, in his father's face.

It may have been curiosity, or a remaining shred of conscience, or a firstborn's inescapable bent toward responsibility that made Lex pack saddlebags and mount up for the road out of Silverton and toward Stony Pass, and La Veta. He questioned the decision with every mile.

Lex heaved the axe up to split one last piece of firewood for the day. His arms burned with fatigue, even though he was strong . . . for a ten-year-old. He could hear Deke Tucker inside, swearing at no one in particular and throwing a pan, a tin cup, turning over something. A chair? Lex locked eyes with Silas, younger by three years, who had emerged from the chicken coop cradling four eggs in his small, dirty hands. They would wait until Pop quieted down to go inside, not that it guaranteed he wouldn't break loose again.

The boys slipped into the one-room cabin. Lex stacked wood against the back wall behind the small stove. Silas fetched the skillet from where it had been flung beneath the table to begin cooking the eggs and a slab of salt pork on top of the stove. Pop lay on the bed, eyes closed but not sleeping. When the cooking smells filled the cabin, he roused, sat up, and reached for the nearly empty bottle on the floor. He took a noisy swig. Lex set the table, dreading the notion of sharing it with his father. Silas divided the eggs and meat onto the plates.

Pop walked past the stack of wood and paused. He stooped to pick up a piece and, with a poker, opened the door to the stove, then shoved the wood inside. He slammed the door hard and it bounced open from the force. Pop swore, drew back the poker and swung at it, clipping the door's edge. It did indeed stay shut, but the iron poker slipped from his hand and flew across the room.

Lex turned his head at the sound of the slamming door, just in time to catch the barbed end of the poker above his left eye. His head snapped back from the blow. Blood streamed down his face and down the front of his shirt. He stood frozen, staring at Pop with the eye not blurred by blood. Pop looked stricken for several seconds, then the familiar dark cloud settled over his face.

"Well, hell, boy. Don't stand there and bleed on our supper. Get outside and wash in the trough."

Lex expected his second crossing of the Rio Grande, where it hooked south at Del Norte, to be uneventful. It was August, and the fury of early summer snowmelt had died down. The Rio was wide but could be temperamental, even on its good days. He gently urged his horse into the current, angling for a shallow bank.

He never knew why the horse went under. Perhaps a leg caught a tree snag, or the river bottom fell away quickly. The sudden dip was enough to throw Lex forward and out of the saddle. He could see nothing, and deep burbling water noises filled his ears. As he scrambled to turn upright, the horse's thrashing front legs pushed him farther under and Lex was trapped beneath the desperate animal as it tried to swim. His head thumped against the sandy bottom, stunning him for a few seconds.

With no sense of up or down, Lex stopped flailing and relaxed. An unexplainable calm settled on him, and he gave himself over to the river, moving with the current, underwater. Surely, only seconds passed, although they seemed like minutes. He felt carried along, as if in unseen arms. Then, he surfaced, face-up, never so grateful to see a blue sky above.

He wasn't sure how he escaped the current, but he was aware of the sound of waves breaking nearby. The Rio washed him up on the opposite shore, a few hundred feet downriver from his intended landing spot. When he was able to sit up, he spied his horse safely on the bank, shaking himself.

Lex took off his clothes and squeezed out the muddy water, then looked the horse over for injuries and, finding none, unsaddled him. They rested for an hour, drying in the sun. When they picked up the trail west toward La Veta, he heard Sarah's voice, sounding for all the world like she was right behind him.

"When are you going to stop crossing rivers and mountains to see what's on the other side, Lex?"

He counted a half dozen saloons as he rode through La Veta, but there were also a number of saddle shops, mercantiles, law offices and other businesses among the storefronts. The tracks of the Denver Rio Grande ran right up Main Street. Lex thought of stopping at one of the saloons for a drink but changed his mind. In order to face Pop after all these years, he needed all his wits about him.

It didn't take long to find the plain, two-story boarding house tucked behind a gunsmith's shop that Pop mentioned in his letter. He tied the reins to the gate post, proceeded to the door and knocked. While waiting, he looked around at the neatly kept porch and yard. A wooden plaque, with burned letters spelling HAAS, hung over the door.

A slight old man, who looked as though he were made of wax, answered. Lex scrutinized the man's face but could see no resemblance to his father.

"Good afternoon. You must be Lexington Tucker," he said, a faint Germanic accent coarsening his words. He held the door open for Lex to enter.

"Yes, sir."

"Ah, it is good that you have come. I am Leo Haas. My wife, Mila, is . . . here . . . in back, I believe. Please, sit. I will tell Mister Tucker you are here." The man disappeared down a dark hall, leaving Lex in the stuffy parlor. He chose a wood bench by the open window and sat.

Lex heard mumbling and shuffling, then Haas emerged from the hallway with his hand supporting Pop's elbow—a frail and stooped incarnation of Pop. Lex wondered which man looked the most likely to collapse.

As Pop settled into a chair, he fixed a milky-eyed gaze on Lex.

"Could you move me closer, my friend?" Leo helped Pop to a half-standing position and walked him forward a few feet, then scooted the chair under him.

"There. Better." Pop resumed his stare. A toothless smile eased the corners of his mouth upward. Lex could not remember seeing Pop smile before. Sneer, perhaps, but smile, no.

"How are you, son?" he said.

Lex squirmed, cleared his throat. "Getting by."

Pop nodded. "Getting by. Meaning things are good. Or . . . meaning things could be a lot better." He dropped his eyes to the braided rug. "I . . . I thank you for making the ride," he said. "You sure as hell didn't owe it to me."

Lex did not care to discuss ancient history. "Silas been here?"

Pop shook his head slowly. "Your brother . . . won't be coming . . ."

Lex worried that something bad had happened to Silas, but he had no desire to ask Pop any questions.

"So I hear," Pop finished.

There was half a minute of silence. Lex was ready to get the meeting over with, now that he had seen with his own eyes that Pop was alive, for now. If he was soon to die, there was nothing anyone could do about it.

"Listen, Lex. I sit here . . . what's left of me . . . the sorriest excuse for a father that ever sucked a breath." At that, he stopped to inhale. Breathing and talking seemed to come hard for him. "Can't blame no one but me, but it was liquor that made me more of a devil than I already was. It was . . . it was the same with my Pop. In the blood, I reckon."

Lex heard kitchen noises, and heard Leo Haas talking—in German—and his wife answering.

"Yeah, well . . . can't change the past. We all live with our choices," said Lex. He'd meant it as a slight, but then he thought of Sarah's front door, closing behind him.

"I won't ask you to forgive me—"

"Good!" Lex interrupted. "That sure ain't what I came for. Hell, I don't know why I came."

Pop sighed and continued as if he hadn't heard. "I won't ask you to forgive me, but . . . I hope someday you will at least try to . . . give some thought to understanding why I—"

"Why you beat the life outa two boys, no matter how hard we tried to be quiet? Why you dragged us across Colorado, from one shit town to another? Left us with, with whoever would agree to feed us for a few days while you—well, we didn't even know what you were doing or where."

Pop was silent. Lex grabbed his hat and rose to leave. He couldn't think of anything more to say, so he just said, "Damn it. All of it."

As Lex walked to the door, Pop said, "Reckon I won't be seeing you again, son, but I want you to know . . . you and Silas were the only good things I ever had anything to do with, and that was mighty little." His breathing was louder and there was a wheeze with each exhale. "Lex. . . you will always be my son, no matter what you say or where you go. You two boys will always be . . . the only treasure Deke Tucker ever found. And lost."

Lex pulled the door shut, stomped down the steps and untied his horse.

When are you going to stop crossing rivers and mountains . . . slamming doors . . . ?

He stood there, breathing raggedly, heart pounding, not thinking. "Damn it. Damn it all," he repeated. He threw his hat down, raising a puff of dust.

He should have already been in the saddle and pointing his horse toward Silverton. Or somewhere. Anywhere. His boots seemed rooted to the ground. When his breathing slowed, Lex wiped his brow.

Then, without warning, something seemed to burble up from a dark, unknown source . . . finding hidden cracks in rocky layers of indifference and detachment. The feeling moved from his gut to his chest to his throat, and finally broke from his mouth in a single sob. Lex leaned his head against the saddle, sobbing quietly, without tears, his shoulders heaving from the release.

He felt like a little boy, and an old man all at the same time.

The sobbing let up. He felt one tear escape and trace down his cheek. Lex kept his head bowed, feeling old weights lift from him, ounce by ounce, then by the pound. Finally, he wiped his face with his handkerchief and stood up straight. He retied the reins and walked back to the front door.

He didn't have to knock. It was Pop who opened the door, and Lex led him back to the chair and took his seat back on the bench. Both men looked at each other.

"Pop. Look, I . . . well, I stand by what I said. We all make our choices. You made some awfully bad ones. But . . . so have I." Lex twisted his handkerchief, untwisted it. "In spite of . . . how it started . . . y'know, I've not had a bad life. Been to Mexico. Been to Frisco. Rode some good horses. Won a sight more hands than I've lost, Pop—you'll be glad to know that. Known some handsome women." He paused. "Known one . . . that I . . ."

Pop's smile was back. "One you can't ride far enough to forget?"

Lex nodded. "Yeah, that's about right."

"Well, I reckon you better turn that horse around and get to riding to wherever that lass is, Lexington."

It was Lex's turn to smile. "Maybe. If it ain't too late. But, Pop . . . I couldn't have done all those things if . . . well, you put me here, I guess. What little you had to do with it. I'm . . . lucky to be alive. Never occurred to me until just now."

"Leo, my friend!" Pop rasped, louder than Lex thought him capable of. Leo rushed into the parlor. "Get me that envelope laid out on my bed." Leo disappeared once more down the hallway and soon returned.

Pop slapped the sealed envelope on his palm, then held it out to Lex.

"You remember that place up in North Park? By the Rabbit Ears Range?"

"Sure, I remember." The memories weren't good, except for the ones of roaming the high meadows with Silas, pretending they were knights on horses.

"Well, by some luck, or by the gods, I hung onto the land all these years. Put the deed in a bank box when I was passing through Leadville, and there it's been, until I had 'em mail it to me once I started wasting away."

Lex reddened with shame. He had not asked about his father's health. "Are you . . .?"

Pop raised an eyebrow. "Well, who's to say how long I'll be here. Damn doctors don't know anything. 'I'm afraid the news isn't good, Mister Tucker,' he told me. Hell, doc, I could look in the mirror and tell ya that!"

Pop shook his head. "Time to pay the band, I reckon. But . . . I made my peace, Lex. With everyone but you. Anyhow, I got no use for a quarter section of nice grazing land with a view of the mountains, but you might. You, maybe and . . . that woman you know."

"What about Silas?"

Pop blinked hard. He said, softly, "Your brother is dead. I didn't want to have to tell you. No fault of his own. Drowned, I heard, down in Texas. On the Rio Grande."

Lex felt the blood leave his face, remembering the strangely peaceful experience of being swept underwater . . . and carried along to safety.

He slid the envelope into his pocket, stood up and walked over to Pop, who braced himself on the chair arms to rise.

"I'll be all right, Lex. Leo and Mila are well paid to look after me. If you find yourself in La Veta again, stop on by. Your son-of-a-bitch father might still be kicking."

Lex held out his hand to shake, but Pop grasped his waist. Lex put an arm around the old man and patted him on the back.

"Goodbye, Pop." He could say no more. The burble from within threatened to rise again.

Lex decided to have that drink. He sat alone, wondering if Sarah would, like the great Gulf of Mexico, agree to receive him, like the filthy, twisting and turning old river that he was. She might not— and he would have to live with the consequence of leaving her in Durango one too many times.

After one whiskey, he asked for directions to the telegraph office. He caught the operator just as he was about to close up for the day. The man slid a pencil and blank form across the counter.

"Ten cents a word," he said.

Lex scratched his head with the pencil, then put it to the paper.

Miss Sarah Blackwell
Durango

Five rivers, six mountains, ten days until all crossings done.
I pray to place a firm hold on the genuine article for good.

Yours truly,
Lex

The Medicine Robe

Michael Zimmer

The government man shoved his chair back from the kitchen table and stood. Rémi knew he was still watching him. Staring down at the top of his head, waiting. The government man's uncertainty hung in the air between them like the ticking seconds following a heated argument, but there had been no harsh words. Only silence. That and Rémi's refusal to acknowledge the government man's demands, to even lift his eyes to meet the younger man's gaze.

Let him stew, Rémi thought. Let him wonder if he was getting through to this old mixed-blood hunter with the wrinkled skin and wild white hair and arthritic knuckles, a relic from a time so far in the past it probably didn't even seem real to a government man not yet out of his twenties.

After a minute, the government man cleared his throat. Rémi tried to remember what he'd called himself when he knocked at the cabin's front door shortly after noon, but the name eluded him. It didn't matter. His message had been clear enough.

"Do you understand?" the government man persisted, repeating a question he'd already asked half a dozen times. "You have to move."

"Yes," Rémi finally relented in a voice that rumbled from deep within his broad chest. "I understand."

"I hate that it has to be this way, but we've already started construction and we'll be moving in this direction by the end of the week."

Rémi nodded and continued to stare at the kitchen table's scarred top. But he understood. He had watched the bulldozers move in last week, less than a musket ball's flight from his front porch. Their grating roar and the stench of their exhaust, the shouts of men in hard hats and the whine of cables, were an incessant reminder of what approached. What awaited him no matter where he went.

Glancing around at the cabin's sparse furnishings, the government man said, "Do you have anyone to help you move?"

"I won't need anyone," Rémi replied. Then he stood abruptly, joints cracking loudly, and came around the table, and the government man backed away.

"You should go now," Rémi said in a voice that belied his years, and the government man nodded and looked relieved.

"Yes, I'll do that."

Picking his briefcase off the floor, the government man started for the door. Then his gaze fell on the robe draped across the top of Rémi's old wooden trunk and he stopped.

"That's . . ."

He paused as if searching for a word that wouldn't offend.

"Large?" Rémi supplied.

"Yes, very," the government said and gave a short, half-embarrassed laugh. "You were a buffalo hunter, right? Back in the old days." He didn't wait for confirmation. "Is that a buffalo robe?"

"It is a grizzly bear's robe," Rémi replied.

"Grizzly bear? I thought your people—the metis, is it?—hunted buffalo east of here, in the Dakotas."

"My people, the *bois brule* of the Red River Valley, hunted buffalo wherever the buffalo were. But the grizzly was killed on Lakota land."

At the government man's puzzled expression, Rémi added, "The Dakotas."

"I've never heard of grizzly bears in the Dakotas."

"Now you have," Rémi replied, his patience wearing thin. Pointing to the door, he said, "You should go now. I have much to think about."

"Yes, of course. You know about the new town of Fort Peck that we're building north of the old town, don't you? If you have any questions, I have an office there. Anyone can tell—"

"I won't have any questions," Rémi interrupted, and the government man nodded and left without further comment.

Standing in the cabin's door, Rémi watched him drive away in a carriage without horses and thought that Old Joe, who had died many years earlier, had been wrong in his belief that the automobiles of the white men would someday vanish, and that the buffalo would come back to replace them. Rémi had known even then that the great herds would never return, but he'd held out hope that the automobiles would eventually disappear, allowing the return of the horse and the ox.

When the dust of the government man's auto began to settle, Rémi moved back into the cool dimness of the cabin's interior and shut the door, muting the sound of heavy equipment tearing at the soil downstream. The government that the government man said he represented was going to build a dam downstream from his cabin, and when it was completed, Rémi Caron's home would sink from sight beneath the surface of progress.

The first eviction notice had come six months ago. Others, too many to count, had followed. They had made fine starters for his morning fires. But now there would be no more notices. Now the government man insisted if Rémi did not leave of his own will, he would return with sheriffs and guns and move him out by force.

On creaky knees, Rémi shuffled back to his chair behind the kitchen table. He tested his coffee with a callused finger and was pleased to discover it still warm. Wrapping his hands around the tin mug, Rémi saet back to contemplate his options. They seemed few and bleak, and he wondered how it had come to this, that he should allow a government man barely able to raise a scrawny mustache to dictate his future.

His eyes roamed the cabin and the memories it generated, and in time they settled on the grizzly bear robe, as they always did. A smile broke through the grim countenance of his face. The hide was old and had been with him since his youth. Its hair was slipping now, and the once supple leather had turned nearly as stiff as rawhide. Probably to someone like the government man, it looked tattered and worthless, but Rémi knew its value. So had Old Joe, before the cancer took him.

Closing his eyes, Rémi let the currents in his mind take him back to the day he'd killed the giant beast.

The day he had become a man in the eyes of the *bois brule.*

They had left their homes in the Red River Valley in June for the summer hunt, pushing southwest onto the wild, rolling plains north of the Missouri River in search of the buffalo they hunted not only for their own sustenance, but for the meat and robes they would take north into the Grandmother's land to sell to the forts of the Hudson's Bay Company. More than two hundred men, women, and children accompanying nearly a hundred infamous Red River carts—greaseless axles squalling like lost souls, the dust rising thick overhead, oxen bawling, children laughing, the men pushing ahead on their best buffalo runners. Everyone eager and excited in spite of the dangers they would inevitably face as they ventured into the homeland of the Sioux.

Among them had ridden Rémi Caron. All of fourteen summers that year, and determined to prove himself worthy of the title of *bois brule*—the people of the burnt wood—named for the dark color of their flesh.

The buffalo had been elusive that year, and the hunters' rambling search had taken them farther west than they had ever before traveled. It was in their second month that they crossed the Missouri, coming in time to the *mauvaises terres,* the badlands, where the Little Missouri flowed north into the Mother River.

In his mind's eye, Rémi saw the barren, lifeless knobs and ridges of the badlands take shape before him, as real as the growl of tractors beyond his door. He saw the valleys, little more than deep, broad coulees twisting like something in pain, and bands of tinted earth that seemed too perfect in their mutations to be natural.

The caravan had stopped at the eastern edge of the badlands to make camp. The next day was Sunday, a time to rest and worship for those who wished, or to hunt and explore for those too young and wayward to slow down.

Rémi had been among the restless ones. Filled with a young man's boundless energy, he and some of the other youths of the camp had ridden into the badlands to explore its wonders. They rode their wild-maned ponies with the ease of natural horsemen, born to the flat, buffalo hair-padded saddles the *metis* preferred, laughing and telling stories, and once in a while mentioning this girl or another who traveled under the watchful eyes of their mothers.

It was in a wide, flat-bottomed valley several miles into the badlands that they dismounted to smoke their pipes, hobbling their ponies on the rich grass carpeting the valley floor. Rémi had been riding a handsome gray stallion his father had purchased the winter before, but which was still too young and undisciplined to be a runner, a mount trained to take its rider into the midst of a stampeding herd of bison. To bring him close alongside the stampeding buffalo until the hunter could empty his smooth-bored musket into the animal's lungs.

It was the gray that scented the bear first. He threw his head up and whinnied loudly, his small ears perked toward the far end of the valley. Rémi immediately dropped the small clay pipe he had been loading with tobacco and scrambled to his feet, pulling his musket up to check the priming. The others followed his example, and one of them, he couldn't remember who, had whispered, "Sioux!" in an awed tone. But Rémi knew it wasn't their age-old enemies who lurked nearby. The gray wouldn't have reacted so violently to another human's presence.

All the ponies had their heads up now, nostrils extended as they sucked in the scent of approaching danger. Rémi quickly bridled the gray and swung into the saddle without using his stirrups. Mounted, they all felt a little braver. When the bear finally lumbered out of a distant draw, their relief was almost overpowering. It was a sow, they would discover later, the first grizzly any of them had ever seen. Too young to remember when grizzlies had roamed the Hair Hills bordering their Red River Valley homelands, they knew only what the elders of their villages told them of the giant bears' swiftness and ferocity.

Some of the older men, the better hunters—and for that reason the ones they admired most—sometimes used summer bearskins as sunshades over their carts. Such skins were considered a coup, a badge honoring their skill and courage.

"Let's kill him," Rémi had urged tautly.

The others instantly agreed. Only Louis Girard voiced caution.

"We can't rush it," he said.

"Why not?" Rémi demanded.

"You've heard the same stories I have. A grizzly can outrun a horse, and it can kill one as easily as a fox kills a rabbit."

"We're not rabbits," Joseph Demer taunted, and the others laughed and mocked Louis for his cowardice. Only Rémi remained silent, absorbing his friend's warning without comment. Of them all, he knew Louis best, and he knew Louis was not afraid of the bear. But he was smart, and that was why Rémi listened.

"How do we do it?" Etienne Bouchard asked.

"Carefully," was Louis' advice, and Rémi quickly seconded it.

By now their ponies were moving nervously under them, sensing the boys' fever but also growing more frightened as the bear ambled in their direction. At Rémi's command they spread out to begin their advance, five young men reaching for manhood. Four of them carried ancient smoothbores, the fifth only a bow with a dozen iron-tipped arrows. Their ponies balked when the boys tried to force them forward, but they had been horsemen even then, and kept the animals in check. The great bear came on in her lazy, rolling gait, her nose dipping into the tall grass every few feet. Rémi knew that, like buffalo, a bear's eyesight was poor at best, and with caution they managed to get within eighty yards of her before one of the horses whinnied and caught the bear's attention. Rising deliberately to her rear legs, front paws hanging down and toward the center of her massive body, the great bear sniffed the air suspiciously, then issued a warning grunt—a sharp *wagh* that caused two of the ponies to go berserk.

Rémi's gray wheeled and tried to bolt, but he sawed back on the reins and kicked the side of the stallion's neck with his moccasined foot until he forced the skittish mount around. The bear was still on her hind legs, still snuffling and squinting almost comically in their direction. Her massive frame tapped some of Rémi's enthusiasm. He had expected something smaller, closer in size to a black bear. Even in the shade of the sow's belly, he could see the long curve of her claws, the rippling muscles of her legs, and he knew what she was capable of. His father's voice came belatedly, a warning issued almost casually some weeks before they pulled out for the buffalo range.

"They are the offspring of the devil, boy. Meaner than a moose and faster than my best buffalo runner. If you see one, ride the other way."

Rémi knew he should, but something within him, some vague sense of invulnerability, refused to let him flee. The gray was nearly crazed with fear, tossing his head and fighting the bit, but Rémi resolutely held him back.

"Let's go, Rémi," Simon Quesnelle pleaded, and there was no hint of mockery in his voice now. His eyes were wide, his mount near to bolting.

"No, I'll stay," Rémi replied stubbornly.

"Only a fool would stand against such a creature," Etienne Bouchard insisted.

Rémi remained unswayed. He tried to force the gray closer, but it seemed a hopeless task. For every step gained, the gray would take one sideways or half a dozen back before Rémi could get him stopped. It was the bear that started to close the gap between them, coming forward on her hind legs, nose wrinkling as she tested the air. At fifty yards she suddenly *waghed* again and slapped the air with a short, powerful swing of her forearm—a warning, Rémi knew, and his scalp crawled.

The gray threw its head up, almost smacking Rémi in his face, and backed off rapidly; it wheeled and danced and raised a cloud of reddish dust in the grass until he and the bear were again separated by nearly eighty yards. It was then that Rémi discovered he was alone, that the others had either made a run for safety or been unable to control their mounts. He should have felt fear. Instead he felt, suddenly and inexplicably, wonderful. Like a warrior with every nerve ending drawn to the surface and set tingling. He and the gray and the giant bear, a dragon from his father's storybooks waiting to be slain, an enemy conquered. And he thought, too, of the young women in camp, and how they would look at him when he returned with the bloodied robe. The valley was his arena, the bear his trial; lifting the musket, he sighted down its long barrel and squeezed off his shot.

The grizzly woofed and slapped at her belly as if stung. Rémi saw the puff of dust erupt from the lighter colored hair covering her stomach and knew his shot had been good, if not exactly true. He wedged the musket's butt between his foot and the stirrup and hitched his powder horn around, filling the antler-tip measure as he blew his moist breath down the barrel to extinguish any lingering sparks. He poured the powder down the barrel as the bear dropped to all fours, unmoving yet, her head held low in pain. The gray had skipped back another twenty paces or so and now stood trembling and taut. Rémi capped the musket's muzzle with a thin square of antelope leather and placed a thumb-sized lead ball over that. He quickly skated the musket's metal ramrod free of the thimbles holding it under the barrel and rammed the patched ball home. He filled the musket's huge pan with a finely-ground powder from the flattened priming horn he carried in his shooting bag and closed the frizzen.

Then he waited. Waited until the grizzly finally lifted her head and started forward, abandoning her former swaying shuffle for a trot. The gray tossed its head and started to back away. He sensed the change in the sow's attitude. So did Rémi. The grizzly was coming toward them now like a bear with business.

At fifty yards Rémi again raised his musket, sighted as best he could from the saddle of the nearly frantic gray, and fired. The ashen cloud of powder smoke obstructed his view for several seconds. Then the breeze swept it clear and he saw the bear lunging to her feet, her right foreleg sheened with blood. With a terrible snarl, the grizzly began to lope toward them, and the gray took the bit in his teeth and fled while Rémi hauled back uselessly on the reins.

Behind them, the bear increased its pace as well, running effortlessly despite her wounds. Panic swelled in Rémi's breast, squeezing until he felt he couldn't breath, and at last he gave the gray its head and let him run.

Within a quarter mile, the valley pinched down to a sandy draw, its steep walls U-shaped, the dirt soft and crumbling. It was the same draw they had followed coming in, and he saw the tracks the others had made leaving, the loose soil churned darker than the red-hued dirt around it. It was a twisting route, he recalled, its banks low enough in places to put a horse over the top if he wanted to. Rémi considered it, attempting to hide rather than try to outrun the wounded grizzly. But instinct screamed for him to run, and he did as it commanded.

In time the winding draw would lead to the plains, and the *bois brule* camp only a few hundred yards from its mouth, but the bear was gaining rapidly. Even wounded, it was obvious she was faster then the gray. Bent low above the gray's neck, Rémi imagined he could hear the angry, snuffling breath of the wounded animal. Often she was within sight when the draw straightened for brief periods. He tried to gauge her speed, to match it against the distance yet to be covered, and knew it was too far. They would never make it.

Rounding a bend, Rémi saw the south bank of the draw swoop low, the land sloping upward beyond, rising toward a series of broken, spiny knobs with passable ridges between, and he and jerked savagely at the reins. The horse took the bank in a single, terrified leap, but its rear hooves snagged the lip, slipping in the loose dirt and sliding back. Rémi shouted and lashed the gray with the ends of his reins. The stallion's rear hooves churned in the loose soil. Then the grizzly appeared. Spotting the gray just yards ahead, it lunged forward. The gray squealed in terror and kicked clumsily over the top of the bank just as the bear pounced. Above the gray's shrill whinny, Rémi heard the wet, ripping sound of torn flesh. Glancing back as the gray stumbled away from the bear's blow, he saw a swath of shredded hide on the stallion's hip, the torn flesh raw and furrowed, running blood. The grizzly was only a few feet away but still at the bottom of the draw. She had one bloody paw upraised yet, and her lips were pulled back to reveal huge teeth, yellowed near the base, a fury of pain and rage in her small, piggish eyes. She wanted to kill, Rémi saw, and began to beat at the gray's croup with the barrel of his musket.

The sterile, bony knobs had seemed close when he first spotted them. Now they looked a hundred miles away. The gray lunged up the steep slope, hooves gouging at the loose soil. The grizzly had lost momentum in taking her swipe at the horse, giving up nearly a dozen yards, but she quickly scrambled over the bank to resume pursuit.

A saddleback opened before them, the knob on the right only head high to a mounted man, but the one on the left towered nearly thirty feet into the blue summer sky. Dropping over the far side, Rémi jerked the gray to the right, guiding him deeper into the labyrinth. There was a trail here. Or at least he thought it was a trail. He reined the gray onto it, pounding the horse's ribs with his heels. The maze grew close. Rémi could never see more than twenty or thirty feet ahead of him at any time. He couldn't see the grizzly either, but he knew it was still following them. He could hear her growling and coughing, and so could the gray.

Rémi wished he'd reloaded his musket after his second shot. He hadn't even thought of it at the time, and now, with the gray twisting and dodging, it was all he could do to stay in the saddle.

When they rounded the last bend and found themselves boxed in, he wanted to cry out in frustration and anger. He had looked forward to this hunt for so long, and now it had turned against him. Through his mind flashed the image of the cabin along the Red River where he had been born. And he remembered his mother and how he'd so foolishly rebuffed her affection only days before when she'd offered him a tidbit from the kettle; how he longed for it now, the quiet comfort and safety he'd always felt when she was near.

The walls rose slick and trackless around him, too steep for the gray to climb. Maybe too steep for him, too, without time to carve grips in the hard earth for his fingers and toes. And he knew there wouldn't be enough time for that. The grizzly's wet, slobbering snarls filled the tiny cul-de-sac, smothering him with its promise of destruction.

Rémi was unable to hold the gray back when the stallion wheeled and plunged back down the trail, which had apparently never been anything more than a track for runoff. Rémi let him go, pushing off with his hands and allowing the horse to run out from under him. He landed against the slope and tumbled down in a heap. Even before he stopped rolling, he heard the abrupt, terror-filled shriek of the gray, the fearsome roar of the grizzly. And above it, once more, the awful sounds of ripping flesh, the brittle snap of bones.

The gray was dead, Rémi was certain of that. The question was whether the bear would stay with the horse or come on. Did she know it was Rémi who had shot her? Or in her small, dim mind did she equate horse and rider as one?

Fingers trembling, Rémi pulled his powder horn around and unplugged it with his teeth. He poured a massive charge down the barrel, then dropped an unpatched lead ball down the muzzle and slammed it home with his ramrod. Tipping the frizzen forward, he sprinkled a hefty charge of priming powder into the pan. He checked the flint with his thumb, cutting it and drawing a thin line of blood, then pulled the hammer back to full cock and brought the stock up between his arm and ribs, bracing the butt against the steep pitch of the ridge.

He could hear the grizzly ripping at the gray's flesh just around the bend, venting its fury on the helpless beast. Then a silence so abrupt and deep it sent a chill down his spine. He closed his eyes for only a second, and when he opened them he saw her standing before him, no more than ten feet away.

Even on all fours she seemed as big as a buffalo. She was working her jaws and tongue against some pink meat lodged in her teeth, her mottled gums red with the gray's blood, the hair around her muzzle matted with it.

Rémi took a deep breath and slowly lifted the musket's barrel toward the bear. His finger curled around the trigger. Now that the moment had arrived, he felt strangely calm and in control, his fear dissipated. The huge grizzly took a tentative step forward, then another, and Rémi smiled coolly. She was watching him curiously, perhaps wondering why he didn't try to flee. Then her eyes met his and fogged in rage. With an earth-tilting roar she lunged forward, her dagger-like claws slicing, jaws yawning, slobbering. Rémi felt the tip of her claws touch his chest and slide across his belly like rolling embers as her mouth closed on the musket's iron muzzle just as he pulled the trigger.

The weapon's report was muffled in the bear's throat, but he could see the look of surprise that crossed her face as the back of her neck and head exploded. She reared back on her haunches, her closed jaws dribbling powder smoke. But she was still slapping, her claws whistling through the air above him. He could never recall exactly how long she pawed at him, but at the time it seemed to go on forever—five minutes, ten?

Probably not, he knew. Probably she hadn't cuffed the air more than a few spastic times before she keeled over dead.

Rémi shivered in the cool dimness of his cabin as he relived that day. He could still feel the tight skin of the old wound across his chest and stomach, and sometimes when the weather was especially cold or damp, there was a little pain, like a distant burning. The grizzly's claws hadn't gone very deep, but they'd left wide, wicked-looking scars from his left shoulder to a spot just above his belt, over his right hip, like furrows turned over by a plow.

"Big medicine," Old John had said when he heard the story.

And Rémi had agreed.

He was sitting on the cabin's porch when he heard the automobiles approaching through the cottonwoods bordering the Missouri River. He couldn't tell how many there were, but thought there was more than one. Maybe two or three.

He had been expecting them for several days now, going out at dawn and waiting patiently until dusk. He had the grizzly's robe draped over his shoulders, taking comfort from its warmth, strength from what the tattered badge represented. Pulling it close, he struggled stiffly to his feet. He wanted to be standing when the government man arrived, not tottering like a stem of autumn grass until he got his knees locked, his balance steadied.

The first car into the clearing was driven by the government man. Close behind came a second vehicle, this one with the county's insignia on the door. Rémi recognized the driver through the windshield. Ed Clark had been around a long time and was a good man, although Rémi had no doubt that he would do what the law required of him.

Rémi didn't know the man riding in Clark's auto, but he'd seen him around, tall and lean with hard eyes and an immutable smirk—a bully always on the prowl for his next victim. Rémi had once watched him pistol-whip Tom Standing Bull for public intoxication and resisting arrest, although Tom had barely been able to stand when the deputy cornered him in an alley behind the Hi-Line Bar.

The government man drove straight up to the cabin and parked with his car's nose pointed toward the front door. Clark stopped some distance away, where the dust from his wheels wouldn't drift forward onto the porch. The government man was first out of his car, gripping a sheaf of papers in one hand so tight he was crumbling the sides. His expression was one of parental exasperation crossed with anger. He started talking before he even got his door slammed shut.

"You were supposed to be gone by now, Caron. What the hell is the matter with you? I know you can speak English, you just don't seem capable of understanding it."

Rémi didn't reply. His gaze moved to Deputy Clark, climbing the gentle slope toward the porch. Clark was looking at the government man with disgust, but didn't try to interrupt his tirade. The other deputy was close behind, his familiar smirk solidly in place. The government man turned to Clark and thrust his papers toward him.

"Here," he said. "He's been warned more times than I can count, and I'm fed up with it." Clark took the papers, and the government man turned back to Rémi. "These are eviction notices, Caron. You're being evicted . . . *today*. Do you know what that means?"

"Easy, Mr. James," Clark said. "We'll handle it from here."

Clark advanced several more strides, until he was standing at the foot of the porch steps. The other deputy stood beside him, his smirk turned up in a taunting grin.

"How are you, Mr. Caron?" Clark said.

"This is my home," Rémi replied. "I have nowhere else to go, and no desire to go wherever this man wants me to go."

"All I want is you outta here," the government man—James—snapped.

"You understand what's going to happen here, right?" Clark asked Rémi.

Nodding solemnly, Rémi replied, "You are a good man, Deputy Clark. I am sorry you were the one they sent."

"Now, don't do anything foolish," Clark replied, but it was already too late.

Rémi's shoulders heaved and the ancient grizzly's robe flew back against the cabin's wall. One corner hooked on the door's latch, but it didn't matter where it landed. Drawing an old Colt revolver from the waistband of his trousers, Rémi eared the hammer to full cock. His thumb screamed in protest, but his hand remained steady. He wanted to laugh at the look on the government man's face as he dived into the dirt in front of the porch. Clark was holding up a hand and telling him not to shoot, and Rémi nodded his approval. Clark understood, and would not pull his own weapon unless Rémi lowered the Colt's muzzle toward him.

But the other deputy, the one who, finally, was not smirking, didn't understand how these things worked. He didn't understand what Rémi was saying when he drew his Colt. He was already snatching his service revolver from a Western-style holster on his hip. Although Clark yelled at him not to fire, the deputy didn't listen.

Rémi saw the service revolver spit a thin cloud of pale blue smoke toward him. He heard the first bullet as it passed his shoulder, but he didn't hear the second one. He felt it, though. Like a carnival strong man's hand pressed flat against his chest, then pushing suddenly. The force of it took the wind from his lungs.

Rémi's shoulders hammered the cabin's door, and his feet flew out from under him. He fell hard to a sitting position, and as he did the bear's robe came free of the door's latch and settled across his shoulders. In the yard, Clark was still yelling at the second deputy, whose face now registered fear, and the government man named James was still in the dirt with his arms pressed tight over his head.

Then the scene faded and Rémi looked to his right, where his name was being called with urgency.

"Rémi, come on."

"Etienne?"

The boy grinned. "Come on, we've been waiting."

Rémi looked past his boyhood friend to where Simon Quesnelle and Louis Girard and Joseph Demers waited with eager expressions. They were all mounted, and Simon was holding the gray's reins in his hands.

"Let's go, Rémi. There are buffalo over the horizon, a big herd, and we want to get there in time to join the hunt."

Laughing, Rémi rose to his feet and strode swiftly across the porch. He left the medicine robe where it lay, draped over the shoulders of someone he no longer knew. In the cabin's yard, he was aware of white men arguing, but their words no longer mattered. He accepted the reins Simon handed him and swung lithely into the buffalo-leather saddle atop the gray's back. Mounted, he shoved his feet into the wooden stirrups, then reached out to catch the old smooth-bore musket Louis tossed him.

"This way," Etienne shouted, and Rémi drove his moccasined heels into the gray's sides.

They rode fast, as true horsemen should, like the wind flowing through the cottonwoods toward the distant horizon where the buffalo still ran free.

Come Necessary

Michael Knost

Tom Delaney wasn't a normal boy. In fact, folks in town said he had the mind of a young'un tucked inside the frame of a full-grown buck of a fella. He might've been slow to catch hold of things, but once he got his grip, he held to that thing like a hellfire preacher clinging to the Good Book, word for word, line by line.

A well-mannered young man, Tom was shorter than most, but his stout build made him appear larger than five-foot six. Even his face told you he wasn't normal. His eyes were sloped and set apart with a gaze that betrayed nothing of what lay behind them. And his nose was just a nub of a thing, short and wide, not much of a feature at all.

"Breakfast is ready," Maddie called from the main room.

"Be right there," Tom said without taking his gaze from the Colt Army single action he'd been cleaning in the parlor. He wiped away excess oil and glanced at his father's photograph on the mantle. "I'd best get to the table, Pa. Maddie's word carries now that she's taken up Ma's duties."

He wiped again, making sure to leave a thin sheen of oil on the metal before wrapping the piece with a care that could only be described as reverence.

"Thomas James Delaney," Maddie said from the doorway, hands on her hips. "Did you not hear me calling?"

"Yes, ma'am. I'm just putting the revolver away."

She shook her head. "You haven't fired that since . . ." Pausing, she stole a quick glance at their father's photograph. "Since your practice sessions. Why must you continue scrubbing the thing like it's been to war?"

"Pa always said there are two kinds of men who fail to keep their piece clean—the greenhorn and the departed."

Bringing her hands together in front of her, Maddie raised an eyebrow. "That thing hasn't seen daylight in three years. It don't gather filth just sitting there."

"A speckless pistol does not suffer from being scrubbed again, Maddie." He laid the rag-wrapped Colt in its place inside their father's officer trunk, along with the holster and belt. "It is neglect that ruins a thing, not care."

Maddie's hard look softened some, enough to pass for the beginnings of a smile. "It's a wonder how much you sound like him." She fixed his collar so it would lie flat against his shirt. "Come and eat. We've got work waiting."

Tom rolled the new barrel of molasses across the store's plank floor, careful not to let it get away from him. "Want this set same as last, Maddie?"

"That will do just fine." She wiped her hands on her apron and stepped closer. "I'll doctor us some beans the way you like with what's left in the old barrel if you'll collect it for me."

"Yes, ma'am," he said, giving ma'am its usual stretch—may-yum—steady and deliberate. "I'm partial to your beans fixed like that."

Out past the open doorway, the sky held that flat white glare of noon, and the hitch rail stood empty but for a swaying saddle blanket.

"When you get that done, bring in the bushel of apples from out back." She raised a hand without looking. "Be sure and sort out the ones with blemishes. Lord knows Mrs. Kensington will be in for pie fixings and will pitch a fit if she spies so much as a bruise. I truly do not know how Mother endured that woman's patronage."

"Does that mean we'll get us a pie too?" Tom asked, his cheeks gone ruddy with the hope of it. "Ain't nothing wrong with the insides of them specked apples, you know."

Maddie laughed and gave a nod. "I reckon I can bake us one as well. Now get on with your work."

"Where do you want I should put the empty barrel?"

"I'll show you," she said, stepping out the door. "Set it at the end of the porch there, where it won't be in folks' way."

"Beg pardon, ma'am," a grimy stranger called out from the saddle of a passing sweat-darkened bay. "But you sure do look like a good reason for a man to forget his prayers." The smile in the rider's eyes was nothing more than measured appetite.

Tom's neck and cheeks turned hot as he stepped in front of Maddie.

"Careful there, Ike," the fella riding next to the man said. "It appears you've riled the lady's rooster."

Ike grinned. "Looks to me like the poor fool got dropped on his head while sucklin' his ma's tit when he was just a pup."

Maddie tugged at Tom's arm. "Let's go inside. We've too much to do to be standing out here gawking about."

The two strangers stopped at the saloon down the street, tied their horses, and went inside without another glance toward the general store.

"Those men—"

"It don't matter none, Tom." Maddie patted his arm and smiled. "Those men don't matter none at all."

"They used ugly talk on Maddie, Pa." Tom held his father's photograph with both hands. "Ain't come necessary yet, but I won't let them treat Maddie ugly like."

The parlor was quiet with his sister downstairs tending the store.

"Made ugly comments about me too, and that don't make no never mind to me." He shook his head. "But I done promised you I would protect Maddie and Ma 'fore you left us. And now that Ma's gone, I reckon I only got Maddie to look after."

His father's uniform showed dark in the photograph, making for a striking figure. "I keep the piece clean and ready, like you said." He nodded toward the officer's trunk. "Scrubbed it again just this morning. You said yourself, a man can't start the day with a fouled-up weapon, not if he means it to work when needed."

"There you are," Maddie said, stepping into the parlor. She paused and leaned forward. "Are you feeling poorly?"

"No ma'am."

Moving closer, she took the photograph from his hands and studied their father's tintype eyes. "You been thinkin' on Pa again, have you?"

Tom nodded. "I talk to him."

Maddie smiled. "You have held closely to his words."

"His words come easy, Maddie. It is his voice I cannot recollect."

She dropped her gaze, not trusting herself to speak.

"Reckon Pa would be proud of how I held to his lessons?" His expression didn't change, but there was something hopeful in his eyes. "You reckon, Maddie?"

Placing a hand to her neck, Maddie cleared her throat and nodded. "Why, those brass buttons on his uniform wouldn't last a day with his pride-swelled chest."

Tom's smile finally broke. "You reckon?"

Maddie returned the photograph to the mantle and nodded. "There is no doubt in my mind. Now, let's get back to our chores."

"I best get to mendin' them shutters like we said. They been left off too long already."

Maddie raised her brows. "Don't get too hot. And mind yourself."

"Yes ma'am."

Tom wiped a gritty sleeve across his forehead as the sun laid heavy. The iron hinges were rusted near through, so he had to drive the new screws hard. Each turn of the hand-crank auger groaned. The sun lit his neck raw, and the back of his shirt clung to him like plaster.

"Well, looky here," Ike said, sauntering up the porch steps like he had bought the land beneath it. "Ain't that just the picture of domestic bliss. Big ol' Tom Delaney playin' house."

Tom kept working, jaw tight, not looking up.

Ike's companion, a stringy fella with slicked-back hair, leaned against the doorway. "We learned all we could about you and your sister at the saloon."

"Hey, Maddie," Ike called inside. "You ever think on settin' up with a real man? One with proper faculties?"

Maddie stepped from behind the counter, arms folded, eyes firm. "What is it you boys want?"

Ike took off his hat and smoothed his hair with one hand. "Heard tell you got some fine preserves. We're partial to sweet things."

"You've had your fun. Now take it elsewhere," Maddie said. "I've got no time nor patience for this kind of foolishness."

"Aww now, don't be like that." Ike sauntered a little closer. "You sure are a pretty thing, Maddie. Shame you got stuck keepin' house for a man that's mostly child."

Tom stood then, slow but straight, and stepped down from the shutter brace. His voice came even. "You two best go. Ain't a place here for talk like that."

Ike snorted and turned, placing both hands on his hips. "That right? And what if we don't?"

Tom didn't blink. "Then I'd do whatever come necessary."

"You hear that, Ellis? Boy says he's gonna do what's necessary." Ike stepped forward again, closer this time, and tilted his head toward Tom. "You ain't your pa, boy. He was a proper soldier I hear. You just play with his boots."

Tom didn't move. "Go."

"Afternoon, gentlemen." Sheriff Lew Harker stepped up onto the porch, pausing with one hand resting on the butt of his sidearm. "Seem like we got a disturbance?"

Ike straightened, then rolled his shoulders like a dog trying to dry off. "No disturbance, Sheriff. Just a friendly visit to a fine establishment."

Harker's gaze moved from Ike to Ellis, then to Tom, and finally to Maddie. "Friendly's a word. Just ain't the one I'd use."

Ellis moved off the wall and started descending the steps. "We was just leavin', Sheriff."

"See that you do," Harker said. "And take your noise with you."

Ike lingered a moment, touched the brim of his hat with two fingers, and turned to leave. "Take care now," he called over his shoulder. "Don't work too hard on them shutters, Tom. Ain't no fixin' what's already broke."

The porch held still for a moment after their departure, a warm breeze washing over Tom and the sheriff.

"Tom, I admire a man willing to stand up for kin." Harker scratched his cheek. "But you ought not try and shoulder that load on your own."

Tom's eyes were still fixed down the street. "I ain't afraid."

"No, I reckon you ain't," the sheriff said. "But bein' unafraid and bein' bulletproof ain't the same thing, son. You leave the hard business to the law, you hear?"

Tom turned and gave a slow nod. "Yes sir."

Harker tipped his hat. "All right then. Maddie, you let me know if them boys come back 'round. They start trouble again, I'll handle it."

"Thank you, Sheriff," Maddie said, voice tight. "I'll be sure."

After Harker stepped off the porch, Maddie came to the doorway and stood beside Tom. Her face was pale, but her mouth was set. "You all right?"

"I'm fine."

"You weren't bluffin' about doin' what come necessary, were you?"

He looked at her, then back at the shutter. "Pa says a respectable man don't bluff none."

Tilting her head, Maddie leaned forward. "You want to come in and have a cool drink?"

"I'll finish this first."

Maddie placed a hand on his back, then left him to his work.

Tom knelt again, took up the auger, and drove in the last screw until it bit tight. The shutter closed with a clean snap. Not loose. Not sagging.

Tom crossed the street, relieved he no longer carried the parcel . . . it wasn't the weight of the items, it was having to face Mrs. Kensington. Of course, the woman had been as disagreeable as always, fussing about the condition of the apples and lecturing him on her rheumatism, which she said came from her husband's disposition and not the weather. Tom had nodded and endured, same as always, because Maddie asked him to be kind, and Tom never could deny her.

By the time he stepped back across their porch, the door to the store was ajar. "Maddie?" he called, nudging it open with a shoulder.

What he saw froze him in place.

There on the floor behind the counter, Maddie was twisted sideways, one arm pinned beneath her. Her hair was loose, her dress yanked at the collar. Ike's full weight pressed on her, his hand over her mouth.

Ellis stood nearby, chewing the corner of his lip. "I told you this was a bad idea, Ike."

Maddie kicked, but Ike only laughed.

"You put your hands on my sister," Tom said, low and even.

"Aw hell," Ellis said. "I told you."

Tom didn't speak again. He stepped forward. Ellis made to block him, reaching for Tom's arm, but Tom caught him by the shirtfront and flung him sideways like he wasn't nothing more than a scarecrow in the wind. Ellis hit a shelf and spilled a row of mason jars before crumpling to the floor.

Ike stood fast, yanking Maddie up in front of him like a human shield. He had a pistol in his right hand, trained at Tom's gut. Maddie gasped, and blood showed at her lip.

"You stay back, mongrel," Ike said. "I'll put daylight through you, I swear."

Tom didn't flinch. "Let her go."

Ike grinned, teeth yellow and spaced out like picket boards. "You best run along. I don't reckon you're fast enough to take this from me."

"I don't need to take nothin'," Tom said. "You let her go and you get outta here. You and your friend. Or I'll end this now."

"You?" Ike laughed. "You ain't got the sand, Delaney. You're simple. You don't know how things are done. You don't—"

"It has come necessary," Tom said.

Ike's smile wavered.

"You bring your pistol and meet me in the street," Tom said. "One hour. Not a minute later."

"Or what?"

Tom stepped forward. "Or I come for you wherever you sleep."

Ellis scrambled up behind the counter, groaning, holding his shoulder. "Let's go, Ike. Now!"

Ike stared at Tom, then shoved Maddie aside. She fell hard against a crate, gasping. Tom didn't move—his eyes were on Ike's the whole time.

Ike pointed his pistol at Tom a final time. "One hour, you say?"

Tom nodded.

"I'll be there. I'll be waitin'. You best make your peace with the Almighty."

The silence that followed the men's departure was worse than any noise.

Tom knelt beside Maddie, pulling her close. "Did they hurt you?"

Her voice was barely there. "No. You got here just in time. He didn't . . ." She looked down. Her dress was torn at the collar, her hair stuck to her cheeks. "Go get Sheriff Harker."

"Ain't no need for that man."

Maddie turned to him quick like. "Tom—"

He shook his head. "You saw what the sheriff did last time. He told 'em to leave polite. He told me to stand down. That don't stop men like them."

"We're not the law."

"Maybe not," he said. "But I gave my word to Pa that I would look after you. I don't break my word."

"You'll get yourself killed."

Tom's mouth went tight. "Maybe. But I'll go to my grave knowin' I tried."

He helped her sit upright. She winced but nodded. "Then I'll come too."

"No ma'am. You stay here."

"I ain't lettin' you walk into a fight like that alone, Tom."

"I need to know you're safe."

She held his gaze. "You can't promise me that now. Not ever."

Tom rose to his feet. His hands were not steady, though it was no sign of fright. It was something else—something rooted deeper. "I'll tend to the shutters by and by," he told her.

Tom just stood in the parlor for what seemed the longest time. He wasn't studying on anything in particular or listening for unheard things. He did not speak to his father or even glance at the photograph. He just stood there with perspiration beading his forehead until his stomach grumbled.

As though awakened from a daydream, Tom moved toward the officer's trunk and opened its lid. Kneeling, he found the belt and holster right where he left them, placed atop the folded cavalry coat along with the pistol still wrapped in the oiled rag. Tom lifted it out and sat back on his haunches.

The Colt felt heavier than it did earlier in the day. It wasn't weight so much as history. Six chambers, single-action, walnut grip worn smooth where his father's hand had curled around it time and again.

He took to wiping it down, slow and methodical like, the same way he'd been taught. The brush of cloth over steel calmed him in a way nothing else could. He checked the sights. Checked the cylinder. Checked the loading gate. Checked it all again.

Downstairs, he could hear Maddie moving through the shop, replacing toppled things. Her steps were careful and precise. She wasn't crying anymore. That somehow hurt more.

Tom gazed at his pa's photograph as though it was the first time doing so. His father stood in uniform, hand resting on the hilt of his saber, face as firm and unreadable as always. Eyes like polished stone.

"It's come necessary, Pa." His voice cracked at the edges, but he didn't clear it. He let it stay that way. "I did like you said. I worked hard, I kept my peace, I looked out for Maddie. I tried every way I knew how to avoid this. But now there ain't another path forward. Ike made sure of that."

He picked up the Colt again, pressed his thumb against the hammer, and felt it click into place.

"All them years you had me clean it, load it, unload it, run dry-fire drills with the hammer back and my heart thumpin'. All the shooting at cans and apples. I didn't know why it mattered. Not until now."

The room felt quiet in the way a church feels with only a few congregants inside.

"I remember what you told me. You said: never point a pistol at a man unless you mean to pull the trigger. And never pull the trigger unless you mean to kill."

His father's voice echoed in his head, low and patient, drawn from another time. He almost smiled at finally recalling what the man sounded like.

"We don't shoot to wound, Tom. You aim center, and you end it. You put a man down clean, or you don't draw at all."

Tom's hands clenched around the grip.

"I hated that lesson. You made me shoot all them bad apples again and again till my ears rang and my hand blistered. You said shootin' a man wasn't no different. You said the nerves would lie to me, that my arm would go soft if I let it. And if I was ever green enough to haul iron on a man and then lose my nerve, that'd be the last foolish notion I'd harbor.

Tom got to his feet slow and steady, worked the belt around his middle, and gave the holster a tug to see it rode firm on his shooting side. The leather was stiff at first, but his movements found the memory of it. He'd worn it before, around the house and in drills. Never like this.

"I remember, too," he whispered. "What you said after. That I should do whatever it took to avoid it. Whatever it took to never have to raise a weapon on another man. But, Pa . . . sometimes a man brings the fight to your front porch."

Tom swung the cylinder out and thumbed in six cartridges, one after the next. He gave it a spin, then snapped it shut and dropped the pistol into the holster with a turn of his wrist that showed he'd done it more than once. It rode on his hip like it belonged there.

He crossed to the mantle and peered closer into the photograph. "I ain't never felt ready. Not one day of my life. But I reckon if I'm ever gonna be, it's now. You trained me for this. All them early mornings, all them times you said I had to learn a thing the hard way . . . it was for this. It had to be."

He stopped short. His throat drew up tight, and near a minute passed before he found words again. "I don't hate him, Pa. Not even after what he did. But I can't let him walk free. Maddie needs to feel safe. I need to feel like I did right by you. And I can't sleep another night knowing I turned away."

He touched the top of the frame with one finger. "I aim to make you proud."

He turned back to the trunk, set the lid down gentle like, then let it drop the rest of the way with a low, empty sound. Gave the room one last look, then made for the stairs.

Maddie looked up from the counter. Her hands were still, resting flat. Her eyes flicked to the Colt on his hip and then to his face.

He gave a single nod.

She looked fit to speak, but nothing came of it.

Tom stepped outside, pulled the door to behind him, and set off down the middle of the street.

The street was lined with folks who'd drifted out from shops and saloons, drawn to the spectacle about to commence. And the quiet was too thick for such a crowd of spectators. Tom Delaney stood in the street with his father's Colt on his hip, eyes fixed down the line at Ike Granger, who wore a crooked grin.

Ike stepped forward with a lazy gait, thumbs hooked in his gun belt, eyes twinkling like he'd already had the story half-told to the boys at the saloon.

Sheriff Harker pushed his way through the crowd and stopped between them. "This ain't happenin'," he yelled. "I ain't gonna see no blood run on Main Street today. This town's got laws, and I aim to keep 'em."

Ike raised both hands as if caught mid-prayer. "Now hold on, Sheriff. I'm just out here stretchin' my legs. Wasn't my notion to fight none at all." He turned to the crowd, voice rising. "But Tom Delaney called me out. That boy said, clear as Sunday morning, to meet him in the street and settle it!"

Harker turned. "That true, Tom?"

Tom nodded once. "It is."

"Then I'm orderin' you to stand down. I know what he done. I don't like it. But we do things by the law here. You let me handle him."

Tom's eyes didn't move. "You tried that. And he just came back."

"Damn it, Tom, you shoot him down in front of a crowd, you'll carry that the rest of your life. I know Randal Delany raised you better."

The mention of his pa's name hit Tom like a thrown stone. His jaw twitched, and behind his eyes he heard it—not a sound, not a dream, but a memory steady as bedrock: *"If there's any way to avoid it, son . . . you find it. You try."*

Tom blinked and took in a breath like he meant to hold it forever. "I don't want to kill you, Ike."

Ike threw his head back and laughed, slapping his thigh. "Hear that, folks? He don't want to kill me." He turned to Ellis. "Boy's got his daddy's pistol and his mama's heart."

Ellis chuckled but held his gaze to Tom's Colt at his side.

Tom took a step forward, voice clear. "How about we settle this so's there ain't no blood."

Ike's grin dimmed a fraction.

"I want to give you a chance," Tom went on. "Fair contest."

Ike cocked his head. "What sort of contest? Spittin' distance? Bible verse recitin'?"

Tom shook his head. "Apples."

"Apples?" Ike squinted like the word had come out in a foreign tongue. "What the hell you talkin' about?"

"You shoot an apple. So do I. Cleanest shot wins."

Ike squinted. "You stalling, boy? Hopin' I get bored and go home?"

Tom just stared.

Ike grinned again, nastier this time. "Tell you what. Let's make it mean somethin'. You're the one wants to prove you got sand, right? So why don't we put them apples on someone's head?"

Before Tom could say a word, a voice rang out.

"I'll do it."

The crowd turned as Maddie stepped past the onlookers, her face pale but determined.

"You put the apple on my head," she said to Tom. "And Ellis can put one on his head for Ike to shoot at."

Ike laughed. "Hell's bells, girl. You'd rather die than take up with a real man?"

"I'd rather die with dignity than live as another man's shame."

The street went still again.

Tom stepped toward Maddie. "You don't have to do this."

"Pa always believed in you, Tom, and since he ain't here, I need to believe in you too."

The apples were fetched. Maddie stepped to the line and placed one on her head with both hands. She stood still, not flinching, not blinking. Ellis, reluctantly, took his place some paces down, muttering curses as he balanced the other apple on his scalp.

Ike looked at Tom, still grinning. "You first, pistoleer. Let's see what kind of fool you are."

Tom walked up ten paces, then twenty, and turned. He locked eyes with Maddie.

She closed her eyes.

And then, like a striking rattler, the Colt cleared leather.

CRACK!

The apple exploded before the crowd even realized Tom had moved. Chunks flew through the air and struck the boards behind her. Maddie stood untouched. The apple hit the ground in wet, broken pieces.

Silence. Then a roar. Shouts. Applause. Half the crowd gasped, and the other half shouted praises to the Almighty.

Tom stood with the revolver already holstered.

Ike's smirk had died somewhere along the way. He looked at Ellis, then back at Tom, whose eyes had not changed.

"You do it," Tom said. "And if your shot is good as mine, then we draw on each other to break the tie."

Ike looked at Tom, then the pistol at his side. His fingers twitched. Sweat bloomed across his brow. "I—I ain't got to prove nothin'," he said.

Ellis, wide-eyed, yanked the apple from his head. "Hell no you ain't!"

Ike cleared his throat and headed down the street. "I ain't got nothin' to prove at all."

Tom watched until the men disappeared down the end of the street.

The sheriff stepped up beside Tom. "You sure are your father's boy."

Tom gazed at him. "Some days I wonder."

Harker nodded, then moved on as Maddie came to Tom, her hands shaking now that it was over. She leaned into him, and he put an arm around her shoulder.

"I wasn't afraid," she whispered.

"I was."

They stood there a long while, the crowd drifting away, the street returning to normal as if nothing had happened.

Folks in town still talk on it to this day—how Tom Delaney stood alone in the street, called out a man twice meaner and three times more sure of himself, and ended it with one clean shot through an apple, no blood spilled, no grave dug.

They say it weren't just the shooting that turned heads. It was the way he stood—calm, rooted, like he'd been planted there by a higher hand for just that purpose.

Sheriff Harker never had to chase Ike or Ellis. Both men rode out like dogs who'd tried the wrong porch.

And Tom? They say he grew ten years older that day, though his face stayed the same and his speech still came slow.

He still had the mind of a young'un tucked inside the frame of a full-grown buck, same as always. Still talked soft and took his time with his words. But once he got a grip on a thing—justice, decency, what was right—he held to it like a hellfire preacher to the Good Book, word for word, line by line.

He didn't become something different that day—just stepped fully into what he'd always been—but then again, Tom Delaney wasn't a normal boy.

Standoff

Johnny D. Boggs

Sweat poured down his face and the sun glared in his eyes, but Private Jedediah Jones refused to blink. Left eye clamped shut, he stared intently down the barrel of his Springfield rifle, braced against a limb of a dead cottonwood, waiting for the slightest movement from behind the pile of rocks at the edge of the butte. He had seen the figure dive behind the rocks and was waiting for the Comanche brave, the last of the war party that ambushed his patrol, to make his play.

Flies buzzed around the ugly wound in his right side, his shirt sticky against the skin with blood. The pain was intense, but Jones bit his bottom lip to keep from trembling and continued his afternoon vigil. He longed for a drink—even the brackish water from the Concho or the rotgut from the Saint Angela saloons—but his canteen was by his dead mount, in the open.

Where is H troop? he thought, and blinked.

When his eyes opened a second later, nothing had changed. He was still somewhere in Texas, and Sergeant Troy, Homer, Luke, Ben—even Jake Lent, the scout—were dead, scattered among the prickly pear and rocks, along with four dead Comanches and six U.S. Army horses, already bloating in the heat.

He wanted to yell at the Comanche behind the rock, but Sergeant Troy had taught him better. Never let up, he had said. Don't move, don't think. Just wait. But that hadn't stopped two arrows from slamming into Troy's back. Jones could still hear the sickening sounds of arrows and bullets striking flesh, shrills of Comanches, smell the stench of black powder. His horse had buckled as he drew his rifle from the scabbard, and he had leaped off and was running for cover when the bullet knocked him near the cottonwood. It had felt like the time Mr. Griffith's mule kicked him in the side, busting a couple of ribs and laying him up for a week.

He hadn't even fired a shot, and it was over.

Only it wasn't over. Not yet. He had seen the quick flash of brown jump behind the rocks. *Maybe he's dead*, Jones thought, but he couldn't risk it. "Comanch ain't never dead," Jake Lent had often said, "till you put that last ball in the back of his head."

It was growing hard to concentrate. He couldn't tell what was real and what was caused by delirium. He thought he heard June bugs, but it had been quiet before the skirmish. *Was that real?* He smelled Mrs. Griffith's cornbread. *That couldn't be, could it?* No, he decided, only two things were real: the bullet hole in his side and the Comanche behind the rock.

"Well, you may got me, but I got you, too," he whispered, his voice dry and cracking. The Comanche had nowhere to go either, not without risking being shot. Just wait, he said, just wait for H troop. He shut his eyes again, this time longer.

Belshazzar? He opened both eyes, searching the distance. Nothing had moved, but he could have sworn he had heard Belshazzar crying out as he would during a thunderstorm. And the smell of Mrs. Griffith's cornbread was heavier.

Ferndale Plantation in South Carolina had been a long time ago, he thought, no longer able to concentrate on the Comanche. He had been just a pup himself when Mrs. Griffith let him have the runt of the litter. "You'll have to take real good care of him, Jed," she had said. "If you don't, he'll die."

He hadn't taken that good care of the hound, though. Once, he had thrown the dog bread crumbs, watching with delight as Belshazzar caught them in his mouth. But the boyish devilment took over, and soon he was alternating tossing bread crumbs with pebbles, laughing uncontrollably when the dog would swallow a rock.

"What you doing?" Sarah had yelled, scaring him out of a year's growth. "Mr. Griffith'll whip the tarnation out of you, Jedediah!"

"You'd better not tell!" he had shot right back. "It's my dog, anyhow."

For once Sarah didn't tell, and Belshazzar grew to be the healthiest dog of the bunch. "Boy, you done a good job raising that dog," Mr. Griffith had said. "Must be feeding it some of Ma's cornbread?"

The thought of rocks almost made him laugh out loud, which would've been grounds for a whipping, but he bit his lip and shook his head, "Nossir, Mr. Griffith."

When he was older, he had tried to train the hound to be a bird dog. He threw a stick in the mill pond and Belshazzar jumped right in the water—and sank like a stone. He had to dive in and fish him out.

"Jedediah Jones, you think of that dog more'n you think of me," Sarah yelled one evening, before the War. "I swear, I ain't never gonna marry you if you keep that up."

That had been the first he had heard of marriage. But it hadn't been the first time he had thought of Sarah as something other than a tattletale. She had filled out nicely, and when he looked up at her that night, he started shaking like he had the fever, his heart beating fast, blood rushing through his head. Sarah sat down beside him, smiling, and kissed him.

Then came the War, and Mr. Griffith's death. And afterward, he found himself a free man. But the Ferndale Plantation had been in Sherman's way, and after the surrender Mrs. Griffith sold the land and moved to Charleston.

"What are we gonna do, Jedediah?" Sarah had asked. He had been sitting in front of his shack, scratching Belshazzar behind his ears the way he liked. Sarah's folks were going to sharecrop, but he had no folks, and he didn't want to farm anymore.

"You stay with your folks for a while," he had said. "I'm going West. I'll learn to write and send for you when I got enough money."

She had said she would wait, and kissed him and more.

He wondered if she had waited, for that had been years ago. Probably not, he thought, for nothing else had worked out. He had enlisted in Louisiana, then found himself at Fort Concho, drilling and drilling and drilling. It had never been that boring on the plantation, and he soon learned to appreciate the patrols.

"Ain't a sign of a Comanch within a day's ride of here," Lent had said. "And that's a bad sign."

Those had been the last understandable words spoken.

He continued to stare across his rifle barrel, but he had lowered his left hand and placed it against his side, using the cottonwood limb to hold up the heavy rifle. He looked up and saw the buzzards circling, then heard Belshazzar again and smelled the sweet skin of Sarah.

Poor Belshazzar hadn't made it to Texas. "Hey, darky!" a man in a slouch hat had yelled on a road in Alabama. "Where'd you steal that mule and hound?"

"I ain't stole this mule, sir. I bought this mule in South Carolina, and this is my dog."

He realized his mistake by the fire in the man's eyes, and he still wore the scar made by the quirt on his forehead. "Don't you sass me, boy," the man had said after knocking him off the mule. The man was riding away, pulling the mule behind him, when he stopped, turned around and shot Belshazzar with a squirrel rifle. Belshazzar hadn't even barked when the man had cut Jedediah with the quirt, hadn't done nothing.

The dog whimpered something fiercely, and he cried some himself, not moving, not caring about his head wound, holding the hound in his arms until it died around sundown. He had buried him by the road, even made a cross out of pine branches, then moved on, cautiously avoiding towns and white men from then on until he enlisted.

"Come on!" he finally yelled. But no reply came. The smell of cornbread was gone, and he no longer felt Sarah's presence, but he could hear Belshazzar's whimpers grow louder, and he felt like crying again.

"I'm sorry about the rocks," he said softly. "Come here. Come back, Belshazzar."

They found him like that, still leaning against the cottonwood, left eye shut, right eye staring sightlessly across the rifle barrel. Apparently, he had been the last to die, for the buzzards were not yet working on his body.

The graves were shallow, but it was too hot for a fitting burial and the smell was already sickening. They searched his haversack for valuables, but only found some hardtack, a few caps and balls, and an old tintype of a young Negro woman. A bugler blew taps, and H troop moved on in silence.

No one found the body behind the rocks, but it didn't matter. Who in his right mind would take time, in the heat of a Texas summer, to bury a Comanche dog that had been shot through the body?

The Bells of Juniper

Vonn McKee

Folks, the name's Ralph Carlisle and my sweet wife here says I need to set this little story down on paper before I go forgetting it. For posterity, she says. But I'm here to tell you that me losing track of this particular memory ain't likely to happen. No sir, not in this lifetime.

You see, that was the day—July the 12th, it was—in eighteen and sixty-nine, that I both killed a man and fell in love with a woman. To be honest, I couldn't tell you which one I done first. Didn't mean to do neither one. Well, I'm already getting ahead of myself.

Anyway, it started like this. I was in the store filling an order. Yep, I'm the proprietor of Carlisle's Mercantile and I reckon I shoulda done told you that. It was shaping up to be a regular old same-as-usual day when, about midmorning, I swore I heard the church bell ringing. Well, I found that curious so I stopped weighing Mrs. Lynch's coffee and cocked my head to listen. There was so much going on outside—wagons rolling by and folks walking on the boardwalks—that I decided I must've been hearing things. I knew for sure it wasn't Sunday.

You see, there ain't but two bells in Juniper, Wyoming, and after a year of working there on Front Street, I guess you could say my ear had got tuned to 'em both. The first bell is down at the train station and we hear it twice a week now that the last spike was drove in at Promontory last May. That opened up the rails all the way to California and turned Juniper into a right bustling little town.

Now, the other bell hangs up there on top of the First Methodist Church and that's the one I was thinking I heard. Preacher Crane's boy, Willie, rings it at ten o'clock every Sunday morning, and on special occasions. The ladies was some proud when that bell came in on the train all the way from Richmond. But I ain't here to tell you about that.

Anyhow, when I got up to the counter to write up Mrs. Lynch's bill, I heard the bell again and I knew something was sore amiss. Weren't no wedding or funeral going on or I would have known it. I saw through the window that people was looking up the street towards the sound. I made my apologies to Mrs. Lynch and excused myself. I yanked off my apron and charged out the door.

There was probably a dozen men running along with me. I didn't see or smell any smoke. Clifford Meeks, the undertaker, passed me like I was a lame mule. I might mention here that Clifford gets more excited about tragic events than is fitting and proper. I said, "What do you reckon is going on, Clifford?" But he was done out of earshot.

When we got to the church, what we saw stopped us all cold there at the front steps. The door was standing open and inside there was a woman slouched down on the floor crying and a big man standing over her pointing a revolver towards the top of her head. I realized that the woman had her arms wrapped tight around the bell rope that hung down inside the door. Every time the man would reach down and try to grab her arm, she would rock her head and shoulders back and forth and moan something—maybe no, no, no—and that would make the bell ring a couple of times.

Daniel Willingham was the first one of us to say anything since I guess all the rest of the men was dumbfounded like me. He hollered out, "You let her go, mister. No need to be a-pointin' a gun at nobody. Let her go, hear me?" But the man just looked at us, real crazy and mean-eyed, and said he'd shoot her if he wanted to, weren't none of our damn business. He said it right there standing in the church house. Well, the woman started wailing like a lamb with no mama and the bell started ringing again from her pulling on it.

"What'll we do?" I asked Daniel since he had kind of put hisself in charge by being the first one to speak out. But Daniel didn't look like he knew what our next move might be.

He said he didn't think we ought to shoot somebody inside the church and, besides that, he didn't have his gun on him. Daniel was still wearing his smithy apron.

That's when I said, "Well, it looks to me like *he's* about to shoot somebody inside the church so we'd best do something quick," and all of the men nodded.

The man with the gun looked nervous and called out, "This here's my wife. I caught her with another man."

The woman shook her head no and looked out towards us. Her face was all red and wet with crying but I noticed she was a pretty girl, maybe a lot younger than the man. It seemed like she put her eyes dead-center on me. "No, no," she was saying but it didn't make any sound. I figured right then the man was lying.

Matter of fact, now that I looked at him, I remembered him coming in the store about once a month to buy a bill of groceries. Nothing fancy, some tobacco and flour and such and, once, a few sewing notions and bolt of calico. I knew that calico wasn't likely for him so I figured he must have him a woman. But I never seen her come in, not even one time. Thought it strange. The man didn't like small talk either. Just paid his bill and left. Kind of man that looked like a mule eating briars, as my ma used to say. Well, he was worse than eating briars there in the church house that day.

Well, back to the story. That big man was a sight—his hair was all mussed up and he was breathing heavy—and he shook hisself sudden-like and turned away from us with a big roaring sound, grabbed the girl by the hair of the head, and twisted her face up towards him. I swear she turned whiter'n a china plate. Then he brought that revolver down slow and careful and pressed the barrel to her lips—almost like a kiss, now that I think about it.

I can't say that I remember just what happened next. All I know is that, in the space of a rattler strike, I was up there tackling that man down like he was a runaway calf. I know I had to have got up those steps somehow but I can't tell you how I did. Must've jumped 'em all in one bound.

Well, that fellow was a beefy one and had a good forty pounds on me but I somehow got a hold of his gun arm and was trying to back him away from that girl. I have thought many a time how lunk-headed I was to run up there with him holding a gun to her face. I can't hardly think about how bad that might have turned out.

Anyhow, I was just durn lucky, I guess, and caught him off his mark. But it wasn't two seconds before he bear-wrapped both arms around me and wrestled me down. Had me on one knee and was trying hard to work that revolver up to my skull.

I didn't think, I just did. Kinda like jumping the church steps. I threw my weight forwards to get my feet under me. Then I jumped up and twisted backwards all at the same time, kinda like a whirligig. He still had me but at least the bulk of him was behind me. I grabbed his wrist—he had big bear-paw hands too—and I was aiming to squeeze it hard enough to make him drop that iron. What an ox he was!

I squeezed and pushed but that barrel kept easing towards me. I could see the muzzle and I was thinking I'd never seen one up that close before and that I might not again.

I was in sore need of a miracle and durned if it didn't show up. Ole Daniel come charging in like a bull through the church door. He was being as fool-headed as me about breaking in on somebody with a gun almost to their head. But I was sure glad to see his homely mug anyhow. His surprise visit was just enough to throw the grizzly man off. His arm loosened up but I forgot to stop pulling and the gun kicked towards us both.

I heard a *boom* . . . and a bell ring!

I was on the floor and when my eyes could look straight, I saw the big man lying maybe a foot away from me. His eyes was open but there was a round hole just under his chin that was beginning to bleed. What I couldn't see until later was the top of his head. Or what there was left of it.

"Ralph, Ralph, are you hearin' me?" Daniel was shaking me.

"Daniel, of course I'm hearin' you and seein' you too, sorry to say. I know that can't be the face of St. Peter. Wouldn't nobody walk past that through them pearly gates."

Daniel pulled me up and started laughing and slapping me on the back. Guess he thought I could have been dead about then. I tell you he wasn't the only one.

We both remembered the girl and saw that she was standing back in the corner quiet and pale. She looked to me like one of them statues of Mary you see in them old missions. I said, "Let's get you outside," and I went over and put my hand on her shoulder. She was a little thing. I led her out the door trying to stay between her and the man's body but I reckoned she'd already seen. When we got out in the daylight, I saw there was a bruise where he'd been holding her wrist. Not only that but there was other dark places further up her arm that looked like they was healing up. Made me sick to my gut.

Well, that's the story—of that day anyhow. Preacher Crane's wife insisted on taking the girl in until things settled down. Some of us offered to escort her back home, which was only a mile from town but hid back in a draw. She got all big-eyed and scared and said she didn't want to ever set foot back in that place again so we went out and got what belongings she said she'd like to have.

I got in a habit of dropping in to check on her now and then. The Cranes began inviting me for supper once a week. I started going to church for the first time since I was a youngster.

Though it wasn't my finger that pulled the trigger, I'll always feel like it was my doing that took a man's life. But I reckon it saved somebody else's too. I leave all the reconciling to the Good Lord.

And it wasn't just the girl's life that was saved neither. It didn't take the Cranes and everybody else long to figure out I was falling for her like a schoolboy. She was the gentlest, nicest human being I had ever met and it riled me to think that someone could ever raise a hand to her.

Sometimes when she's standing by the window, I still think she looks like a pretty church statue. Even prettier now that she smiles. Her name isn't Mary though. It's Emmeline. And I was one happy storekeeper the day the Juniper church bell rang for us on our wedding day—happy in spite of the fact that I had that blockheaded Daniel Willingham for a best man. I reckon he'll do though.

Oh, and what we figured out later was that the bullet, the one that lead-poisoned her stinking excuse for a husband, went straight on up into the belfry. Willie Crane saw the hole in the ceiling and climbed up to investigate. He said there was a skint mark up the side of the bell. I knew I wasn't hearing things!

If you want to hear more than that, you'll have to come on by the mercantile and get it from Miz Emmeline. My story writin' ends here, folks. You all have a fine day now.

Regards,
Ralph Carlisle

Showdown at Timberline

Michael Zimmer

The square-bodied ex-army ambulance was the first vehicle over South Pass that spring. It took two days to cover those eight perilous miles, twenty-plus hours of skidding and lurching, bucking drifts almost belly-deep to the mules in a few spots, while the clouds hung low between the gray peaks, spitting a pebbly snow as if to mock their efforts.

At the bottom of the pass the road leveled out for the town of Swift Water, a dozen miles to the north. The big man handling the lines breathed easier on flat ground, and his team of bay mules stepped out with a renewed confidence now that the world had ceased its crazy tilt. The hounds, four of them, romped through the green grass and short sage like pups until the driver called them back.

He was a tall man, broad through the shoulders and solidly girthed. His thick black hair was cut straight at the collar, and a dark stubble covered the near inflexible thrust of his jaw. His hands were large and blunt and scarred across the knuckles, his feet like small shovels inside a pair of low-heeled Wellingtons. He wore a flat-crowned gray hat, a nearly new store-bought shirt, wool trousers, and a heavy sheepskin coat. Strapped around his middle was a Frontier Model Colt and a large hunting knife, both sheathed in plain black leather. His rifle, a .50-95 Winchester, hung from a scabbard on the wagon's front panel, at his back, and a heavy cartridge belt lay curled beside his feet like a dozing snake. His name was Thomas Jefferson Bodine. He was a hunter.

It was edging onto dusk when Bodine reached his destination. Coming in from the south, he raised quite a stir among the citizens of Swift Water, several of whom stopped what they were doing to follow his rig down the street to the Congress Saloon. Hauling up in front of the two-story log structure, Bodine eased his long frame to the ground, paused a moment to work the stiffness from his bad leg, then fastened a tether weight to the bit of his near-side mule and climbed the muddy steps to the saloon.

The crowd of men and boys who had tagged along behind the wagon were quick to move aside when Bodine's four big hounds scampered up the steps after him, offering warning growls to anyone who stepped too close. The dogs ducked unhesitantly under the wide double doors, and, although Bodine heard a few aggravated curses thrown at the pack for its apparent aggression, he didn't pay them any heed. Speaking quietly, he sent the leggy trailers into a corner, where they immediately rumped down in fresh sawdust to keep a wary eye on their surroundings.

Moving to the bar, Bodine said: "Rye," in a voice that seemed to rumble up from deep in his chest, and a slim man wearing an apron nearly to his ankles silently poured. The first sip was harsh after two weeks on the trail, with only river water and coffee to slake his thirst. The second went down smoother, and Bodine's lips twitched in satisfaction as the whiskey's glow spread through his tall frame. For a while, coming over South Pass, he'd wondered if he'd ever feel warm again.

"Another?" the barkeep asked.

Bodine shoved his glass forward. "Pour."

The bartender tipped the bottle, eyes narrowing as he watched the gentle swirl of amber in the clean glass. "The snow must be melting fast," he remarked quietly, without looking up. "Either that or you've found another way over the mountains."

"The snow was deep enough," Bodine admitted. "My wagon sits high."

The bartender nodded, topped the glass off at the rim, then poured a round for himself. "My name's Hamilton, in case you're curious." He leaned familiarly against the bar. "I own the Congress. I own the store next door, too. If you're passing through, you ought to stock up on supplies before you pull out. It's four days to the next town by wagon."

Bodine glanced up stoically. "You a fisherman, Mister Hamilton?"

Chuckling, the bartender replied: "It goes with the job, I guess, but I'll confess to wondering." His gaze shuttled briefly to the hounds. "I was tending bar in Durango a few years ago when you were hunting mountain lions in those hoodoo canyons south of there. I'd see you around town from time to time. If my memory ain't totally shot to hell, you're T.J. Bodine, in which case I'd have to speculate that you're here for the five hundred dollar reward the local cattlemen have posted on the lion that's been killing their beeves."

"I'm Bodine," the big man acknowledged, and after a pause, added almost casually: "Is it true what they're saying about that cat?"

"Likely, depending on what you've heard. She's been raising hell over havoc ever since she showed up last summer. Goes kill-crazy every few weeks and'll bring down three, four, five beeves a night, then kill a calf for eating."

Bodine's dark brows furrowed. "She sounds like a troublemaker, all right, but the reward puzzles me. I've never known a bounty to go that high on a cat."

"Ain't nobody ever had to chase a she-devil like what we've got up here. She won't tree."

Bodine met the bartender's gaze levelly. "All cats'll tree if you push them hard enough."

"This one won't, but you ain't the first bounty man to come through that's thought that way. Was a couple hunters here last fall, before the Stockmen's Association raised its bounty. They left a month later with a lot fewer dogs than they showed up with. Good, solid hounds, too, but that lion wasn't afraid of 'em. Folks who've seen her say she ain't right, like maybe she's got something bad wrong with her, or she's just plain off in the head, like some people'll get before you have to lock 'em up in a hatch somewhere. She whelped a litter of kittens last spring, which is how we know she's a queen, but then she abandoned 'em before they were fully grown. The young ones were easy to catch, but their mama didn't seem to care."

A faraway look drifted into the bartender's eyes. "Bob Stutz . . . he runs a few hundred head of beeves toward the upper end of the valley . . . he got a real good look at her once. Damned near face to face, he claims. Said lookin' into her eyes sent a chill down his back all the way to his socks. Said if he was superstitiously inclined, he could easily imagine she was something come straight outta hell. Now, ol' Bob ain't overly superstitious, but I notice he won't head for home anymore if he doesn't think he can make it before dark, and he carries his rifle across his saddlebows nowadays, too, instead of booted, like he used to."

Bodine was silent a moment, considering Hamilton's story. Then he drained his glass and scooted it across the bar with a flick of his finger. "I ain't yet gone after prey I couldn't tree one way or another."

The bartender shrugged. "I got my doubts, friend, but I'll wish you luck, just the same."

Bodine called his hounds as he left the saloon. He loosened the near mule's tether, then paused to stare quietly at the distant peaks where the cat roamed. The dogs swirled around his legs like flowing water, sensing they were close and eager to hunt.

"Bodine." Hamilton stood at the saloon's doors, one of the batwings swung partway back, held in place with his shoulder.

"Yeah?"

"Thought I'd let you know you ain't the only one hunting that lion. Glenn Tucker is here."

"Tucker!" Bodine's hand moved subtly toward his Colt, and the muscles across his stomach drew taut. "Are you sure?"

"As sure as I was of you. Came through three days ago, along the river road from the east."

"Where is he now?"

"Somewhere near timberline, I'd guess. They say the lion's got a den up there she uses during the summer. It's early yet, but the south-facing slopes are mostly clear."

The ache deep in Bodine's hip seemed to intensify as he studied the high, toothy contours of the divide. So Tucker was here, and after all these years, they were again pursuing the same objective. Only this time it wasn't a woman's love they were vying for. Somewhere up there where the winds blew cold and the law belonged to the primitive, lived a vicious lion, and the only man Bodine had ever hated enough to want to kill.

Thunder crackled like shattering glass, and a streak of lightning sizzled across the face of the slope below him. Braying in terror, the mules lunged into their collars, the off-side john swinging a wicked, roundhouse kick that missed whatever invisible target it thought had strayed into range, and immediately wrapping its leg in the harness' sturdy leather trace.

Bodine swore and jumped to the ground, yelling for the mules to settle down. Then another blue-white bolt of lightning cleaved the sky, and his tongue tingled unpleasantly. Twenty yards away, a wind-twisted evergreen exploded into oblivion, and a pungent, vaguely metallic scent flowed warmly over him. Seconds later an icy rain began to fall, scattered, plopping drops at first, then swiftly increasing, until it was as if a gate had been knocked wide open.

The rain hammered at Bodine's shoulders as he stumbled forward to grab the near-side mule's bridle. He'd barely wrapped his fingers around the cheek piece when the tall jenny whinnied, then reared without warning, yanking Bodine effortlessly off the ground. Cursing the mule's rankness, he wrapped a powerful arm around her neck and grabbed an ear, twisting the flapping appendage painfully to the side and hauling her back to earth. They both went to their knees in the rain, and remained that way for the duration of the storm, the near-side mule eared down, the john so hopelessly snarled in harness he couldn't have bolted if he tried.

From beginning to end, the storm didn't last twenty minutes. When the final roll of thunder had tumbled off toward the lowlands, Bodine relaxed his grip on the jenny's ear and scrambled out of the way. The jenny snorted and flicked her ear experimentally, but with the storm past, both animals seemed willing to behave.

Bodine straightened the harness along the mules' steaming backs with chill-numbed fingers, having to unbuckle it in places to get the thick leather straps to lay right. Then he looked around for the hounds. He spotted Gyp first, slinking out of the trees as if embarrassed by his flight. The others followed sheepishly, grinning Daisy and Tick with his missing eye, and finally Nameless, not quite a year old and still pup-clumsy, all gangling legs, too-big feet, and slobbering enthusiasm—the clown of the pack.

Bodine called them back, then awkwardly hauled himself into the wagon and shook out the lines. The team moved out docilely, and the hounds stayed close. They came to a little mountain park just below timberline shortly before dusk, and Bodine set the brake and chocked the wheels. After picketing the mules next to the wind-ruffled waters of a glacier-fed lake, he set about making a more or less permanent camp at the meadow's edge. Although the grass in the open spaces was green and lush, there was still a lot of snow under the trees, as tinted as week-old dish water from its dusting of gray granite and dried pine needles.

At dawn he turned the jenny loose, then saddled the john. He packed enough grub to last three days, then slung his bedroll over the skirting and wedged the heavy cartridge belt under it. His nose was already dripping from the cold as he stepped into the saddle, and his hip ached with a dull, persistent throb.

It was a savage land up here, bleak and wintery for much of the year, untrammeled and generally untouched. Although such an encompassing isolation cowed a lot of men, Bodine had never been particularly intimidated by it. Still, he knew it took a special breed to survive long in such an unforgiving environment. Someone who scabbed easily, and learned to keep his mind occupied with the business at hand. It had been a long time since he'd allowed his thoughts to drift so far into the past, but it kept doing so now, prodded there by the knowledge that Glenn Tucker was somewhere nearby. No matter how he tried, Bodine couldn't keep his mind from returning . . .

. . . by mid April at the latest. All he needed was one more good hunt. One more season chasing the big shaggies, then he and Sarah could be married, and Bodine could shed himself of the stink of death. If the market held, he stood to clear four thousand dollars by spring. Added to what he'd already saved and it would be the start of a nice little business somewhere, either a ranch or a small freight outfit. They could buy a house right there in Dodge if that was what Sarah wanted, and her father could stop grumbling about how life married to a professional hunter would be nothing but a steady procession of cheap boarding houses and lonely campsites.

Bodine left Dodge in September, riding a bonnet-faced black gelding and blazing trail for the two wagons that followed. With him was a Creole from New Orleans named Jean Paul, and a Choctaw Indian who went by the unlikely handle of Sammy Biscuit, each promised a salary of sixty cents per animal as skinner and camp tender for every hide brought safely to market.

They traveled south from Dodge through Indian country and on into the panhandle of Texas. For a while they hunted along the Canadian, and brought in a fair amount of hides with no other outfits nearby to spook the herds, but then one day in early December, the buffalo vanished. Bodine moved his crew south to the Red, where the buffalo were thicker, but so were the hiders.

It was better in a way, though. Hunting alone like they had been, they were all feeling the strain. At least on the Red there were other outfits they could visit with from time to time. And, as usual, where there were buffalo, there was a hide town, a place where merchants, gamblers, and whores from places like Dodge and Fort Griffin could rendezvous with the buffalo hunters. It was in Hidetown that Bodine learned Tucker had brought an outfit south for the season. The discovery burned in his gut like hot brass, straight from the breech of his Sharps rifle.

Glenn Tucker was a hometown boy as far as Sarah's father was concerned. The son of a Kansas Redleg and a New Englander mother, he'd made a fair living during the war by supplying horses to the Union Army. He'd also hunted some in the early years, but when the railroad reached Dodge in '72, Tucker set himself up as a merchant, catering to the hide trade. He made good money, and wasn't shy about flaunting it. He had a big, two-story clapboard house on the north side of town, a high-stepping buggy horse and a carriage to hitch it to, and three fine suits to choose from when out on the town.

Bodine had his wagons and an ill-tempered saddle horse, and only a time-worn broadcloth suit, shiny in the elbows and permanently stained at the cuffs, for courting. He was as clumsy as an oaf around fine china and delicate parlor furniture, and had to constantly remind himself not to wolf down the meals Sarah and her mother prepared for Sunday dinners and Saturday picnics. He knew his presence around the Evans' household was an affront to Sarah's father, who considered the towering hunter as little better than a savage, wind-burnished and rough talking, without prospects.

But Sarah had seen what her father hadn't—or wouldn't. There was a darkness hovering over Glenn Tucker's soul, an iciness in his every action that, despite his best efforts, he could never keep entirely hidden. Bodine was the man Sarah Evans wanted, and her mind wouldn't be swayed. Tucker had finally realized the impossibility of marrying her. Eventually, her father had, as well.

Tucker was standing near the dusty rear wheel of a massive freight wagon when Bodine spotted him in Hidetown. He approached cautiously, his greeting reserved. Tucker's eyes, over the rim of a tin coffee cup, were as brittle as flint. They spoke briefly, exchanging small talk, then parted ways. Bodine figured he'd seen the last of Tucker for a while, but a few days later, while reloading cartridges in his camp on one of the Red's shallow tributaries, Sammy Biscuit looked up from where he was mixing bug poison and said: "Someone's coming, T.J."

It being the heart of Comanche and Kiowa country, Bodine didn't take the announcement lightly. Shoving to his feet, he gathered up his Sharps and a leather bag of ammunition, then stepped out from under the canvas awning set up between the wagons. His eyes narrowed as he studied the lone horseman calmly watching their camp from a knoll several hundred yards to the southwest. A few minutes later, he heard the distant creak of a wagon straining under its load, and knew it wasn't Indians who approached, but he still didn't relax his guard. Out here, a man didn't last long without a certain amount of distrust.

Even though he wasn't expecting trouble, Bodine called Jean Paul in from the staking grounds, and told him to bring his rifle. It was a large outfit that rolled toward them. Four lumbering, high-wheeled freight wagons rigged for hides, and a smaller wagon with a hooped canvas cover to tote their supplies—five vehicles altogether, each with its own driver, and three others flanking the small train on horseback. The man they'd first spotted on the knoll was Glenn Tucker.

"Bodine," the merchant greeted as he rode up. His gaze quickly took in the camp, but lingered longest on the staking grounds, where a little over two hundred hides were curing in the winter's sun.

"Hello, Glenn," Bodine replied grudgingly. "Fall off and have some coffee . . . unless you're in a hurry."

Tucker laughed expansively. "Naw, I've got plenty of time." Twisting partway around in his saddle, he motioned toward a flat piece of ground downstream from Bodine's camp. "Set up over there, boys. We'll sit awhile and visit."

Bodine ordered his crew to start putting a meal together. Jean Paul went out to fetch meat from the drying racks, while Sammy Biscuit smacked bug poison from his fingers, then started the coffee. Tucker hunkered down close to Bodine's hide wagon and lit a cigar.

Swallowing back his irritation, Bodine squatted nearby, although he refused Tucker's offer of a cigar.

"You're a far piece from your usual grounds, aren't you?" Bodine asked pointedly.

"Some, but with a reason. You hear about the trouble they've been having on the Brazos?"

"Hide thieves?"

Tucker nodded. "Killed Chip Preston's camp help and made off with over a hundred hides. Did the same to a couple of other outfits out of Fort Griffin a month ago, then last week they hit Bud Sanderson's camp on the Washita."

"The Washita, huh?" Bodine chewed thoughtfully at his lower lip. "That's hitting pretty close," he admitted.

"It's pretty close to where I was hunting, too. That's why I'm here. Figured we might throw in together. No sense working our tails off, then having some mange-infested gang of hide thieves slit our throats for the profit."

Bodine glanced to where Tucker's crew was setting up camp, caring for the stock, spilling bedrolls and picket ropes from the back of the supply wagon. It looked like a tightly run outfit, and he couldn't help wondering why Tucker thought he needed more men than he already had.

"What's in this for you?" he asked bluntly. "Hide thieves wouldn't tackle an outfit the size of yours."

"I'd hate to bet my scalp on that," Tucker replied. "I trust you, Bodine. That might be all I can say for you, but it's enough for now. Since I don't know how big of a gang we might be dealing with, I figure having a few extra men around would be smart." Jettisoning a stream of blue tobacco smoke toward the sky, he added smugly: "It'd sure as hell help a tiny outfit like yours."

Bodine ignored the slight as he considered the merchant's offer. Although Tucker's motive seemed suspicious, Bodine had to acknowledge that he didn't know the man well, and Tucker was right about one thing. If hide thieves were working the area in a gang large enough to strike Bud Sanderson's camp, then having

Tucker's men around could be a real benefit to him and Jean Paul and Sammy Biscuit. Nodding reluctantly, he said: "All right, let's do it. How do you want to work it?"

"There'll be twelve of us altogether. We'll pair up on the ranges, and keep at least four guards posted around the camp day and night."

"What about you?"

"Me?" He grinned crookedly. "I'll partner with you, Bodine. I promised Sarah I'd keep an eye on you."

Despite some tension early on, things soon smoothed out. They kept their camps separate, but worked together for a common cause. It didn't hurt that someone from Tucker's camp had smuggled a five-gallon keg of whiskey along in the supply wagon. Although Bodine was generally opposed drinking on the range—he preferred his crew sharp-eyed and clear-witted—he knew it wouldn't do any good to try to impose limits on alcohol already in camp. Buffalo men were notoriously rough-barked, and both Jean Paul and Sammy Biscuit would probably have quit if he attempted any kind of prohibition. He contented himself with demanding a full day's labor from his crew, no matter how badly their heads were pounding from too much snakehead the night before.

Hunting was good, and they managed to keep the same camp well into January. After that, it was a short move to the Pease, and almost more hides than they could handle. Bodine's estimate of four thousand dollars for the season was seeming more and more likely.

The remained on the Pease through February and March, and then, on a bright and pleasantly warm day in early April, it all fell apart. He and Tucker had just made a stand, their best yet. Nearly a hundred cows, bulls, and kips, scattered across a flat valley less than half a mile wide. While Tucker rode back to bring up the skinners and their wagons, Bodine leaned his rifle against a bull to cool and began skinning on a nearby cow. He was on his second carcass when he noticed movement from the corner of his eye. At the far end of the flat, a wounded bull had lurched to its feet. It wobbled uncertainly for a moment, then began its escape.

Bodine sheathed his knife and swung astride his horse, leaving his rifle behind. He raced after the lumbering beast, but the bull had a long lead and was quickly gaining strength, and it was several miles before Bodine was able to close with it. He reined alongside, keeping the buffalo between himself and the banks of a swift flowing stream on the other side, its roiling waters silted from upstream melt. The bull was wheezing loudly, bleeding from its nostrils. Its small, red-rimmed eyes looked wild with fear, and Bodine felt regret for not having made a clean kill. Drawing his Colt, he swayed easily from the saddle, seeking a clear shot, an end to the chase. That was when the bull charged. Bodine's horse dodged nimbly to the side, but Bodine lost his seat, and for one sickening moment, he hung as if suspended above the bull's curved horns.

The shock of the impact—of tearing cloth and snapping bone and the sharp cold of flesh ripped wide—was like a sledge hammer's blow to the back of his skull, dumping him headfirst into darkness. His last image was of the buffalo's trampling hooves, slashing the ground on every side.

He was alone when he came to. Neither his horse nor the wounded bull were anywhere to be seen. He felt strangely detached, lost in a world he only vaguely recognized. When he tried to move, nothing seemed to function properly. Although there was pain, it remained distant and inconsequential. Mostly he felt lazy and uncaring, and after a while he allowed himself the luxury of slipping once more into the comforting embrace of unconsciousness.

It was evening when he awoke next, the sun down and the air turning cold. The pain was more pronounced, too, washing over him in patterned waves that mimicked the beating of his heart. His head felt full and swollen, his throat parched. Close by, he could hear the swift flow of deep water, and there was a dampness against his cheek from that same direction, although it seemed far too far away to reach.

There were sounds from above him, too, the thud of a horse's hooves, the soft creak of saddle leather. At first he thought it was his own mount that had returned. Then a dark form hove up against the purpling sky and stopped a few feet away.

"Well, hell, look what I found."

"Tucker."

"You still alive, Bodine?"

"Hurting . . . pretty bad." The words came slowly, as if they had to be nudged out of his mouth with his tongue.

Kneeling at his side, Tucker struck a match and passed it over Bodine's body. He whistled softly at the damage. "That old boy sure tore hell out of you, didn't he?"

"How bad?"

"Bad enough. Your hip is gored and your leg's broke. I couldn't say what else he might have wrenched or busted."

"Get help, Tucker. Get Jean Paul, he'll know what to do."

Tucker hesitated, then pushed to his feet and looked around. He was silent a long time.

"Tucker . . . get help. Get Jean Paul."

"Well, I don't know that I want to do that," he replied hesitantly.

"I need . . . need help."

"Yeah, you do, you sure do." He pushed his hat up off his forehead, and a surprised smile flashed across his face. "Well, hell, ain't this a blessing come slipping through the back door? Tell you the truth, Bodine, I'm needing a little help myself. You likely don't know this, but I got my tail wedged under the rocker last summer playing poker with a gent from Wichita. I slipped in a little too deep and lost the deed to both my house and my business. The house doesn't worry me too much, but I've worked hard to build up my business, and I'd hate to lose it because I got so damned moody last year when Sarah said she wouldn't marry me. Didn't just say no, mind you, but told me straight out that she loved you, instead. That was tough meat to chew.

"The news ain't all gloomy, though. The fella I lost it to is what most folks would call a fine, upstanding, church-going type, and he's admitted he'd rather have the cash than the property. That's how I talked him into holding onto the deeds until I got back in the spring. The way things stand now, I figure I'll clear between four and five thousand dollars from my hides. That's profit, mind you, but it's still not going to be enough. But here's the kicker. If I married Sarah, then her daddy would be almost honor-bound to loan me the rest of the money. Sort of a dowry, you see?"

"I'll loan you the money," Bodine said hoarsely. "Just . . . get help."

"And there's the fly in that ointment, at least as far as you're concerned. Money borrowed has to be paid back, but with you gone and Sarah's daddy pushing her to marry me, I'd say she'd be as good as mine before the summer's half done, wouldn't you?" He chuckled, his mind working. "Think about it, Bodine. When I tell your crew I found you gored by a buffalo, and that I buried you out here, say, under a cut bank, they wouldn't have any reason at all not to believe me. Especially with the tracks you left behind when you rode out after that bull. And with their old boss gone, it's not going to take much to convince them to throw in with me. Hell, I'll even pay what they earned skinning for you." He shook his head slowly, as if in awe of the opportunity fate had presented him. "This just might work, hoss. I'll move camp first thing, and chances are, no one'll ever find where you died." He looked at Bodine, his dark eyes like liquid in the gathering dusk, without emotion. "And you will die. As tough as you are, you'll die." He took a step back. "Goodbye, Bodine. I hope you rot in hell."

"For God's sake, man, give me a chance. Leave some food, water."

"No, I won't help you." He turned to his horse, and Bodine groaned. "At least . . . give me some water."

Tucker hesitated, then smiled. "Sure, hoss, I'll do that much for you." He came back to slip the toe of his boot under Bodine's side. Bodine's head whirled as he was lifted and turned. Pain shot through him like hot lava in his veins. He barely hung onto consciousness when Tucker turned him a second time. He sensed emptiness opening beneath him, the cool dampness of the river rising up to gently bathe his sweating face. His fingers clutched at the loose soil but the bank was too steep, and he struck the deep water with a . . .

. . . scream, torn from the pinnacles high above. Wild and shrill, it sent a shiver coursing down Bodine's spine. He yanked the

Winchester from its scabbard and levered a round into the chamber. The mule bobbed violently under him, tossing its head in fright. Bodine's gaze raked the looming mountainside, but there was nothing to see except for snow and rock and the rich, dizzying blue of the sky.

The mule settled down after a bit. When it did, Bodine could hear the far-off howling of his dogs. He listened intently for a moment, then heaved a relieved sigh when he recognized Gyp's deep, bass wailing. It was reassuring to know the old man was leading the pack. Gyp had more dog sense than Daisy and Nameless combined, and a lot more gumption than Tick, at least since Tick's mauling a few years before, when he'd lost his left eye and most of his ear to a cat that had turned too soon.

Another high-pitched scream tumbled down off the high pinnacle, and the mule jerked to a spraddle-legged stop and blew loudly, its entire body trembling. Bodine suppressed a shudder, as well. Lord, how that sounded like a woman, mad and grief-stricken, a sound torn straight from the soul.

Bodine's expression was taut as he guided his mule across a patch of bare rock, heading for a low saddle between two jagged peaks where Gyp's voice still sounded at regular intervals. He followed by track and sound all day, through the rocky saddle and down the other side. By dusk he was so far behind the pack that he had to step away of his mule, with its heavy breathing and creaking leather, to hear the dogs at all. There was just three of them now. He'd come across Nameless shortly after sundown, wandering among the rocks looking lost and forlorn, although he'd perked up quickly when he spotted Bodine and the mule.

He made a cheerless camp that night on a narrow shelf of rock. After sharing a piece of cold venison with Nameless, he pulled a buffalo robe over his shoulders and settled back to wait for dawn. His sleep was fitful, checkered with bad dreams and disturbing images, and when he awoke a few hours before first light, he felt as exhausted as when he'd laid down.

Hearing the distant baying of the pack brought him instantly to his feet, and he moved to the edge of the shelf. He could tell from the sound that the chase was returning to the cat's home range. Although the dogs' howls were laced with fatigue, they didn't seem to be slowing down yet. At Bodine's side, Nameless whined deep in his throat. The cries of the pack were calling him, and he might have attempted to rejoin the pursuit if Bodine hadn't reached down and reassuringly rubbed the dog's hackled neck.

He was riding back through the shallow pass as soon as it was light enough to see, the tracks of the cat plain before him. Although the trail was a couple of hours old, he wasn't worried about catching up. He was certain that, sooner or later, the cat would tree. Either that or she would keep running until exhaustion overtook her, at which point the hounds would finish the chase for him.

The trail wound along the base of the peaks just above timberline. Although the sky was clear and the sun was shining, the wind was cold off the snowpack, and it never stopped blowing. From time to time the baying of the hounds would grow so faint that Bodine feared he might lose it altogether. When that happened, he would stop and wait and listen until he picked up the sound again, then push on determinedly. It was midafternoon when the cries of the pack suddenly sharpened, their tenor becoming more frantic. Anticipating the end, Bodine urged his mule on at a faster pace. He wasn't surprised when he caught up with his dogs shortly before sundown.

Gyp and Daisy were standing with their front paws braced against the face of a nearly sheer sixty foot cliff, baying in frustration. Tick paced anxiously behind them, throwing frequent glances toward the top of the bluff. Bodine's gaze trailed upward until it arrived at a narrow ledge, almost invisible from below. The small, black opening of a cave, set at the far end of the protruding sill, reminded him of a punctuation mark.

Bodine's grip tightened on the Winchester as he eyed the thread-like trace cutting almost diagonally across the upper end of the bluff. He could see where the lion had accessed the ledge—one long, fifteen foot leap from the ground to a rocky knob protruding from the side of the cliff, then another, shorter jump to the lower end of the ledge—but he had to think hard before deciding he could make the same climb. Even then, he knew it was going to be a bloodied-fingers and scraped-toes effort.

Dismounting, he pulled the heavy cartridge belt from under his bedroll and draped it over his shoulder like a bandolier. Then he slid the rifle under that and snugged the belt tight. He left his hat wedged in the saddle's gullet. Where he was going, he didn't want anything blocking his vision.

All four hounds were on the job now, howling furiously as Bodine approached the base of the cliff. They clawed at the rock, scrambling part way up, then sliding back again, jumping and stumbling over each another. Bodine let them go. He wanted to keep the cat's attention occupied with the hounds' baying while he made his way up the cliff's face.

It took twenty heart-thumping minutes before he was able to flop across the lower portion of the ledge, then squirm onto solid footing. Still on his stomach, gasping and wiping sweat from his eyes, Bodine studied the narrow shelf that wound along the face of the bluff. Its surface near the bottom was marred with shallow gouges, white against the gray stone; apparently it wasn't an easy climb for the lion, either.

Pushing cautiously to his feet, Bodine freed the Winchester, then checked his revolver and knife. Satisfied that everything was in place and ready to grab, he started up the ledge. With his path so narrow—less than a foot in some places, no more than two feet anywhere—it took another ten minutes to cover the thirty or so yards to the cavern's low entrance. He paused at its mouth, his pulse racing. The opening was even smaller than he'd anticipated. Crouching to peer inside, it appeared as if the cramped passageway cut straight back into the mountain. Taking a deep breath, Bodine eased a few feet inside, then stopped again to listen. Although the only sound he heard was the low moaning of the wind, the smell was execrable, and unmistakably feline. With his lips pressed tight, he pulled his bandanna up over his nose to filter the stench of rotting carrion.

With the Winchester cocked and his finger firmly on the trigger, Bodine edged deeper into the mountain. The light was poor, and it grew steadily worse the farther he went. He'd made a mistake by not taking that into consideration, but he wouldn't back out now—not yet. Then something cracked sharply under him and his left foot rolled. He cried out hoarsely as his balance deserted him. His knuckles rapped the cave's walls and the Winchester flew out of his hands. Panic rose like bile in his throat. He clawed desperately for his Colt, and didn't breathe easy until he had it in his hand, the hammer rolled back, muzzle pointed into the darkness. At first the laughter puzzled him, and he put his back to the cavern's wall.

"That's not the way I learned to hunt cats, Bodine."

He swore loudly, and tipped his head back until it was pressed tight against stone.

"What's the matter, hoss, did you think it was the lion talking to you?"

"Tucker." Bodine's voice was flat and hard.

"Yeah, it's been awhile, hasn't it?"

"Where'd you come from?"

"I came in through the back way, you dumb ox. You should've figured a cat with a five hundred dollar bounty wasn't going to let itself get cornered this easily. I was setting up a deadfall trap when your dogs forced him through. Thought the damned thing was going to jump me at first. We met eye to eye, and not twenty feet apart."

"Too bad she didn't," Bodine replied, and Tucker chuckled.

"I see your feelings toward me haven't mellowed, although I can't say that I blame you. I'll tell you, hoss, I could hardly believe it when they said you were still alive. When I heard you were hunting out of Durango, I rode down there to see for myself, and damned if it wasn't like looking at a ghost. I wanted to call you out then, but there were too many people around. Then I heard about this lion, and I knew you'd come after it. Figured this would be the perfect place to settle the bad blood between us. Strange country to both of us, and about as far from the law as a man can get anymore. Just the two of us, Bodine. What do you say?"

"Come on out into the open and we'll finish it now."

"No, not today. Tomorrow, maybe, or the next. Just you and me . . . and that damned lion."

"This isn't a game, Tucker."

"I never considered it as such, but I don't have an urge to finish it just yet. I wouldn't think you would, either. Hell, I can see you against the cave's entrance plain as day."

Bodine cursed and tried to flatten himself against the wall. Tucker laughed, the sound fading as he backed deeper into the cavern. "Don't worry, Bodine," he called. "Not today, not here. I want you to know it's coming. I want you to think about it."

"Where's Sarah? What happened after you two left Dodge?"

There was no reply.

"Damnit, Tucker, where's Sarah!"

The silence continued, and Bodine swore helplessly. Pushing away from the wall, he retrieved his rifle, then made his way to the cave's low front entrance. Stepping into the open, the sun . . .

. . . stabbed through him like white hot iron as he pulled the tattered cloth, ripped from the bottom of his shirt, tight over the gaping wound in his hip. If the crude poultice of mud and peeled cactus pads stopped the bleeding, Bodine thought he stood a fair chance of making it to the next camp. Not his own. That was upstream and would require too much effort, but the next one down couldn't be more than ten miles away, and by staying with the river, he'd have plenty of water to help sustain him, if not food.

He crawled some, but was able to float for long stretches, pulling himself along with his hands when the current weakened. He moved steadily downriver all that first day, then all the next. The sun hammered the land without mercy, while fever gnawed at him from within. On the second day he caught some crawdads and cracked them open with a rock, sucking the wet, raw meat down whole. Buzzards wheeled curiously overhead, but he suffered no trouble from them, nor from the wolves that passed on their way to the killing grounds. They were getting enough meat by following the hunters, and had no need to stalk their own.

On the third day he came to the hiders' camp, or what was left of it—a smoking fire pit and a couple of acres of flattened grass where the skins had been staked. There was no sign of an attack, and he almost gave up then, knowing that if this outfit had moved on, the chances were good that the others had, as well. The main herd had been migrating north for a couple of weeks by then, following the warming temperatures of spring, and the buffalo men would be quick to pull their pins and follow. Yet even as he contemplated surrender, of rolling over and allowing death to overtake him, he remembered the expression on Tucker's face as he wished Bodine an eternity in hell, and his resolve hardened.

He floated on, moving downstream at an agonizingly slow pace. He ate another crawdad the next day and took time to change his poultice. The wound looked ugly, the color of charcoal, but there was no sign of an infection, and he took comfort in that. The sun fried his skin through the tattered remnants of his shirt, and its reflection off the water was like iron spikes drilling into his eyes. He took to holing up during the hottest hours, then pulling himself forward through the shallow waters by moonlight. Twenty pounds dropped quickly from his frame, then thirty, until on the sixth day, when a peddler fished him out of the river near the forks of the North and Middle Pease, he looked more like a skeleton stretched with wrinkled hide than a human being.

His savior was a skinny little man named Ossie Hawthorne, a trader in some of the smaller items a hunter's camp might need or want—salt and coffee and candies to satisfy a man's sweet tooth, extra shirts and socks. He carried medicines, too, and after wrestling Bodine into the shade of a tilted cottonwood tree and pitching camp around him, he'd dug the appropriate pharmaceuticals from his wagon and set about repairing his catch. He set Bodine's broken leg as best he could, then cleaned and stitched together the torn flap of skin over his hip. The numerous others cuts and abrasions were minor enough that he didn't mess with them.

Bodine remained mercifully unconscious throughout process, and Hawthorne kept him so filled with laudanum afterward that, when he did awaken, there was never much pain. It was nearly a week after pulling the emaciated hunter from the river before

Hawthorne confessed he'd thought at first he'd been dealing with a corpse.

"I was just gonna see was they anything sellable in ye pockets," he explained to Bodine one evening over coffee. "Liked to shat me britches proper when ye opened ye eyes and looked at me."

Hawthorne chuckled at the recollection, but Bodine didn't crack a smile. He stared silently into his cup, the memory of Tucker's grating laughter and smirking face filling his mind.

They spent two weeks at the forks of the Pease before Bodine was finally able to hobble around with the aid of a crutch Hawthorne fashioned for him from a cottonwood limb. Then they packed up and moved on, going first to Portales, in New Mexico Territory, then on up through Santa Rosa and Taos and Trinidad. It was on the Purgatoire River in southeastern Colorado that some Kiowas tried to steal their harness stock. Although they were able to prevent the theft, Hawthorne caught a musket ball in his thigh during the fray, and they had to return to Trinidad until he could heal.

Bodine stayed with the trader until he was on his feet again, then borrowed enough money from a hider he knew to outfit himself with a horse and rifle and a few supplies. He reached Dodge City on the fourth of August, six weeks after the marriage of Sarah Evans to Glenn Tucker.

Tucker had been too late to buy back his Dodge City enterprise, but with the hide money he'd made over winter and Sarah's dowry, he'd considered himself well set. With his bride in tow, he left Kansas for parts unknown less than a week after the wedding. Bodine tried to worm their whereabouts out of Sarah's parents, but her father refused to divulge any information, and even her mother, who had originally sided with Bodine over Tucker, insisted that what might have been no longer mattered.

"They're married," she'd stated firmly. "Can't you understand that, Mister Bodine?"

His rage had burned like a coal-fueled fire. He'd wanted to tear the Evans' house down with his bare hands, to chew it up and spit it into the wind—but he'd kept his temper in check, at least until he got down to the saloons on Front Street, where he'd gotten roaring drunk and tried to take apart the Longbranch with a six-gun and a heavy-heeled boot. When he finally woke up, hungover and behind bars, he'd had to sell his newly acquired horse and rifle to pay for the damages. Luckily, his credit was still good and he was able to put together a small hunting outfit on tick. He pulled out for the buffalo ranges near the end of August, just himself and a Mexican skinner named Manuel Valdez. He was dead broke, riding another man's horse and shooting another man's rifle, but knew that until he was able to dig himself out of debt again, he'd have to stay with what he knew best. But someday, by God. Someday . . .

. . . that damned hound was going to choke herself to death, Bodine thought irritably, watching Daisy steal a chunk of raw venison from between Nameless' paws and wolf it down, while the gangly pup stood back and whined.

"Damnit, Daisy," he grumbled, but let it go at that. If Nameless hoped to survive out here, he was going to have to learn to fend for himself, and that included standing up to the pack's only female.

Leaning back against the iron rim of his wagon's rear wheel, Bodine studied the gnarled pinnacles above him. Although the opportunity to exact revenge from Tucker was a pleasant balm for his troubled mind, he couldn't keep his thoughts from returning to Sarah. Was she still with Tucker, perhaps hovering over their fire right now, in a mountain meadow similar to this one? Or was she somewhere down below, waiting for her husband's return? He wondered what she was like after all these years, and if her smile could still brighten the dimmest room. After a while he rolled up in his robe and lay down to sleep. The answers he sought were still somewhere above him, but he intended to find them. Tomorrow . . . finally.

He was in the saddle again before dawn, guiding his mule toward the cliff where he'd lost the cat's trail the day before, and found Glenn Tucker's. He left the hounds in camp, tied to the wagon with leather leashes they could chew through if he didn't return, and plenty of food and water close by for the short term.

It was a bitterly cold, overcast morning, with a strong wind blowing out of the northwest. Bodine let the john pick its own path through the rocks, and only corrected him when the mule seemed to be turning away from the direction of the mountain lion's cliff-side refuge.

It was full light by the time they reached their destination. Bodine stepped warily from the mule's back, bringing the Winchester with him. Staring overhead, the cliff seemed to stretch on forever, towering into the gray belly of the sky. Behind him, dark clouds were spilling through the rocky saddle where he and Nameless had spent a cold night waiting for the lion's return. Thunder rumbled threateningly. After double-checking to make sure he had a round chambered, Bodine shoved the rifle under the cartridge belt draped over his shoulder and pulled it tight. Across his chest, the massive .50-95 rounds glinted like stubby brass cigars lined up side by side.

Having already made the climb once, it was easier this time, and faster. Wiggling onto the narrow ledge, he took a moment to catch his breath, then unlimbered his rifle and cautiously approached the den's low opening. The strong odor of decay that wafted from the cavern's mouth on a faint downdraft reminded Bodine of Tucker's explanation that the cave had a rear entrance, although he didn't remember the smell being quite so overpowering yesterday. As he moved deeper into the cavern, the musky tang of the cat grew stronger, and Bodine's scalp began to crawl. He jerked to a stop when a low, warning snarl floated out of the darkness toward him, and his heart made a leap for his throat. He began backpedaling quickly, but wasn't near fast enough. He heard the scuff of the lion's approaching pads just a heartbeat before a rage-filled cry erupted from the den's interior. Movement—black against blackness that turned first gray, then tawny yellow—streaked toward him.

Bodine's startled shout was lost in the cat's piercing scream. He pulled the Winchester's trigger at point-blank range, and the rifle's heavy recoil, along with the brushing impact of the cat, knocked him backward. He slammed into cavern's wall, and the rifle was jolted from his hands. The lion writhed before him, its nerve-numbing cries filled with more fury than pain, its claws flashing wickedly. Bodine stumbled sideways and fell when his leg gave out from under him. Frantically yanking the Colt from its holster, he thrust it before him and fired once, swiftly, then twice more, and the big cat shrieked loud enough to set his teeth on edge, before hurtling itself back into the cavern's darkness.

His breath as ragged as tearing cloth, Bodine shoved clumsily to his feet, then began moving backward toward the den's entrance. A raspy gurgling flowed toward him from the cavern's deeper recesses. He hesitated with his revolver in hand and thought about going back for his rifle, then changed his mind when the cat's breathing seemed to swell and draw closer. Outside, he put his back to the cliff's face and eased along the narrow ledge until he was out of the lion's sight. As he did, the lion's heavy wheezing also seemed to retreat, until finally only the low moaning of the wind was all that disturbed the cliff's silence.

Bodine straightened slowly, and after a moment he lowered the Colt's hammer to half-cock and quickly reloaded. He dreaded going back inside, but knew he'd have to. He wanted his rifle, and he'd need the cat's pelt to collect his bounty. But he wasn't in any hurry, either. If the cat had a rear entrance, as Tucker claimed . . .

Tucker!

The bullet struck just him below the shoulder, spinning him full circle and dropping him face first along the narrow ledge. The sky slammed into the cliff and a roaring filled his ears. He tried to move and couldn't, tried again and managed to bring up one leg. He groped for his revolver, then remembered seeing it spinning out over the side of the cliff as he fell. Cursing softly in frustration, he rolled onto his back.

"What I want to know is, did you kill that lion?"

The voice seemed to float out of the rocks. Bodine's gaze searched the ledge, the face of the cliff, the mouth of the den. All appeared empty, and Tucker laughed as if delighted.

"You're losing your touch, hoss."

Bodine raised his head to sight between his toes. Tucker stepped, seemingly, from the face of the cliff itself, but as Bodine's vision steadied, he saw what appeared to be a crevice near the far end of the ledge, past the den's low mouth.

Tucker advanced carefully, the still smoking muzzle of his lever gun trained on Bodine's chest. "I guess you didn't know I went back in yesterday and closed off the cave's rear entrance." He stopped a few feet away and chuckled. "They say a cornered mountain lion is one of the most dangerous animals out here. I was afraid for a while that cat was going to take away the pleasure of me seeing you die from my own hands."

"You tried that before and failed."

The smirk disappeared from Tucker's face. "This time I'm going to make sure you're dead."

Bodine inhaled deeply, gathering his strength, his wits. He didn't know what kind of chance he might get, but he knew that if an opportunity did present itself, he'd have to move fast. "Where's Sarah?" he asked.

Tucker hesitated, frowning. "Huh?"

"Sarah, where is she?"

"Her? Hell, I don't know. We split trails years ago."

"Where?"

"What difference could that make to you, Bodine? You're never going to see her again." Then he laughed. "You're never going to see any woman again."

"Where, damnit!" Bodine roared, and Tucker flinched and swayed back.

"Denver, you son of a bitch. I left her in Denver."

Denver—less than two hundred miles away. Bodine's hand moved to the hilt of his knife. He'd never been very good at throwing a blade, but right now it seemed like his only option. It was a hope quickly dashed. Tucker yelled and jumped forward, the butt of his rifle swinging in a tight arc. Bodine grunted loudly as the brass butt plate struck his wrist. The knife jerked free of its sheath, polished steel winking as it disappeared over the ledge. He grasped his wrist tightly as waves of pain surged up his arm. Tucker stood above him, seemingly blocking out the sky, and for a moment it was as if Bodine was reliving the past—the foot sliding beneath him, lifting, pushing, the yawning emptiness below. But something was different this time. It was the scream.

At first Bodine thought it was himself, then Tucker, until his eyes passed the length of the ledge to where the cat had ventured from its den. It was crouched low, ready to spring, and Tucker yelled and whirled and brought his rifle up, firing without sighting. The lion screamed again, twisting under the slug's impact. Then Tucker fired a second round, aiming this time, and his bullet caught the big cat square. Bodine watched in awe as she slid silently off the ledge, leaving a bright crimson smear over the smooth stone. It seemed like minutes before he heard the distant thud of her body striking the rocks far below.

Tucker turned back to Bodine, the rifle sagging in his hands. His eyes were wide with a lingering fear, unseeing as Bodine used his good hand, the left one, to unbuckle the cartridge belt from over his shoulder. He sat up suddenly, swinging the heavy belt like a club. The buckle took Tucker across the face and he reeled backward with a strangled cry, a spray of blood fanning across the sky from his crushed nose.

Tucker screamed once as he tumbled over the edge. A lower sound than the lion's, it trailed behind him like a tattered banner. Laying back quietly to ease the dizziness wrought from both his wrist and the bullet in his shoulder, Bodine barely heard the body strike the rocks sixty feet below.

The climb down was a nightmare. His wrist was swollen and tight, and his shoulder continued to weep bleed through the makeshift bandage he'd tightened over the wound. But he made it, just as he had all those years before in Texas. Just as he'd continue to do, down off the timberline into Swift Water with Tucker and the cat wrapped in the same heavy canvas atop his wagon. And then, finally, on to Denver, to see what his future held.

Below him, the clouds were whipping about in a frenzy, and thunder rattled off the peaks. Gritting his teeth, Bodine dragged himself into the saddle. He paused a moment to stare at the pile of rocks where he'd covered the bodies until he felt well enough to return. Then he reined away from the cliff, starting down the mountain in a misting rain.

Perdition's Yard
Michael Knost

Martha Wilmington raised the coffee to her lips and closed her eyes, hoping to somehow quell the saloon's piano clangoring. "Must you maltreat that contraption before the nooning?"

"My apologies," the bartender said, abruptly moving from the upright Hallet & Davis. "Don't usually spot one of you gals down here this time of day."

"I emerge, not out of choice, Vernon, but in retreat from the ungodly snoring that currently plagues my room."

He slid a wedge of sourdough in front of her and smiled. "Are you saying you have an ore-chaser lingering in your bed?"

She offered a coin from her reticule, but he waved it off.

"Not exactly a common miner, but yes. And he paid extra for the privilege."

Vernon's smile widened. "I might he did."

Sunlight spilled through the front window, bathing the tables and walls with a reddish warmth.

"I can roust that fella out to the livery if you'd like."

"Leave him be. Besides, I'm already up and about."

Faint shouting echoed from the street, growing louder until a boy rushed inside in a breathless state. Bracing hands on his knees, he locked his gaze on Vernon's face.

"Well? Spit it out, son."

The boy swallowed hard and scanned the room. "I'm looking for Sheriff Bartrum."

"I'm afraid it's a mite early for bending elbows, even for Bartrum."

"Where can I find him?"

"Most likely the jailhouse, if I were to hazard a guess."

The boy was turning to leave when Vernon took hold of his arm. "Just a minute, son. What's the trouble?"

"Somebody's killed Captain Oakley." Strength drained from the boy's voice as he pulled away and backed toward the door. "They found him gutshot over an hour ago, said it must have happened during the night." And with that, the boy was back on the street.

"*James* Oakley?" Vernon made a beeline for the bar. "Dear God," he said, pouring from a bottle. "Every pick-wielding bastard on the Oakley Smelting payroll will bring hellfire and fury fit for Revelation when word gets out." He downed the whiskey and poured again. "And I don't even want to think about . . ." He shook his head and drank again.

Coldness fluttered in Martha's stomach. "On second thought, Vernon, maybe rousting that fella out the door is not a bad idea after all." She placed a hand on his forearm. "But you need to know . . . that man snoring up there in my bed is the captain's brother, Bill Oakley."

Martha trimmed the final stitch on one of the knee patches and held out the canvas trousers to inspect her work.

"Why leather patches?" Lucille seemed to have the uncanny ability to enter a room as quietly as moonlight crossing a parlor floor.

"Leather's durable," Martha said, folding the material into a neat square at the end of her bed. "It reinforces the areas that take the most wear, especially for miners crawling around in those tunnels."

Picking up the britches, Lucille held her gaze to the fabric. "You still aiming to leave us?"

"I . . ." Martha cleared her throat and gently retrieved the folded bundle as heat rose in her cheeks. "I'm planning to go back east. I just need to save a little more money. You know as well as anyone, working as a soiled dove barely gets a roof over your head and food in your belly."

"Is that why you're doing all this sewing on the side? To save enough money to leave us?"

"I'm not trying to leave you girls, Lucy. I just want to go back home."

"I thought you said you ain't got nobody left where you're from?"

The heat spread to Martha's neck and chest. "That's true, but I want to go back to a place where people know me, so that I might open my own milliner shop."

"Can't you do that here in Georgetown? Everybody knows you here."

"People back in Massachusetts regard me as a seamstress, while the folks in *this* territory only see me as the woman I was forced to become in order to survive." She shook her head. "And that's all they'll ever allow me to be."

Lucille offered a crooked smile that didn't quite reach her eyes. "I reckon that's all they'll ever let any of us be."

Martha moved to the window and stared out onto the sparsely populated street. "Did I ever tell you how I ended up here?"

"In Colorado?"

"Well, yes. Colorado." She returned her attention to Lucille. "But also here in our little dove cage as a sporting woman."

"I don't recollect ever hearing your account."

"Mother succumbed to consumption just after I'd turned sixteen. And my father was gone long before that." Movement from the street captured Martha's attention as Bill Oakley and Sheriff Bartrum came together near the boardwalk. "I was the youngest in the family, so when I met a suitor who took an interest in me, I fear I took the relationship far more genuinely than he did."

"Well, that part sounds all too familiar."

"Matthew was raised in this territory and convinced me to journey west with him so his family could witness our nuptials.

"But days before the ceremony, he decided he'd rather chase cattle in Texas than be married in Colorado. And with his family living in Leadville, I was left alone without any means to support myself."

"His family wouldn't take you in?"

Martha shook her head while focusing her attention on the dozen or more men gathering around Oakley and Bartrum on the street. "They wouldn't even reply to my letters."

"So joining us here at the dove cage was your only option."

"It was either that or starve." Martha moved from the window when she noticed Sheriff Bartrum leading the band of men toward the saloon. "Come with me," she said, taking Lucille's wrist. "It appears a posse is forming downstairs."

Most of the men brought the mine into the saloon with them, its dust still clinging to their faces as though death had already staked its claim.

Martha and Lucille moved quietly to the bar as Vernon raised his eyebrows at them and draped a towel over his shoulder.

"All right," Sheriff Bartrum said, settling the crowd. "The captain was shot in the stomach by a scattergun, about as close as one could get, by the looks of it. Found him near the powder shack out on Red Rock. That's where we'll start searching for the killer."

Bill Oakley scrambled to his feet. "And nobody touches the son of a bitch until I tighten the noose around his neck myself."

Grumbles of agreement filled the saloon.

"Best not let those tempers outrun the law, gentlemen." Judge Waggoner had obviously slipped through the door unnoticed. "Justice is served in a courtroom, not out there in perdition's yard."

The grumbles now filling the saloon were not those of agreement.

"It was your courtroom that gave the damn dust rats access to properties *we* developed," Oakley practically barked. "Do you realize how many workers lost everything because of your so-called *justice*?"

"You have no issue with justice, Bill Oakley. Your issue is with the laws that do not suit you."

"That's where you are wrong. *My* issue is with the men who make the laws, then change them when it no longer serves their interests. They'll lock up a man for trying to protect what's his while allowing a cheat and a liar to take something he's never worked a day for in his life."

The judge shook his head. "I might not have seen eye to eye with your brother on a number of things." He removed his hat and held its underbrim to his chest. "But James and I wore the blue together. Rode beside him at Glorieta Pass and watched him drag boys out from under fire." He stepped closer. "Believe me, I want the killer brought to justice as much as anyone . . . but it has to be done legally, in a way that protects each and every one of you."

Oakley didn't move, didn't speak, just continued to glare.

"Let the law find him guilty first, Bill. Then the noose will be in your hands to deliver the sentence. I give you my word."

Martha met Vernon's gaze but remained silent.

"A few folks out that way tell us a rider has been spotted near the powder shack," Sheriff Bartrum said. "He's no doubt left the area by now, but we can start our tracking there."

"That's right." Oakley never pulled his gaze from Waggoner's face. "And that man fits the description of one of the very dust rats that threatened James and me."

Bartrum cleared his throat. "We can sit around here and argue if that's what you want to do, but the best light's already slipping away." He gestured toward the door. "I suggest we get moving."

As the men made their way outside, Oakley stepped toward the bar and tipped his hat to Martha. "During the rush of this morning's excitement, I'm afraid I may have left a few personal items behind in your room." He glanced at Vernon and Lucille before removing his hat. "I wonder if you'd be kind enough to hang on to those things for me until we get back into town?"

Martha stared at him for a moment. "Of course."

"For your trouble," he said, handing her a silver dollar. He gently pressed it into her hand when she tried to refuse it. "I insist," he said, returning the hat to his head and moving to join the others.

Vernon leaned into her. "I told you, did I not?"

"What in God's name is a dust rat?" Lucille looked as though she'd just had her first taste of wild persimmon.

"Independent miner." Vernon poured a whiskey. "Men who won't sell out to the big land companies, blocking folks like the Oakleys with lawsuits over claim-jumping and land disputes."

"I don't know what any of that means."

"They're folks who want to dig for silver on their own and don't like big companies telling them what to do." Martha retrieved her makings from her handbag and began rolling a paper of tobacco. "Sometimes they get into fights over who owns the land,"—she struck a lucifer and lit up—"and sometimes they argue over how much silver is in their ore, which determines its worth."

Vernon slid the whiskey in front of Martha. "How do you know so much about mining?"

"God knows I've heard enough talk about it."

Martha followed a man still tucking his shirt into high-waisted trousers as he clomped down the stairs into the smoke-filled saloon. While he made straight for the door, Martha veered toward the bar.

Vernon lifted his chin to her. "Parched?"

"Give me a rye."

He took down a bottle from the top shelf and shook his head. "Hope to hell those fellas get back soon," he said, pouring a glass. "There ain't been enough business in this place to float a gnat in vinegar."

Sliding a coin across the bar top, Martha raised an eyebrow. "What in God's name does that even mean?"

"No idea. It's just one of those things the old man would say when . . ."

Martha turned to follow his gaze and found two miners from the posse making their way toward them.

Leaning to the side, Vernon peered past the men. "Where's the rest of your party?"

"They'll be along directly," the one in front said. "Sheriff Bartrum sent Huey and me ahead to make sure the jail was ready."

Martha stepped aside to make room. "Does this mean the killer is in custody?"

"Yes, ma'am. That fool was passed out drunk when we stumbled upon him . . . exactly where they said he'd been seen."

Martha pushed a few coins to Vernon. "Get these men something to drink."

"Thank you, ma'am." The miner removed his hat as though the thought had just occurred to him. "We could sure use a beer."

"Or two," the other man added, removing his hat as well.

Vernon placed the mugs in front of the two. "Did the fella say why he killed the captain?"

"He's suffering from barrel fever right now . . . but swears he doesn't know a thing about the captain's death."

"And yet," the second man said, holding the beer near his lips, "we found Captain Oakley's pocket watch in the low-down cur's coat."

Vernon toweled something unseen from the bar top. "That gaudy thing with the captain's insignia on the case?"

The man nodded. "The captain always said it was one of a kind. But Bill Oakley confirmed that fella was a dust rat. Said he'd been threatening the captain for months after losing a legal dispute."

The second man took a drink and wiped his mouth. "As far as I'm concerned, the blood on the muzzle of that fella's shotgun told me everything I needed to know."

Martha and Lucille joined the gathering crowd on the street, making their way toward the jailhouse in hopes of catching a glimpse of the killer once the posse brought him in.

Martha could feel their eyes, especially the women in their stiff

Sunday bonnets, clutching their children close as if she and Lucille might contaminate them with some errant glance.

"What do you reckon will happen to the mining company?" Lucille asked, either blind to the judgment or just too used to it to care.

"I'm not sure I follow your meaning."

"Do you suppose Bill Oakley will now be in charge? Or do you figure they'll just sell to someone else?"

A woman bumped Martha in passing, then turned with an apologetic smile, one that quickly faded as recognition settled in. "Aren't you the saloon seamstress?"

Surprised that the woman's tone was void of malice or disgust, Martha adjusted her shawl and nodded.

"I've seen your work on a number of miners. Your stitching is second to none."

Trying not to stare into the woman's reddened eyes, Martha cleared her throat and dropped her gaze to her feet. "Thank you."

"Do you work on other garments, or just mining gear?"

"Martha can do anything, Mrs. Oakley," Lucille said with a smile.

"Mrs. Oakley?" Martha's chest tightened as she gazed deeper into the woman's face. "I am so sorry about your husband."

"Here they come!" someone yelled from down the street.

"If you will excuse me," Mrs. Oakley said, moving toward the commotion.

The crowd fell silent as the riders drew near, their horses shifting from a canter to the measured cadence of a trot.

Bill Oakley led the procession, sitting tall in the saddle, his face cold and blank like that of a moneyed gambler.

Martha rose onto her toes, craning her neck to see past the horses, past the line of riders, even past the men who always managed to shove their way to the front.

Then she saw the figure slumped in the saddle, wrists bound, face weary and smeared with dirt. Something in the way he held his shoulders made her flinch.

And then he lifted his head.

A sourness clenched Martha's gut. The face was thinner, older, but there was no mistaking the brown eyes that had promised her everything.

Martha pressed a hand to her mouth, certain she was about to empty her stomach. She staggered back from the crowd as voices, boots, and dust swirled into a single, roaring blur.

"Martha?" Lucille stepped quickly to her side, reaching as if to steady her. "Are you unwell?"

"Lucille," Martha said, gesturing toward the killer. "That's my Matthew."

Martha sat on the edge of her bed, relieved that the sourness had finally left her. At least it had left her stomach.

Matthew.

She had caught a glimpse of his face between riders, his mouth bloodied, eyes distant.

Her Matthew.

No. *Not anymore.*

Rubbing her temple, Martha took a deep breath and slowly released it. Part of her wanted to stay tucked away in her room, but another part couldn't bear another minute in the confining space. Rising stiffly, she stepped to the small bureau to check her mending basket. She needed thread and patches. Nothing urgent, but enough of an excuse to get away and clear her mind.

She noticed the drawer to the left wasn't fully closed, and the sight of it reminded her of Bill Oakley's belongings, bringing back a pang of sourness in her stomach. She didn't want to face him. Didn't want to see him. Not now. Not in her current state of emotions.

"Oakley and his brother ruined my family, Martha. That whole damn company's built on fraud."

Opening the drawer, Martha removed a coarse gunny sack. Curious as to the faint clink within the bag, she loosened the drawstring and rummaged through a tangle of objects, her fingers closing around a small bottle. Turning it over, she recognized it as laudanum, nearly empty.

Figures, she thought. She didn't want to know if it had been for pain, for sleep, or maybe even both.

After tying the bag shut again, Martha headed downstairs where the posse had regrouped—this time, apparently plotting to capture drunkenness from the sounds of it.

Vernon looked up from stacking glasses behind the bar top. "Feeling better?"

"I believe so." She placed the sack on the bar top and glanced toward the miners. "If Bill Oakley takes a break from his imbibing to look for me, give this to him. I'd prefer to keep my distance for the next few days."

Vernon nodded, wiping his hands. "I'll take care of it."

Martha turned left as soon as she stepped onto the boardwalk, even though she knew the general store was to the right. She kept telling herself she had no business in the direction she was walking, but that did not stop her from continuing on her way.

The street had emptied, with most of the crowd now inside the saloon. It didn't take long before she was lingering at the jailhouse door, still trying to convince herself she should just walk away.

"Miss Wilmington?"

Startled by the voice behind her, Martha turned quickly to find Sheriff Bartrum closing the distance.

"I wondered if you'd be coming by," he said, tipping his hat.

"Oh? Why would you wonder that?"

"Lucille told me about your past relationship with the prisoner after you took your fainting spell." He looked away, either out of courtesy or unease. "If you ask me, the man doesn't have a soul."

She glanced down the street and let out a long breath. "I would like a few moments to speak with him."

"Don't you think that's a bad idea?"

"It wouldn't be the worst I've had."

Nodding, Bartrum made his way to the door. "I don't reckon I can argue with that. Come inside."

The building was cooler than expected, yet the air felt oddly warm and stale, thick with the smell of coffee and tobacco smoke.

"Through there," Bartrum said, pointing the way. "Just don't get too close to his bars."

Martha stepped into the narrow corridor, gathering her skirts to keep them from brushing the rough plank walls. Her heart thumped in her ears.

Then he came into view.

Perched on the edge of a scrawny cot, Matthew hunched forward, shoulders slumped, his face buried in his hands.

He looked up with bloodshot eyes and slowly rose to his feet. "Martha."

For an instant, she wanted to weep for the man she remembered, but instead, she closed her eyes and shook her head. "You damned fool."

"I can explain—"

"You left me," she said. "You took everything I was and buried it out on that cattle trail. You knew I had nothing. Nothing! And still, you turned your back. Now you come slinking into town, killing a man who *never* once raised a hand to you."

"I didn't—"

"Don't you dare lie to me!" She stepped close enough to whisper. "You left, forcing me to become something no woman *ever* wants to be. I had to scrape and crawl and trade every scrap of decency just to keep from starving in this godforsaken place." She paused long enough to swallow back a sob. "And you expect me to believe you didn't murder Captain Oakley?"

His eyes softened. "I swear to you, Martha, I don't know how it happened. I woke up at my camp with my skull feeling split in two. Somebody hit me. I swear it. I never touched a drop that night, but I was drunker than I've ever been in my life when I woke up."

Martha crossed her arms over her chest. "Convenient."

"You remember me telling you about my grandfather. The accident. I've never owned a scattergun. I never even wanted one near me, and you know it."

She recalled him telling her about the boom he'd heard, about finding the old man slumped across the kitchen floor, the shotgun still smoking, half his chest gone. "I also remember all those nights you spat your hate for the Oakleys. How you kept saying they stole your father's claim. That they ruined your family."

"They did. But that doesn't mean I killed him."

She focused on the bars between them. "Why did you bring me here, only to abandon me?"

"Martha, I loved you more than—"

"Just stop it! I did not come here for more lies."

She turned before he could say another word, rushing past the sheriff, through the door, and down the street.

The bell above the door jingled as Martha stepped inside the general store. She drew a steadying breath and moved to the counter, fixing her gaze on bolts of calico and tidy rows of threading spools.

"Morning, Miss Wilmington," Mr. Harlan said, giving her a pleasant smile. "Need more stitching supplies?"

Martha touched her neck, worried that vexation still colored her face. "Mending patches," she said. "And some blue thread if you have it."

He began gathering the supplies when his wife emerged from the back, waving a slip of paper.

"Bernard," she said. "I cannot read your handwriting on this ticket you wrote last week for the Oakley brother."

Martha's fingers went cold on the counter's edge.

"Oh, hello, Miss Wilmington," the woman said with a smile. "I apologize for interrupting. I'm doing the books and can barely decipher Bernard's scrawl."

"He bought laudanum," Mr. Harlan said before Martha could reply. "Said he had a touch of the ague. Odd, though. Never knew Bill Oakley to take anything stronger than whiskey. He also bought one of those cheap tin flasks. And you'll be happy to know he bought the one I dropped in the storeroom."

"And here I thought that one would never sell because of the dent in its bottom."

Martha tucked a loose strand of hair behind her ear. "What kind of flask?"

"Same as those." Mr. Harlan gestured toward a shelf by the door. "He bought it cheap because of the dent."

Martha paid for her items and smiled. "I won't keep the two of you any longer," she said, making her way toward the door. "But I thank you for your kindness."

She had barely stepped out the door when shouting erupted down the street.

Pushing her way through the crowd, Martha saw that the posse had returned from the saloon, bringing with them the haze of drunken reasoning. Sheriff Bartrum and Judge Waggoner stood in front of the jailhouse as the crowd churned around them, faces flushed, voices raised.

"You'll not take him," Bartrum said, one hand on his Colt, the other raised. "He stands trial in this town, same as any man."

"Trial's weeks away," Bill Oakley said, his face blotched red. "We've waited long enough."

"Waited?" Judge Waggoner stepped forward. "You just brought him in two hours ago."

"That's long enough," Oakley said, slurring his words. "The evidence shows he did it."

Waggoner lifted an eyebrow. "What *evidence* do you have that's so certain you're willing to hang him before his day in court?"

"He was seen near the shack, drunk as a lord. He had my brother's watch in his coat, and his shotgun had James's blood on the muzzle."

The judge signaled to a deputy. "Bring out everything you found at the man's camp. And someone pull that chair over here." He returned his gaze to Oakley. "How much have you had to drink?"

"Drinking against the law now?"

The deputy returned carrying the bloodied shotgun and a bulging burlap sack. "Everything he had on him or in his saddlebags is in that sack."

Martha watched as Waggoner set out each item on the seat of the chair.

"This all you have, Bill?" Waggoner's voice was firm. "He could have found the captain's watch somewhere, and how do you know that's not animal blood on the scattergun? Why, with so little evidence, any man here could be accused as the killer. Even you, Bill."

Oakley's face paled. "I was with a whore the night my brother died. All night, until morning. Ask her yourself." He turned, scanning the crowd. When he spotted her, Oakley pointed. "There she is. Ask Martha Wilmington."

Acid rose in Martha's throat as she turned and stumbled away.

They had Matthew outside the jail when Martha returned. He stood behind Sheriff Bartrum and Judge Waggoner with wrists bound, his face as gray as ash.

"It's true," Martha said, raising her voice while forcing her way to the front of the crowd. "Bill Oakley *did* spend the night with me."

Murmurs and chuckles grew.

"But the flask you found on Matthew . . . this one,"—she lifted the object over her head—"wasn't his."

The chuckling fell away, but the murmuring continued.

"Mr. Harlan. Martha held out the flask to show the dent on the bottom. "Do you recognize this?"

The shopkeeper stepped forward, hat in hand. "I do."

"Who did you sell it to?"

He looked up, his face pale. "Bill Oakley."

Gasps now joined the murmurs.

She turned to Judge Waggoner. "Bill left this gunny sack in my room," she said, handing it to him. "Inside is an empty laudanum bottle." She turned back to the shopkeeper. "And Mr. Harlan, how often has Bill Oakley purchased laudanum from you?"

"That was the first time."

"Bill Oakley drugged this man," Martha said to the crowd. "He planted the flask and the captain's pocket watch on him. Even left the bloodied shotgun he'd used to murder his own brother. And then he led the posse straight to the man."

"That's a lie!"

Judge Waggoner's eyebrows came together over his nose when he removed a gold pocket watch from the gunny sack. Just the sight of the cover's etched pick and shovel weakened Martha's legs.

Waggoner held up the timepiece. "I've never seen you carry this, Bill. Is it yours?"

Oakley's face lost all color. "Of course it's mine! And the laudanum was to help with the ague I suffered."

"The pocket watch is mine," Matthew said.

"He's lying. I bought the watch when James purchased his."

"Bill," Martha said, "what's inscribed inside the cover?"

He glared at her. "What are you talking about?"

She drew a folded slip of paper from her reticule. "This is the bill of sale. I bought that watch for the prisoner when we were to be married." She turned to Matthew, her voice softer. "Tell them what's inscribed inside."

Matthew blinked. "Hebrews 13:5."

The judge flipped open the case, squinting in the fading light, and frowned. "Sheriff, put Mr. Oakley in custody."

Oakley began to shout, but his words were lost as the men around him took hold.

Waggoner opened a document from the gunny sack and squinted at its contents. "This is the reason you killed your brother, is it not, Bill?" He handed the letter to Bartrum. "Captain Oakley was selling out, and you didn't own a shovel in the company."

Oakley just stared at the ground.

"Take him inside," Bartrum said.

Martha turned to Matthew, her voice barely a breath. "Let your conversation be without covetousness; and be content with such things as ye have: for he hath said . . ." She stepped closer. "What is the rest of the scripture, Matthew?"

He cleared his throat and closed his eyes. "I will never leave thee, nor forsake thee."

The next day, Matthew stood beside a saddled roan, adjusting the straps while Martha waited.

"You saved my life," he said hoarsely. "After everything I did to you, you could have turned away. You could have let them hang me right then and there."

Martha shook her head. "I'm not the same girl you left behind."

He stepped closer, searching her face. "Come with me, Martha. We can start over. Somewhere far from here."

She looked past him, toward the jagged blue shoulders of the mountains rising beyond town. "Captain Oakley's widow saw fit to reward me. Enough to open a shop."

"So you're leaving?"

"I was saving to go back east," she said, taking a long, steady breath. "But I think I'll stay and open a seamstress and milliner's shop right here in Georgetown."

He removed his hat. "I did you wrong, Martha." His smile was strained. "But we had some good times, did we not?"

"It's true," she said, pressing Oakley's silver dollar into Matthew's hand. "But I'm afraid goodbye is all we have left."

"Here." He held the pocket watch out to her.

Coldness sank in her stomach. "I don't want it."

Dropping his gaze, Matthew nodded, swung into the saddle, and let out.

Martha waited a moment before turning back toward the dove cage. She had things to mend, but first, she needed to pack.

The Man Who Sneezed

Johnny D. Boggs

He didn't look like a killer. Too young, too pleasant. But Dad Stratton had seen enough gunmen in his days, and he knew this man was more than a passing cowhand. He carried a short-barreled .45 low on his right hip, sat facing the door to the way station with his back to the wall, and used his left hand to eat his eggs and drink his coffee. His right hand stayed near the Colt.

Karen Russell came to the stranger's table with a coffee pot in her hand. "More coffee, Mr. Valentine?" she asked. Stratton looked up from mending his spur strap and saw the young man politely decline his granddaughter's offer. *Valentine*, Stratton thought, *Jacob Valentine*. It wasn't a name you forgot, and he had heard it before.

Karen disappeared, and Valentine suddenly tensed, his blue eyes staring at the door. Stratton finally heard the sound of shuffling feet. "That would be Homer and Phillip," Stratton said, standing up and walking to the door. "Any luck?" he asked.

"Not a bite all day, Grandpa," Phillip Russell said, handing him a fishing pole. Karen was back inside, collecting Valentine's plate. Homer Waddell entered the station complaining about the heat, the lack of fish, the low water and Phillip's constant chattering. Homer had been complaining since he and Stratton served together in the Mexican War. Thirty years without a compliment.

Jacob Valentine sneezed, and Phillip and Waddell noticed him for the first time. "God bless you," Karen said. Valentine sniffed and thanked her.

"Oh," Stratton said, leaning Phillip's pole in a corner. "This is Homer Waddell, my partner, and my grandson, Phillip, Karen's brother. This is Jacob Valentine."

Valentine was walking toward Waddell, extending his hand when the curmudgeon said, "Jacob Valentine? From Cimarron?" Valentine frowned and instinctively lowered his right hand over his gun.

"Yeah," he said.

"Good Lord," Waddell said. "Dad, this feller gunned down Buck Colbert and two others at Lambert's Saloon about three years ago. I remember reading about it in the *Cimarron News*. Buck Colbert had a shotgun on him, and Valentine's gun was still in his holster, but he got it out and sent all three to their reward before any of 'em got off a shot."

Valentine sniffed. "You shouldn't believe all you read," he said.

"I believe graveyards, and I've seen where Colbert is buried."

"Is that true, sir?" Phillip asked.

Valentine looked down at the boy, probably nine or ten years old. Valentine's blue eyes brightened and he relaxed. The kid was probably captivated by tales of fast draws and daring-do, of Clay Allisons and Jacob Valentines. "They're dead, and I'm alive," he said.

"Tell me about it, please," Phillip said. Valentine heard Karen sharply call her younger brother. And then Waddell began, "Valentine here was a deputy in Colfax County, and Buck Colbert, he was meaner than a Ute, when he was in his cups. He and two guys robbed a stage, then went to Lambert's to drink. Yes-sir, I remember that all right."

"But how did you get all three?" Phillip said.

Valentine smiled. "I sneezed," he said. "Hay fever."

Waddell was at it again. "Shoot, Phillip, he's joshin' you. He's faster than a prairie fire. Three shots, three badmen died. Wisht I could've seen it."

"Well, maybe you'll get another chance," a voice said from the doorway. Waddell and Stratton quickly turned around to see a black-mustached man cock his pistol and casually walk inside. Stratton glanced at his Spencer rifle in the corner, but heard a pistol cock behind him, then felt the barrel of Valentine's .45 against his back.

A fat, gray-bearded man in a butternut slouch hat and two other men, one pockmarked, the other the spitting image of the fat man, entered the station. All were armed, but Stratton recognized only one. The fat old man's face was postered throughout New Mexico Territory.

"Horace McGillycuddy," Stratton said.

"I am flattered," McGillycuddy said. "Now, if y'all would kindly sit at the table, maybe this'll pass quickly and we'll be out of your hair in no time."

"There's little money here, and only a few horses," Stratton said.

"Horace McGillycuddy doesn't waste his time robbing stagecoach stations in the middle of nowhere," the fat man said. "Just sit down. Ma'am, fetch us some coffee."

"Do as he says," Stratton said, and Karen disappeared.

"Maybe I should go help her along," the pockmarked man said, revealing a toothless grin. McGillycuddy chuckled. "In time. In time. Right now, go watch for the stage."

As soon as the pockmarked man was gone, McGillycuddy said, "Sean, search this place for any guns. Grandin, find that girl and make sure she doesn't get any fool woman notions. Valentine, keep our hosts company. I gotta find the privy."

Valentine sat at the table with the hostages, while McGillycuddy, Grandin and Sean kept taking pulls on a jug and looking outside for a swirl of dust that would mean the stage was coming.

"Sean would be McGillycuddy's boy," Waddell whispered. "Don't know the one outside, but if that Grandin is George Grandin, then he's a bad one. Used to ride with Clay Allison, and killed a couple of soldiers at Fort Union last month just because they was Black."

"He says they insulted him," Valentine said, then sniffed.

"Why, Mr. Valentine?" the boy asked. "If you were a deputy, why do you side with them?"

Valentine avoided the boy's eyes, then poured himself a cup of coffee.

"Stage don't carry hardly nothing," Stratton said. "Maybe a couple of passengers. Can't figure out why they want to rob it."

"Me neither," Waddell said.

Horace McGillycuddy staggered over to the table. "Mr. Jed Wright will be on that stagecoach, stationmaster," he said, slurring his words. "Mr. high-and-mighty Jed Wright of the Flying W, carrying his payroll for his hired cowboys. We aim to relieve Mr. Jed Wright of that money."

"Oh, Lord," Karen said softly.

"Jed'll have a guard with him," Stratton said. "He's not a fool."

McGillycuddy laughed. "Ain't no guard a match for either Jacob Valentine or George Grandin," he said. "And Wright wouldn't expect trouble at this station." He staggered back toward Grandin and his son.

"They keep drinking, they'll be passed out by the time the stage comes," Waddell said.

"Don't count on it," Stratton said. "Besides, Valentine ain't drunk. Never thought an ex-lawman would stoop so low."

Valentine's eyes turned cold, and for a moment, Stratton thought he was going to draw. But instead, the gunman relaxed, sniffed, then sneezed.

This time, Karen did not bless him.

They had stopped drinking for about a half hour. Grandin was checking the shells in his revolver, the metallic click of the rotating cylinder the only sound in the station. McGillycuddy walked over to the table and looked at his watch. "About that time," he said.

"Stage could be late," Stratton said.

McGillycuddy laughed. "Not with Mr. high-and-mighty Jed Wright aboard. Not hardly."

"What have you against Mr. Wright?" Karen yelled. Valentine glanced at her, then stared at his employer.

McGillycuddy frowned. "Mr. Wright strung up my brother six years back," he said acidly. "He kicked me off his spread like he was God."

"Your brother was rustling and you were helping him," Stratton said. "You're lucky he didn't hang you, too."

"Shut up! Don't you preach at me! Mr. Jed Wright is gonna walk through that door, and I'm gonna take his payroll and put a ball in his belly. And he's gonna know it was me who done it."

Valentine coughed, then cleared his throat. "This was supposed to be a simple robbery. You didn't say anything about killing that rancher."

The table shook under McGillycuddy's fist. "You're bought and paid for, gunman! You do what I say, when I say!" McGillycuddy turned and stormed to the jug, took a final pull and sent it crashing against the adobe wall.

"Easy, Pa," Sean said.

Grandin laughed, then holstered his Remington. "Valentine turning yellow? Maybe the man who took Buck Colbert would like to try my hand."

Valentine calmly wiped his nose.

There was a minute of still silence, broken by the pockmarked man's cry. He stuck his head in the door, panting. "The stage's coming, boys. About five minutes away."

Horace McGillycuddy grabbed his shotgun and threw it to his son. "Watch 'em. Grandin, you and Lee and Sean stay inside. I'll cover 'em from the privy. And remember, Wright is mine." He stumbled through the door, then yelled, "Grandin, make sure Valentine doesn't have a change of heart!"

George Grandin smiled. Sean McGillycuddy cocked his shotgun, and the pockmarked man sat on a stool to catch his breath.

"They'll kill us all," Waddell said. "McGillycuddy'll gun down Jed in cold blood and won't want any witnesses."

"Shut up!" Sean yelled. "I'll blast you all if you don't shut up."

Sean was pouring sweat, Valentine noticed. He sniffed, then looked at Karen Russell, her azure eyes pleading. "You can take 'em, Mr. Valentine," her brother said.

Waddell wouldn't do anything, Valentine thought, but Stratton would die trying to warn the rancher. Slowly, Valentine stood up and walked away from the table.

George Grandin drew his pistol, cocked it and brought it up to his shoulder, the barrel pointing at the ceiling. Sean McGillycuddy aimed the shotgun at Valentine's stomach. The pockmarked man stood up and let his right hand rest on the butt of his Colt.

"Try it, Valentine," Grandin said. "Always knew you were too soft for this. Come on. Tough gunman like you wouldn't be afraid of us three. I'll give you a chance." He uncocked the Remington and smiled.

"Don't," Karen said softly. "They'll kill you."

"Take his gun," Grandin told the pockmarked man.

The man started toward Valentine, but the young gunman motioned for him to stop, then brought his right hand up under his nose and took a breath, leaning his head back.

Sean McGillycuddy laughed as Jacob Valentine sneezed violently, jerking his whole body down forward. But McGillycuddy wasn't laughing when he saw Valentine straighten, the Colt .45 in his right hand. The gun thundered and McGillycuddy fell against the wall, dropping the shotgun on the floor. Valentine had turned in an instant, cocking the .45 and firing again. The bullet struck George Grandin in the center of his chest. Grandin fired his Remington, but it was the act of a dead man. The bullet hit the wall above Valentine as he turned toward the pockmarked man. Valentine's gun spoke again before the pockmarked man's gun was halfway out of his holster. The man groaned and dropped to his knees, clutching his belly with both hands.

The station filled with black-powder smoke. The stench and noise was too much for Phillip, who was screaming, and through the corner of his eye, Valentine saw Stratton dive for McGillycuddy's shotgun. Karen's hands covered her mouth; Waddell sat spellbound.

"What the —" Horace McGillycuddy yelled as he ran in the station, firing his pistol at Valentine when he realized what had happened. Valentine went reeling to the floor, and McGillycuddy was thumbing the hammer back on his pistol when Valentine fired twice. Horace McGillycuddy staggered back, then brought his pistol up again. The hammer of Valentine's Colt snapped on an empty chamber.

McGillycuddy was smiling went Dad Stratton blew him through the door with a shotgun blast.

Valentine rested his head against the adobe wall as Karen ripped his shirt and probed the wound in his left shoulder. Dad Stratton began checking on the dead outlaws, and sent Waddell and Phillip outside to greet the stage.

"It's a clean wound, Mr. Valentine," she said quietly. "I think you'll be all right." She looked toward the loft. "I should have some old sheets for a bandage."

Jacob Valentine softly sneezed. Karen Russell and Dad Stratton both turned and stared at him.

"That one was for real," Valentine said softly.

Karen smiled and wiped the gunman's nose with his bandana.

"God bless you," she said.

The Run for Ruby Camp

Vonn McKee

Hey, Ma. It's Billy again.

It's a funny thing how a fella can be a-ridin' hell for leather like this and talkin' to his mama at the same time. After so many miles and so many weeks, I got to talk to somebody or I . . . well, I don't know how I'll keep a sound mind.

There's somethin' unsettlin' about this valley anyhow. Ruby Valley. It's a big lonely place, Ma. I always feel like there might be ghosts in them far-off hills. Or maybe down here waitin' behind a rock or a bush. I'm grateful this pony runs like his tail's afire. He knows where we're a-goin' and knows we ain't got no time to waste. Well, you ain't gonna like hearin' this, Ma, but there's been plenty of trouble with the Paiutes on this trail, mostly on account of them brothers that run the Williams Station. Two of them, in particular. Couple of hungry Paiute girls showed up askin' to be fed and got themselves locked up as prisoners and I hate to think what else.

Their Indian kin didn't take kindly and they've been houndin' us riders ever since. Attacked a couple of stations. Killed them two Williams fellas.

I know you think it's dangerous work, what I'm doin'. Well, I reckon it is, at that. But the money's good, Ma. A hunnerd bucks a month! So when I saw that Pony Express poster wantin' "young, skinny wiry fellows, not over 18, expert riders," I signed right up. "Orphans preferred," it said. Well, you know better'n anybody I fit every last one of them requirements, sad to say.

You know, Ma, I dreamed of the attack just the other night. Always the same. What's it been now? Three years? Four? I just remember shots bein' fired back and forth for a few days. Us hidin' in the wagons. Then warriors and some other men ridin' in, tellin' us to give up our weapons and they'd not only spare us but make sure we got out of Indian country alive. And Papa and all the others give in to 'em! Only they wasn't all Indians, we came to find out. Blasted Mormons dressed up in deerskins and a few feathers stickin' up on their heads.

Mountain Meadows. It sounds like a right peaceful place, don't it? But them Mormons and maybe a few Paiutes left nothing but a bloody mess. Well, you know the story. I just still have trouble believin' it myself. Killed all the men and women, you and Papa included. Wasn't but seventeen of us young ones left alive.

Might be why I don't fancy these open places. Trouble can show up out of nowhere.

You know why I run off from that family I got give to. They never treated me like their own. Besides, they was Mormons, too. Them Brigham followers ain't likely to talk Billy Tate into convertin'. No, ma'am. Well, I'm still Billy Miller in my mind. The Tates hung their name on me since I had no other kin. Wished I could change it back but now Billy Tate's what I'm known by.

And last spring they wanted to send me back to Arkansas to some far-off relation. Fourteen years old, what was I to do? So I run off and joined the Pony Express. Be sure to let Papa know I'm one of their fastest, I'm proud to say. They give us a revolver and California ponies to ride. Them Californias can outrun a Paiute mustang, I can tell you that.

I ride like the dickens from station to station, changin' out my horse at each one. Get to the end of my line, rest up and do it backwards. Hardest thing is stayin' awake sometimes. But I will say that knowin' there might be Indians waitin' along the trail sure encourages me to keep my eyes open. And I talk to you whilst I'm ridin'. Sometimes there ain't but a few envelopes in this *mochila* and I wonder what's so important inside 'em. Seems awful risky to life and limb to haul a couple of letters through this kind of country.

Well, criminy. Speakin' of that, I just heard war whoops behind me. Don't worry, Ma. My pony's a quick one. I can't say I'm too surprised. Ruby Valley is the worst stretch of the entire trail these days. Them Paiutes ain't scared of nobody and I reckon they know we ain't too well armed. It's our horses they're after. And vengeance too, I reckon.

I believe this pony's named Star. Come on now, fella. Stretch out and get ahead of them devils.

There's a pretty good bunch of 'em. Ten, maybe twelve. I got six shots in the revolver and an extra chamber of six in my pocket. Well now, that's just enough, ain't it, Ma? That is, if I can't outrun 'em.

Sure wished I could get across this open ground and find some cover. This pony was already 'bout givin' me his all. Ruby Camp station is up ahead but it ain't as close as I'd like for it to be. Kick up them heels, Star, ole buddy. Seems like them Indians is closin' in a mite.

It's a strange thing to mention right now but I sure do miss you, Ma. I still picture that dress you always wore. Blue with the little flowers. We was all goin' to California. Oh, the stories Papa told about how life was gonna be once we got there! A land full of rich, black dirt and streams shinin' with gold nuggets. And a new dress for you. Maybe two or three dresses, he said, and you could throw away that old faded blue one that you'd wore all the way from Arkansas. But I miss that faded dress, and you and Papa.

Them Paiutes'll kill you, they say, and take your mount and guns. Then scalp and cut you up just for the meanness of it. My hat blew off just now and I'm sure them fellas is thinkin' they'll own this yellow hair of mine 'fore the day's out. But I got some sad news for 'em. I'm a survivor. Not only a survivor but a fighter, too. Learned that at the Tates. So don't you worry, Ma.

Twelve bullets. Reckon I won't waste 'em shootin' from here. Not likely to hit anything, aimin' behind me at a dead run.

They're closer, but not by much. But it's all right, ain't it?

Ahhh! Shucks, Ma. Star's been hit. Blasted Paiute arrow, right in the flank. Come on, boy. Let me see if I can reach back and—*Christ*! Sorry, Ma, didn't mean to say that but they got him again. Ahhhh . . . sorry, fella. Can you keep . . .? No, no . . . this ain't good.

I know you got to slow down, boy. You're a good one, you are. Hey, now. You think we can make them rocks up ahead? Come on, Star. You can do it. You got to.

Oh, Ma. There's arrows rainin' down on us, all around. A California's faster'n a Indian mustang—oh, lordy, that was awful close—but not faster'n their arrows, I reckon. But I'm Billy Tate, used to be Billy Miller. I made it outa Mountain Meadows alive and I'm sure gonna get outa Ruby Valley.

Hey! What in—? Guess I took an arrow but it's just above my boot. I can pull it out when we get to them rocks. They're further off than I thought, them rocks are. This pony is slowin' down. Can't blame him.

You might say a prayer for us, Ma.

Oh, lordy. Never been so glad to see a pile of rocks. There, Star. You're a fine pony. I'm gettin' off you now. Get us hid and see if we can't pick us off a few Indians. I'll have to prop my gun up in this crack, I'm shakin' so bad. Don't even know when that arrow hit my arm. Here they come, Ma. Here they come.

Aim. Squeeze. There you go, you devil. That'll teach you to ride in front. Teach you to get close to Billy Tate.

Gotta mind my shots, Ma. Eleven left. One Indian down though. Here comes the rest of 'em. Maybe twenty yards back.

Aaaggh! Christ, they got me good. Aaahh. 'Tween the ribs, Ma. Sorry . . . for the language . . . I just . . .

Alrighty, Star, this ain't . . . lookin' so good for me. But you got mail in that *mochila* that's gotta get to Ruby Camp. I want you to run, fella! Don't let these . . . mangy coyotes catch you. Hate slappin' you when . . . you got arrows stickin' out of yer rump but . . . *run*! Hyaaaahhh!

Yeah. You run, boy. You run. There ya go. You know . . . the way.

Alrighty. Who wants . . . to be next? How 'bout you on that stumpy roan? Easy, Billy. Aim. Squeeze. Well, hell's fire. Missed. Try . . . again. Leg shot. Well, that'll . . . do for now.

I'm bleedin' bad, Ma. Not . . . breathin' so good neither. Gotta keep shootin'. Aim, Billy. Right at his chest. That one . . . on the gray. Just like that. Die, you devil. Yep. Just . . . like that.

Make them shots count, Billy boy. Two left, then I'll fish out .. the extras. Damn hand . . . is shakin' so. Clipped him! Ahh. Can't afford . . . just try . . . again. That one, ridin' by . . . right there, where his heart . . . oughta be. If he has one . . .

Just like that. Die, will ya? Ha!

Thank you, Ma. I know you're a-prayin'. I gotta get to . . . my pocket. Hands shakin' . . . all of me, shakin'. Get the . . . chamber out. Just . . . pop that one out. Other one . . . in. Here we go. Aim. Squeeze. Ha! I'm doin' good, Ma. Is Papa . . . smilin'?

They're mighty close. Ridin' all around me. Shoot 'em all, Billy boy. Shoot 'em all. Aim, squeeze. Aim . . . squeeze.

Aaaaahhh. Oh, Christ. Two more arrows. I don't even . . . know where they . . . come from. I think I done killed . . . six, maybe seven of them devils, Ma. But I sure do hate to tell you . . . I'm plumb .. . outa bullets. But not . . . outa Indians.

It's alright, Ma. It ain't . . . your fault. I know . . . you was prayin'. Reckon the Good Lord's . . . answer . . . was *no*.

"Well, he's gotta be out here somewhere," said Fred Hurst. He glanced at "Uncle Billy" Rogers, who rode alongside. Both men turned even more grim with the unspoken . . . *If there's anything left of him.*

They'd been searching ever since Billy Tate's horse limped into Ruby Camp station with two arrows lodged in his hindquarters. The *mochila* was still across the saddle, precious contents still bundled inside.

"How long we gonna keep looking?" Hurst asked.

Rogers rubbed his eyes with a dirty blue handkerchief. They'd both grown fond of the boy.

"Till we find him."

They rode east toward Egan Station, where Billy would have last changed horses. Some of the wounded pony's tracks had survived the Nevada winds so they searched the trail for sign, only seeing hoof prints in sheltered dips and between rocky passes.

"Look there!" Rogers pointed ahead and drew up his mount. Hurst did the same. In unison, the men let out a deep sigh.

A column of vultures rose up through the pale sky. It did not take long to find the reason for their gathering.

"God in heaven," said Rogers. Like the shared sigh, he and Hurst removed their hats at the same time. "How many arrows you reckon . . .?"

Hurst looked away. His eyes swept across the corpses of the Paiute warriors, counting aloud, ". . . five, six . . . seven! What a stand that boy made! From the looks of it, he didn't get 'em all but, lordy, what a fight."

Rogers reached down and touched the top of Billy's head. "He looks . . . like a little child, don't he? I reckon he is." His voice choked. "*Was* a child. Had the biggest blue eyes I ever saw. Wonder why they didn't take that yellow hair of his? Didn't desecrate his body neither."

Hurst knelt. The smell of death was growing heavy around them but he kept his handkerchief at the corner of his eye instead of over his nose and mouth. "You know how Indians are. They take notice of bravery, even an enemy's. Reckon it was their way of honoring a brave man."

Rogers nodded. "And, for his years, Billy Tate was a man. If he wasn't, he became one right here behind these rocks."

They stayed there, silent, for a few more minutes.

Hurst stood. "Them Paiutes'll be back for their dead." He took a long look at the boy, whose cornsilk hair ruffled in the wind.

"Reckon I'll get the shovel." He had brought it along, fearing the worst.

Look at that, Ma. That's old Uncle Billy Rogers and Fred Hurst from Ruby Camp. I told you all about 'em, remember? When I was ridin'. Well, well. They're takin' care of what's left on earth of Billy Tate. That's awful kind of 'em. If they only knew how I'm a-doin' right this minute, they wouldn't look so sad, would they?

Say, Ma, is that a new dress you're wearin'? Well, Papa, you made good on your word after all, didn't ya? You sure did.

And this place is sure better'n California ever thought about bein', ain't it?

The Trading Post

Michael Zimmer

The old man was fleshing a hide when movement on the southern prairie caught his eye. He paused to study the distant horizon, twisting his head slightly to the side to avoid the cataract haze that blurred his straight-on vision. A faint smile lifted the corners of his mouth when he recognized the man riding out front. Well, not the man, not yet, but the white mule, for sure.

"Woman," he called into the nearby doorway, leading into the side of the hill at his back. He kept his scraper pressed firmly against the wolf's pelt, stretched tightly over a willow frame braced against one knee. "They have come."

The sounds from within ceased, and a moment later he heard her at the dugout's door, could picture her standing there with one brown hand propped against the frame, watching the line of approaching carts. "They are late this year," she said in Cree, the language of her people.

"Late or early, they're here now." He straightened slowly, ignoring the ripple of twitching muscles along his spine. "There looks to be half a dozen of them," he added after a moment. "Better put some more meat in the pot."

"Do you think I do not already know this?" she replied, turning back into the dugout.

The trader chuckled and went back to his labors. The little caravan was still a few miles away. There would be plenty of time to finish the gray wolf's pelt before they arrived.

He worked the hide with practiced ease, scraping away the excess fat and meat until only the milky underside remained. He was putting away his tools when the man on the mule splashed across Cutbank Creek and trotted his white jenny into the hard-packed dirt yard fronting the tiny trading post.

"Ho!" he called in greeting.

"Ho, yourself, old friend," the trader replied, tossing aside the thin antelope hide he'd used as a rag to clean his scraper, before walking out to shake the agent's hand. "You had a safe trip?"

"A quiet trip," the agent replied gratefully, his gaze wandering past the old man's shoulder to take in the condition of the post – the unlocked door to the storeroom, the empty corral down by the creek.

Although the trader didn't speak, he flinched inwardly at the agent's silent appraisal. He knew the trading post made a poor impression when compared with the fur trade company's larger forts farther to the west. There wasn't much to Cutbank Post anymore, just the trade room and living quarters for him and the woman, hollowed out of the side of the hill, and the storeroom to the west, also a dugout, although with its own entrance. In front of these burrows was a crude fur press held together with rawhide and hand-carved wooden pegs, and a cottonwood fleshing beam for the larger hides, like buffalo and elk, that sometimes found their way downriver.

At one time, Cutbank Post had handled a good portion of the robe trade among the eastern Cree, and even some from the Ojibway and Santee, but those days were long past now. The buffalo had been drifting steadily westward for decades, away from the pressure of the Red River hunters, and in recent years it sometimes seemed like it was hardly worth the effort to keep the place supplied.

The trader supposed it only made sense to shift the Company's satellite posts in the same direction, moving them farther west with the migrating herds, but he'd lived on the Cutbank for nearly thirty years by then. He'd seen his children play among the towering cottonwoods along the creek, had watched them learn the skills not only of their mother's people, but of his own —reading and writing, conquering the complexity of numbers so that someday his sons could manage posts of their own. His daughters were even now married to other traders, living along the far-off Milk and Musselshell rivers, while his sons hunted for big outfits like Hudson's Bay and American Fur.

The trader's life here had been a good one, and he was happy with the way it had played out. He cared deeply for the woman who had shared his robes these many years, and still had good friends among the Cree and Ojibway, old men like himself who had stayed when others moved on. The trader wanted to stay, as well, but he knew the decision wouldn't be his to make. Or the agent's, for that matter. Cutbank Post's future rested in the hands of the Company's superintendent at the big fort on the Missouri, a decision based in no small part upon the agent's yearly assessment of the post and its profitability.

The old man's lips thinned in quiet despair as he reflected upon the nearly empty storeroom. He'd taken in fewer than a hundred buffalo robes over the summer, along with fifty or so wolf pelts, and not even enough beaver, muskrat, and other furs to run through the press for baling.

The heavy carts rolled ponderously into the yard, spokes dripping from the shallow waters of the Cutbank, ungreased hubs squealing like frightened hags in the act of being robbed. One of the *engagés'* came up to take the agent's mule, while others lifted heavy maple yokes from the necks of their oxen and turned them loose to graze. The woman appeared at the dugout's entrance, and the agent swept his hat from his head. "M'lady," he said graciously, then switched to Cree. "It is good to see you again."

"There is food for all, if food is sought," she replied simply, but the trader knew she reveled in the agent's gallantry. It was often lonely along the Cutbank. Especially now, with their children gone.

"I will see to my men first, then clean up at the creek so that I don't offend your table," the agent promised, eliciting the flash of a smile from the woman's dusky features. She turned back into the dugout without further comment, and the agent's expression sobered. "I have heard from your sons," he told the trader.

"They are well?"

The agent nodded. "The youngest sent a letter. I'll fetch it from my kit before we eat."

The trader didn't reply. He was watching a stranger standing to one side of the carts, holding the reins to a leggy sorrel horse, several cuts above the average Indian pony one usually found at fur trade posts; an expensive, double-barreled rifle was cradled against his chest with his free arm. He was young, with a neatly-trimmed mustache and sideburns, and wore a new, hooded green capote, although the temperature hardly seemed cool enough to warrant such a heavy article of clothing.

"The factor's nephew," the agent explained, following the direction of the older man's gaze. "He was sent along to learn the ropes."

The trader turned a curious eye on the agent. He didn't ask the question he most wanted to. Instead, he said, "Maybe someday the boy will take over your job, eh? So you can be given your own fort to manage."

After a pause, the agent placed a gentle hand upon the older man's shoulder. "Come along," he said. "We can talk while I wash up at the creek."

It was night, but the trader couldn't sleep. He'd tossed and turned atop his rope-sprung mattress long after the others had retired to their robes. He'd muttered and kicked and ground his teeth, until the woman finally jerked at their blankets in exasperation.

With an uncharacteristic curse, he rolled out of bed, dressed in the cavern-like darkness of their living quarters, then pushed aside the blanket that served as a door between home and store. He paused at the dugout's single window, peering through the thick, wavy glass. The *engages'* were scattered around their carts, oblong forms in the moonlight. A faint red glow marked the location of their evening fire.

The *engages'* had eaten on their own, a stew of tender buffalo from the trader's kettle, with carrots, squash, and onions from the woman's garden, and bread from the last of their flour. Only the agent and the factor's nephew had shared the makeshift table the trader had set up in front the dugout, eating off the woman's best bone china.

They had talked of many things that evening. The agent wanted to know about the summer's trade, and why it had been so poor, and his brows had furrowed in concern as the trader explained how only the older men had come in to trade.

"The younger men want guns and whiskey, and go to posts that give them these things."

The agent knew about the whiskey, but the superintendent refused to use it in the Company's bartering. Not because of its impact on the tribes, but because it was illegal, and the superintendent didn't want to risk the Company losing its license to trade with the Indians along the Missouri.

The agent had asked about the empty corral, too, his scowl deepening when the trader told him about the Santee's raid in the Month When the Grass Turns Brown. The agent hadn't seemed impressed when the trader related how he thought he'd wounded one of the thieves.

"You should have horses," was the agent's curt response. "Get some when the Crees and Ojibways come in to trade."

Their talk moved away from business after that, the woman hanging on the agent's every word when he told them what he knew of their children, all of them safe and healthy, the last he'd heard. He'd shared what news he had from downriver as well, of the growing unrest in Kansas and Nebraska over slavery, of rumors of gold being found in the Beaverhead Valley, and of Fremont's efforts with the newly formed Republican Party.

Neither the agent nor the trader had mentioned the plans for the factor's nephew to the woman. The trader had intended to do that later, when they were alone, but he hadn't been able to find the words when the time came, nor the courage to answer the questions he knew she would ask.

The *engagés'* had unloaded their carts before sunset, exchanging crates of trade goods for the meager piles of robes and furs in the storeroom. The trader had seen the disappointment in the agent's eyes as the summer's take was heaped into the carts. There had been no need to stomp the loads down tight; when the *engagés'* were finished, the carts were barely a third filled.

Standing alone and discouraged at the dugout's solitary window, the old man rubbed tenderly at his watery eyes. He told himself that he should go back to bed, so that he could be sharp and on guard when the little caravan pulled out the next morning for its return journey to the big fort. But he couldn't face the darkness of the post's living quarters, the guileless presence of the sleeping woman, and after a while he took a new blanket off the shelf behind the counter and made himself as comfortable as his old bones would allow on the trade room floor.

He told her after the caravan had left the next day, the three of them standing in front of the dugout, watching the carts struggle up the far bank before striking out to the south. It was not his decision, he explained in Cree, strangely relieved that the factor's nephew didn't understand her native tongue.

"He is the factor's nephew," he emphasized. "The second-in-command. His sister's son. The factor wants his nephew to learn the ways of a trader's life, here, where the tribes are not as hostile as they are farther west. It was the superintendent, the Company's chief, who insisted that we take the boy in and train him over the winter."

"He is trouble," the woman said simply.

The old man nodded. He had sensed as much himself, but his hands were tied. It was what the superintendent wanted. He didn't mention his fear that he was training his successor, that someday the kid in the green capote would take over Cutbank Post, and that he and the woman would have to find somewhere else to live. He thought he would rather see the post closed permanently than have it taken away like that, turned over to someone else.

That afternoon, the nephew saddled his horse and rode out to the west. The trader was in the storeroom, sorting inventory, while the woman puttered over the evening meal in her kitchen. He had ordered the youth to help him as he broke open crate and box and barrel, but the boy had ignored him.

"We need fresh meat," the nephew had declared, pulling his double rifle from the little stack of personal belongings the *engages'* had piled beside the dugout's entrance.

"We have plenty of meat," the trader countered firmly. "I want your help here, so that you can learn the ropes."

But the nephew had turned his back on the older man. "I'll be back before dark," he stated confidently, thumping his heels against the sorrel's ribs.

The trader watched him go, eyes glinting with anger, then quietly returned to his chores. Darkness came without the boy's appearance, but they didn't wait for him. They had their evening meal, and afterward sat outside and smoked their pipes, talking about the children, happy that they were still safe on such an uncertain frontier. They left the nephew's gear, his sacks and satchels and a heavy cowhide trunk, outside, and when the kid returned well after dark, knocking on the door and demanding his supper and a place to sleep, the trader went to the window and told him that the evening's meal was finished, and that there was only the one bed in the post's cramped living quarters.

"There is a hut in the trees where our children used to sleep in the summer," he said. "I'll show it to you tomorrow, and let you fix it up for your own quarters."

"Where did your kids sleep in winter?" the nephew demanded.

"They slept on the floor beside our bed, but you'll have to sleep in the hut . . . unless you want to dig your own shelter." He smiled, picturing the kid hacking at the unyielding soil with a pick and shovel. "I can show you how to do that tomorrow, too, if you prefer."

"No, don't bother," the nephew replied. "I'm sure a bed will open up soon." He turned away, laughing derisively, and went to his personal belongings, where he dug out his bedroll.

The trader returned to his bed, but his smile had disappeared.

"What did he want?" the woman asked as he slid under the blankets at her side.

"He wanted to be fed."

She started to get up, but he pulled her back. "The boy is not ours. He can find his own food, or be here when a meal is served."

He sensed the woman's reluctance to let someone go away hungry, but kept his hand on her shoulder until she finally relaxed. He found an odd measure of accomplishment in that. He was still in charge of this post. The woman knew it, and the nephew would have to learn it. Either that or return on his own to the big fort.

They settled into an uneasy truce after that. The factor's nephew moved his gear into the children's hut after rechinking the cracks with a batter of mud and grass from the creek bank, then adding a fresh layer of sod over the roof. The trader and his woman returned to the life they had known before the boy's arrival, preparing for the coming winter while readying themselves for the flurry of late-season trading that always preceded the heaviest snows. Soon, small parties of Cree and Ojibway would descend upon the post, bringing with them the furs and robes they had held back in the spring. Luxuries like sugar and tea and chocolate would fetch a commanding price in robes, and the trader placed those items prominently on his shelves. Blankets for the coldest months, along with powder and shot for the hunters' *fusils*, would also be eagerly sought. The trader would dicker hard for these items, but he would be fair, too, and next summer, in the Moon When the Ponies Grew Fat, the Indians would return with their winter's catch of prime plews and fresh robes.

For a while, the nephew's presence was like a gentle breeze—there, felt, but seldom acknowledged. After that first day, when the trader had ordered the boy to help in the storeroom and he'd refused, the trader seldom approached the youth. The nephew seemed satisfied with that arrangement. He came and went as he pleased, hunting regularly and bringing back fresh venison or pronghorn that he shared freely, accepting bread and vegetables from the woman in return, coffee and tobacco from the trader. But after a few weeks, the trader began to sense a change in the youth's demeanor, a growing arrogance in his stride. The woman noticed it, too, and commented on it one night in bed.

"He is becoming bold," she said.

"What do you mean?"

"I mean that he is becoming bold," she replied, but would say no more.

After that, the trader began keeping a closer eye on the factor's nephew, and soon he noticed it, too. The boy was young. No doubt he missed the companionship of others his own age, especially the attention of the opposite sex—a young's woman's coquettish look, the sweet fragrance of her perfume. Startled, the trader began to look at the woman differently, to see her as others must. He remembered the appreciative glances of the *engages'*, sitting around their fire while she ladled stew into their wooden bowls, and the charming formality of the agent, the way he removed his hat when she came near, or remained standing until she was seated.

He still remembered the day he'd gone to her father's lodge to leave a trio of fine horses hobbled outside, along with several blankets and a new Leman rifle. Not to purchase, as some thought, but to prove to her family that he was a capable provider, and could support a wife and children. He'd been a trader even then, and quite a catch in any Indian woman's eyes; his trading post, with all of its European imports—its kettles and beads and good Sheffield knives—like a mansion compared to a hide lodge.

He'd been thirty-seven at the time, she twenty years his junior. He tried to recall how many years ago that had been. Twenty-five, at least, and maybe even more that that. She was no longer young, but it occurred to him that she wasn't old, either. And she was still attractive. A shapely figure, long black hair only lightly sprinkled with gray, a willowy grace as she moved about the yard or tended her garden.

The trader's anger began to simmer as he observed the nephew watching her with hungry eyes, following her every move from the shelter of the trees surrounding his log hut. He confronted the youth the next day.

"We are getting low on meat. We need to hunt."

The factor's nephew appeared startled by the older man's declaration. "We have plenty of meat," he protested. "You tell me that every time I go out after fresh game."

"Now we need more, to dry, and for pemmican for the winter, when we can't hunt because of the deep snows. Tomorrow we'll go out together. You can follow the Cutbank downstream. I'll go upstream. We'll be gone two days, and use your horse to pack in the meat we harvest."

A smile crept across the boy's face. "All right, you'll go upstream, and I'll go downstream." His grin continued to spread, and the trader turned away before the youth spotted the motive in his eyes.

Tomorrow, he grimly promised himself. *Tomorrow, I'll know for sure.*

That night he cleaned his rifle before the crackling flames in the fireplace. The woman was piecing together a pair of mittens from scraps of leather she kept in a small box beside their bed, the smoked deerskin gleaming richly in the pulsating light.

"I did not know I needed a new pair," the trader said quietly.

"These are not for you. These are for the boy."

A frown creased his brow.

"He is young and inexperienced, and did not think to bring along a pair from the big fort," she explained.

"Is he paying you for your work?"

She glanced up in vexation. "He is young, and does not always think ahead, but he will learn."

"He is bold. You said so yourself."

"His eyes are bold, but his hands will be useless if they freeze."

"Maybe that would be for the best," he murmured.

She smiled in response. "Not if you had to care for him until the agent's return in the spring."

He let it go after that. He trusted the woman, and knew she would have made mittens for anyone the superintendent sent to them if they didn't have a pair of their own. It was the nephew he didn't trust, but that would soon change. By tomorrow he would know the youth's intentions, and if they were bad, then the boy would learn. It was why the superintendent had sent him to Cutbank Post—to learn.

They left shortly after dawn, the trader walking because the Santees had stolen his horses, the boy riding because the Santees had not yet returned to steal his.

Upstream from Cutbank Post was northwest, toward the divide that separated the Missouri River drainage from that of the Saskatchewan. It was higher ground, although not by much. Yet by following the ridge above the creek, the trader was able to keep an eye on the factor's nephew for a good long ways, the boy's bright green capote standing out sharply against the late autumn tans. The nephew kept his sorrel to a walk, following the meandering course of the creek's left bank until the timber farther down seemed to close in around him like a shroud.

With the youth out of sight, the trader dropped over the far side of the ridge, into a ravine that would take him back to the post. He hurried now, knees protesting the rough terrain, lungs straining over ground he had once been able to fairly leap across. Despite the cool temperature, he was sweating by the time he reached the rear of the hill where the dugouts were located.

He crossed the brow of the hill in a crouch, then dropped heavily to one knee when he spotted the sorrel tied firmly to the hide press. Up until that moment, he hadn't realized how much he'd privately doubted the boy's resolve. It couldn't be denied now, though, and his jaws tightened as he ran a callused thumb over the rifle's lock, checking the cap he'd placed over the nipple the night before. It was still there, and he rocked the hammer back to full cock as he closed the gap to the dugout's entrance.

The trade room was empty, but he could hear them in the post's living quarters, behind the worn blanket door. He eased along the empty space between the front wall and the wide trade counter where he received his customers' furs and robes. His moccasins barely whispered over the hard-packed dirt floor, but there was a deep roaring in his ears, and the blanket's colorful stripes seemed to blur even more than his cataracts could account for. The harsh, eager grunts of the boy and the protesting cries of the woman seemed distant and unfamiliar as he stretched his trembling fingers toward the blanket. Then the youth cried out in pain and panic. There was a loud crash from within, followed by a clatter of tin and iron.

The trader froze, one hand stopped mere inches from the heavy curtain, the other holding his rifle level, its muzzle centered on the door. He jumped back when the blanket was ripped aside. The factor's nephew stood before him, wild-eyed and panting, his left hand pressed tightly against his side. Blood poured through his fingers, soaking the dark green wool of his capote.

Lunging forward, the boy slammed into the trader's chest, sending the older man down hard, the wind gushing from his lungs, the rifle dancing free of his grasp. He saw the boy stumble outside, but was too weak to go after him. He lay where he'd fallen, one arm and shoulder squeezed against the front of the trade counter, his free hand flat, covering the hollow curve between his stomach and chest. The flesh there burned as if on fire, and he gritted his teeth and squeezed his eyes shut until the pain gradually subsided.

With effort, the trader rolled onto his hands and knees, then struggled to his feet. His rifle lay on the floor nearby and he scooped it up on his way to the door, checking that the cap hadn't been jolted loose in the fall. Sidling up to the door, he eased an eye past its frame. It was midday and the sky was clear and bright, but the yard was empty. He inched out a little farther, until he could see the trees along the creek, the hut barely visible between the thick trunks.

It was there, also, that he spotted the boy, crouched behind a waist-high fallen log just inside the timber. The log's bark had long since been stripped for kindling, its wood a smooth, pale gray. The boy saw him in the same instant and raised his rifle, but the trader jerked his head back before he could pull the trigger.

Leaning back against the inside wall, the trader sucked in a deep breath to steady his nerves. He could hear the woman in the other room, muttering darkly as she began cleaning up the wreckage. He considered going to her, asking if she was all right, but knew she wouldn't appreciate his concern. She was too angry yet. Besides, he couldn't leave with the boy lurking outside, waiting for him to lower his guard.

He moved to the window, where he could just make out the deep forest green of the youth's capote, the lad's hunched shoulders where he knelt behind the log. The twin muzzles of the double-barreled rifle stared back dully, like the empty black sockets of a sun-bleached skull.

Returning to the door, the trader cautiously poked his head around the frame, then pulled it back when the boy moved his rifle to cover the entrance. Raising he voice so that it would carry into the trees, he said, "You cannot stay out there forever."

"Nor can you stay in there forever."

The trader smiled at the boy's skewed logic. "We have plenty of food, and the water keg is full. You have nothing but the creek, and you'll have to leave your hiding place to go to it."

"I'm not thirsty," the boy shouted.

You will be, the trader thought fiercely, then moved back to the window to stare at the distorted patch of green, showing among the bare trunks of the cottonwoods. He thought briefly of firing through the window, but decided the target was too small, the odds too great that the thick glass would deflect the muzzle loader's round ball just enough for him to miss. He didn't want to do that, not yet. The trader didn't care about the youth, but he didn't want to be shot himself.

The hours passed slowly. Although the nights had been cold recently, often with a light frost by morning, the afternoons were still comfortable. Inside the dugout, the air grew warm as the day progressed. Bees buzzed at the door, and a fat black fly explored the shelves against the rear wall. The trader ignored these tiny distractions and kept his attention focused on the patch of trees along the creek. From time to time he would move from the door to the window, then back again, and each time the youth's rifle would shift just enough to cover him.

The boy's vigilance began to annoy the old trader. More and more as the afternoon waned, his gaze would shift to the sorrel, hitched snugly to the fur press with a length of sturdy hemp rope. Toward evening, the horse began to nicker longingly, its big, soulful eyes on the Cutbank's purling waters. The animal was thirsty, but the trader couldn't do anything about it. Finally he shouted, "Take care of your horse, damnit!"

"And get a bullet in my back when I try?"

"I won't shoot."

The boy laughed. "You go take care of it. I promise I won't shoot."

The trader cursed loudly, and the youth laughed harder.

"I can wait here all day if I have to," he told the trader. "All week, if that's what it takes."

Moving swiftly to the door, the trader cocked his rifle, then stepped brazenly into the opening. The boy yelped when he saw him, and ducked out of sight. Then he popped up again, the double rifle shouldered, its single front sight like a stout finger poking at the old man's chest. The trader hesitated only a moment, then jumped back out of sight.

"Hell will freeze over before you win this one," the factor's nephew bellowed.

"Hell and heaven, both," the old man vowed.

Darkness came, but the trader remained alertly at his post. He could hear the kid moving around in the trees, the crackle of dried leaves like scratching rust. Yet when dawn arrived, the green patch of the youth's capote was still visible. The trader tipped his head past the door, thinking the boy might be trying to fool him, but the twin muzzles of the kid's rifle followed him out and back, and the trader's lips thinned in frustration.

It went on like that for the rest of the day, the old man moving from window to door, door to window, the kid staying low behind the fallen log, yet never failing to have his sights on whatever location the trader chose to peer from. From time to time the trader would hear the woman in the other room, the clang of a pan or the scrape of kindling pulled from the wood box, but she never came to check on him, and he was afraid to abandon his position even long enough to look in on her. He could tell she was still angry, though. There was a harshness to the sounds emanating from their living quarters, like she was throwing the wood on the fire, or the spoon in the kettle. He knew she must be growing as weary of this stand-off as he was, yet she would also understand that his hands were tied, that it wouldn't end, couldn't end, until the boy surrendered.

The trader thought the scales might tip in his favor when the Indians showed up. There were three of them, Ojibways from the north, although coming from the south, from the buffalo lands along the Missouri River. He recognized Crow's Beak and Standing Bear, both of them old friends, and cried out a greeting. He didn't know the third man, but hoped he soon would. More important was the dust that feathered the horizon, the women and children and old ones. The whole village was coming in to trade, before moving on to their winter camp in the Turtle Mountains.

A smile lit the trader's face at this unexpected aid. He moved quickly to the door, although he didn't dare step through it. When he peered past the frame, he saw that the Ojibways halted on the far side of the creek, staring uncertainly at the trading post.

"Be careful, my friends," he called to them. "There is an enemy in the trees."

The kid immediately popped up, but this time his rifle wasn't pointed at the dugout. It was aimed at the Ojibways. "Get back," the factor's nephew ordered.

He spoke in English, and the trader could tell that the Indians didn't understand him, yet the boy's words and his intimidating gestures with the double rifle had an immediate effect on the Indians. They pulled their horses around and started to ride off, throwing quick, frightened glances over their shoulders every few rods, as if afraid the kid might come after them.

"Don't go," the trader shouted in a panicking tone, but the Ojibways only slapped their heels harder against their mounts' ribs, the ponies' hooves kicking up little clouds of dust that the wind carried away. When they were gone, the old man stood in the doorway, trembling with rage.

Chortling gleefully, the boy said, "No help there, old man."

"They'll be back," the trader replied, but in his heart, he knew they wouldn't. He feared no one would, once word of what the Ojibways had encountered spread to the other villages.

The breeze strengthened as the day wound down, and the temperature began to plummet. The trader could see the sorrel's breath in the star shine, until clouds rolled in from the northwest and obscured the light.

There was snow on the ground by morning, and the sun remained hidden behind an overcast sky. Wind snatched at the falling flakes, swirling them through the air like tiny dancers. Despite the snow and the cold, the kid remained alert and on guard, his gaze seemingly never straying from the dugout door and window. The trader knew this couldn't go on forever. Sooner or later, one of them would have to make a move. But he also knew that the odds would favor the man with the most patience, and that he would need all the help he could get against the youth's speed and agility, and especially the sharpness of his vision. The trader rubbed at his tired eyes, softly cursing the boy's stubbornness.

The snow continued to fall all day, drifting in front of the dugout like mounds of the purest cotton, and in the timber, a tree split from the sub-zero temperatures with a sound like a gunshot. As time wore on, the trader began to experience a grudging respect for the youth's tenacity, his endurance against such frigid elements, but after a few days the weather changed once more. The sun came out and the snow melted. The trader tipped his face to the sun's warmth, although he was careful not to expose himself to the kid's rifle.

The grass turned unexpectedly green in the snowmelt, and a faint, emerald mist clung to the bare limbs along the creek. The trader was standing at the window, brooding and cranky, when he heard a sound from the prairie. Moving to the door, he felt a mixture of dread and relief at the sight of an ox-yoked caravan approaching the post. The agent rode out front on his white mule, a red-headed clerk astride a scrawny buckskin at his side. From the trees, the factor's nephew hooted cheerfully.

"You're in trouble now, old man," he shouted. "They're going to close this post for good after this, and turn you out to feed the wolves."

There was a crash from the living quarters, followed by the sound of slamming skillets and pieces of flying firewood. The trader's shoulders slumped as he turned away from the door and put his back to the wall. The rifle sagged in his hands. He knew the kid was probably right. The superintendent had sent the boy here for training. Instead, they had become embroiled in a feud that was driving away their customers.

Hearing the devilish screech of ungreased hubs from the yard, he squared his shoulders and returned to the door. But he didn't venture outside. The kid was still standing in the trees, grinning broadly with his rifle clutched in both hands. Eyes narrowing in suspicion, the trader remained where he was. He noticed the agent and the clerk staring at the sorrel's feet.

"It's a damned shame," the clerk was saying. "That was a good horse."

"We'll pull the saddle," the agent said as he dismounted. "We can replace what's rotted and still use it."

The carts were circled in the yard, the *engages'* milling nervously, their eyes shifting from the trader to the nephew. The clerk made his way through the trees to the boy's hut, bending at the waist to peek inside, while the agent came toward the post in measured strides. Observing the granite-like cast of the man's face, the trader moved behind the counter. The agent paused in the door, his gaze resting briefly on the floor in front of the counter, his expression darkening. "You damn fool," he snarled, then moved on to the living quarters.

The trader didn't reply to the agents words, sensing that now wasn't the time. He would speak up later, after the agent's rage had lessened.

Brushing the blanket to the living quarters aside, the agent peered inside for only a moment, then spun on his heels and stalked back outside. The trader moved to the window to watch.

"Found him," the clerk said, coming back to where the buckskin and the white mule were standing ground-tied in front of the trading post, tails switching lazily at summer flies.

"In the hut?"

"No, hiding behind that log over yonder. Still has his rifle, too." He tipped his head toward the dugout.

"Yeah, they're still in there," the agent acknowledged darkly.

"You know we've got to shut it down, don't you? The tribes will never come back after this."

The agent spat. "Just as well, I suppose. The place has barely broken even the last couple of seasons." There was sadness in his words, though. Cutbank Post had been one of the Company's earliest efforts to stretch its wings beyond the immediate vicinity of the big fort on the Missouri. There was history here that even the thickest-skinned employee had to appreciate.

"The *engages'* won't go into the trade room," the clerk said.

"That's all right," the agent replied. "I'll take care of that. You get 'em started emptying the storeroom. I want to pull out of here as soon as we're loaded."

The clerk's lips thinned to a hard, razor-sharp line. "You feel it, too, don't you?"

"Let's get to work," the agent said curtly.

He came back into the trade room, and the old man moved out of his way. He started to speak, but when the agent looked at him, the words died in his throat. The agent went into the living quarters first, coming back a little later with an armload of bedding and cooking utensils. He was almost to the door when the woman slammed a pot to the floor with a loud bang. The agent jumped and whirled, his eyes going wide.

"She didn't mean it," the trader said quickly, but the agent wasn't listening. Didn't even seem to hear him. He went outside, and the trader followed as far as the door. He could see the kid down by the fallen log, standing with his rifle butted to the soil between his worn boots. He was watching a pair of *engages'* digging a hole in the dirt. Others were scurrying back and forth between the storeroom and the carts, practically throwing the untraded goods into the vehicles.

The agent returned and began emptying the shelves behind the counter. The trader hung back, feeling utterly worthless. It seemed to take only a few seconds to strip the post clean. When he was done, the agent ordered one of the *engages'* to bring up a team of oxen.

"You're going to leave them there?" the clerk asked, his brows furrowing.

"It's their home," the agent replied. "I doubt if they'd want to leave." He pried the window from its frame and handed it to the clerk. "Glass is too expensive to leave behind," he added, then ran a length of rope through the opening and out the front door.

After securing the rope to the center ring, the *engage'* shouted for the oxen to move out. The large beasts leaned into the yoke, the rope tightening until it seemed to hum. The front wall of the trading post bulged toward the straining cattle, and the trader cried out in alarm. As he darted behind the counter, he caught a glimpse of something familiar lying on the floor, pressed firmly against the footboard as if it had been there a while. But he was moving too fast to get a good look at it, and wasn't sure he wanted one.

There was a dull, rumbling groan just before the ceiling caved in, filling the empty trade room with a suffocating cloud of dust. The trader huddled against the rear wall with his arms over his head, his eyes squeezed shut. He didn't look up again until the dust began to settle. Rising awkwardly, he made his way to the front door. A scowl formed on his face as he watched the little caravan crawl out the far side of the Cutbank, moving south toward the big fort on the Missouri. He wanted to call after the agent, to ask what he was supposed to do, but then he spotted movement in the trees, and jumped back just in time. He went to the window, staring through the thick glass to where the kid stood behind the log, his rifle held firmly in both hands.

Picking up his own gun, the trader returned to the door, peering cautiously around the frame. The kid had ducked back behind the log, but the twin muzzles of his rifle were still visible, and in their living quarters, the angry clatter of the woman's spoon banged against the rim of a kettle. The trader's gaze went to the green prairie, but the caravan was gone, swallowed by the empty distance. Like ghosts.

JOHNNY D. BOGGS has worked cattle, been bucked off horses (breaking two ribs last time), shot rapids in a canoe, hiked across mountains and deserts, traipsed around ghost towns, and spent hours poring over microfilm in library archives—all in the name of finding a good story. He was won a record ten Spur Awards from Western Writers of America, a Western Heritage Wrangler Award from the National Cowboy and Western Heritage Museum, and has been called by *Booklist* magazine "among the best western writers at work today." He also writes for *True West, Wild West, Boys' Life* and *Western Art & Architecture,* speaks and lectures often, studies old movies, and even finds time to coach and umpire Little League. A native of South Carolina and former newspaper journalist, he lives in Santa Fe, New Mexico, with his wife and son.

Learn more at www.JohhnyDBoggs.com

MICHAEL ZIMMER is the author of twenty novels. His work has been praised by *Library Journal, Booklist, Publishers Weekly*, the *Historical Novel Society*, and others. *City of Rocks* (Five Star, 2012) was chosen by *Booklist* as one of the top ten Western novels of 2012. *The Poacher's Daughter* (Five Star, 2014) received a starred *Booklist* review, and was selected winner of the National Cowboy and Western Heritage Museum's prestigious *Western Heritage Wrangler Award for Outstanding Western Novel* (2015); both were finalists for the *Spur Award* from the Western Writers of America, and his short story, "The Medicine Robe," won the *Spur Award* in 2019. Zimmer resides in Utah with his wife, Vanessa, and their two dogs.

Learn more at www.Michael-Zimmer.com

VONN MCKEE entered the Western writing scene in 2014 with "The Songbird of Seville," a Spur Award finalist from Western Writers of America. That same year, "The Gunfighter's Gift" was a Peacemaker Award finalist from Western Fictioneers. Her short story "Wren's Perch" earned another Spur finalist nod in 2019, and in 2023, "The Run for Ruby Camp" won the Peacemaker Award for short fiction. McKee's stories blend rich emotion, historical realism, and vivid portrayals of a beautiful yet unforgiving land and its hardy settlers. Although she grew up in the Red River Valley of Louisiana, she now makes her home in Tennessee. She continues to write short fiction—her collection *Comanche Winter* was released by Wolfpack Publishing in 2020—and is currently at work on a historical novel.

Learn more at www.VonnMcKee.com

MICHAEL KNOST is a two-time Bram Stoker Award®-winner and has written in various genres and helmed dozens of anthologies. Michael received the Horror Writers Association's Silver Hammer Award in 2015 for his work as the organization's mentorship chair and was recognized as the 2021 Mentor of the Year from the organization. He also received the prestigious J.U.G. (Just Uncommonly Good) Award from West Virginia Writer's Inc. and was recently inducted into the inaugural class of the Imagination Hall of Fame in July of 2025. His novel *Return of the Mothman* has been filmed as a movie adaptation, and he has taught writing classes and workshops at several colleges, conventions, online, and currently resides in Chapmanville, WV with his wife and daughter.

Learn more at www.MichaelKnost.com